Praise for *Redneck Opera*...

In Redneck Opera, *Margaret Mooney casts a knowing and amused eye on the roughnecks, wildcatters, and swindlers who thrived in Texas oil fields half a century ago. They still do.*

—JAN REID
Author of *Commanche Sundown* and
Let the People In: The Life and Times of Ann Richards

Margaret Mooney's debut novel, Redneck Opera, *is one flat-out hilarious romp. It's clever and reckless and is written with brio and grace. So, dear reader, strap on your seat belt and hold on to your Stetsons—this is one wild and bumpy ride you're going on, and there are turns up ahead that you won't see coming. This is a story so big, a tale so tall, it took the great state of Texas to hold it all in place.*

—JOHN DUFRESNE
Author of *No Regrets, Coyote*

Mooney tells an authentic East Texas tale with keen insight. No matter how unlikely the plot, it's the way we do things down here.

—STEVE RAMSEY
Two-term mayor of Caledonia, Texas,
population seventeen

A real history lesson about Texas characters told with belly laughs throughout.

—JOAN BROOKS BAKER
Award-winning writer, photographer, and videographer of
The Black Madonna

Written like a Texan Dostoyevsky.
—SHARON ELIASHAR
Writer and composer of *Return of the Horse*

A hilarious tale of the early days of oil discovery and the men who would stop at nothing to get rich. Mooney gives us an unforgetta-ble cast of characters that could only be grown in Texas.
—M. G. GRANA
Winner, 2000 Willa Cather Book Award

Redneck Opera

Thank You kindly

Margaret

REDNECK OPERA

~ A Novel ~

Margaret Mooney

**KIDDROSE
PUBLISHING**

CERRILLOS, NEW MEXICO

Kiddrose Publishing
PO Box 357
Cerrillos, NM 87501
www.redneckopera.com

Editor: Ellen Kleiner
Cover and interior art: George Lawrence

"Gusher! Gusher!" lyrics reprinted with permission of the families of Dr. Joseph Carlucci, Conductor Emeritus of the Symphony of Southeast Texas, and Mrs. Violet Newton, Poet Laureate of Texas.

Printed in the United States of America

Publisher's Cataloging-in-Publication Data
Mooney, Margaret (Margaret R.), 1948-

Redneck opera / Margaret Mooney. -- Cerrillos, New Mexico : Kiddrose Publishing, [2016]

pages ; cm.

ISBN: 978-0-9864150-0-5 ; 978-0-9864150-1-2 (eBook)
Summary: A mostly true sweeping tale about the early days of oil discovery in East Texas. Dirt poor cotton farmers became overnight millionaires when they drilled for water and hit oil. The book follows a crooked wildcatters' escapades of greed and those who ultimately exact revenge from him.--Publisher.

1. Texas, East--Fiction. 2. Oil fields--Texas, East--History--Fiction. 3. Petroleum industry and trade--Texas, East--Fiction. 4. Swindlers and swindling--Texas, East--Fiction. 5. Revenge--Fiction. 6. Historical fiction. 7. Humorous fiction.

PS3613 .O5519 R43 2016   2015931405
813/.6--dc23   1506

1 3 5 7 9 10 8 6 4 2

*To the memory of my parents
and Upper East Texas*

Acknowledgments

Numerous people have provided encouragement and valuable input during the development of *Redneck Opera:* my family, Larry Davis, John Dufresne, The Friday Write Group—Tori, Joan, Bruce, Jack, Colin, Marigay—Ann Church, Anne Shannon, Barbara Hooper, Steve Ramsey, Susan Meredith, the Bloombergs, Skip Hollandsworth, Marilyn Abraham, illustrator George Lawrence, Ellen Kleiner with Blessingway Authors' Services in Santa Fe, New Mexico, and a few other Texans out there.

Contents

1. The Tornado Trial 1

2. Weldon (Not So) Christian Camp 21

3. Wooing Wealth 41

4. The Gulf Coast Cares Caper 71

5. The Mr. Alabama Deception 79

6. Wedded Bliss with Priss? 87

7. The Teasles 99

8. The Cherokee Lake Oil Swindle 109

9. A Teasle Goes Offshore 123

10. The Grand Petroleum Shannon Hotel 133

11. Talford and Sloots Go Hollywood 143

12. Casa Mer Offshore Dinner Theater 151

13. A Teasle Comes Onshore 171

14. Wildcatter Speakeasy 183

15. The Sermon of Shame 189

16. The Our Lady of Guadalupe Scheme 197

17. Social Rejection Revisited 203

18. A Little Respect 209

19. Gambling on Gushing Oil 217

20. Shaping Up and Preparing to Ship Out 229

21. The Casa Bella Dinner Theater Fiasco 243

22. The Will 251

23. Circle of Deceit 259

Chapter 1
The Tornado Trial

 Before the deadly tornado of 1931 tore through Enid, Oklahoma, before Leland Peck Sr. was sentenced to life in prison, and before his wife Daisy went crazy twice and moved into the train depot, life in Enid was somewhat predictable.

The population of 18,342 was supported mostly by grain companies, owing to the large wheat crop. Some of the menfolk worked the harvest, while others made a living managing grain silo operations or held shipping jobs on the Rock Island Railroad. The wives tended to their vegetable gardens and enjoyed various quilting, baking, and canning competitions put on by the Enid Baptist Church.

Every spring Daisy Peck's mornings began at sunup. She worked in her garden and swatted at the new crop of mosquitoes buzzing in her ears. This time of year the weather was usually calm. The sky was a crisp robin's egg blue, cloudless with light winds blowing through the thick pine tree forests spreading their clean scent and helping diffuse the stifling humidity. However, one such day Daisy stood up, swiped the sweat from her forehead with the crook of her elbow, and noticed that the sky had changed. She couldn't know how much her life, too, would soon change permanently.

The gathering of flat white clouds was the first sign of impending danger. The cows in her neighbor's pasture stampeded for no apparent reason, all stopping under a grove of trees facing the same direction—into the wind. Then there was a dead calm and an ominous dark gray cast to the sky. Within minutes, the clouds themselves turned dark, almost black. They produced a heavy rain accompanied by a rapid temperature drop, causing unseasonal hail that bounced off the tin roofs of barns, making a pop-pop-pop sound. The sky turned an eerie yellow. A long twisting funnel curled down from the clouds and struck the ground with a deafening crack. Powerful winds blew so much dust and debris you couldn't see your hand in front of your face.

Daisy knew the warning signs of a tornado, having grown up in what was known as Tornado Alley, a broad swathe of land stretching from East Texas up through Oklahoma and Missouri. She knew to take immediate cover and ran into her basement, slamming and bolting the wooden door. As she lit kerosene lamps, she thought about how she was now totally alone. She took some comfort in knowing that her husband Leland was on a construction job twenty miles away and that she had sent their only son, Junior, away to Weldon Christian Camp for the summer.

The rest of the townspeople in Enid also knew to take cover. They quickly moved underground—under houses, into the basements or root cellars, anywhere to escape the horrifying 190-mile-per-hour wind causing total destruction in its serpentine path.

Most of the high school students had heeded the warning bells rung from the church and gone home to be with their families. But that day enthusiasm for competitive sports clouded the judgment of Dora and Gussie Nell, two of Enid's most popular teenage girls, who had decided to stay in the new high school gymnasium to practice their cheerleading routines for spring sports events.

"Dora, what are you doing up there on the bleachers?" yelled Gussie.

"I thought I'd try that flip off the first row. I could do two cartwheels in a row and land down on the sidelines of the court," replied Dora, looking out the window and hiking up her skirt in preparation. "Oh, my Lord. Get up here and look out, Gussie Nell. You won't believe what's happening outside." The tornado had hit swiftly. It had moved across the plains surrounding the town, ripping up the grain crop and tearing off roofs from the downtown mercantile exchange and the abandoned movie theater but skipping the hardware store as if it knew the town would need that to rebuild. Roof shingles, car tires, tree limbs, pasture gates, stock tanks, and all other manner of debris was swirling sideways outside the gym in the gusting, howling wind.

In the gym, the walls heaved in and out like a giant lung. The glass from the clerestory windows crashed to the gym floor, and the wooden bleachers fell in a pile like a bunch of popsicle sticks. Before the horror of what was happening could register with the girls or they could even think about an escape, the west wall of the new gymnasium collapsed, killing them instantly.

Its horrendous damage done, the tornado retreated into the sky. The hazy setting sun illuminated the devastation it had left behind. The Enid Police and Fire Departments put out a call to nearby towns to send over emergency vehicles and personnel. Townspeople alongside the rescue crews worked feverishly throughout the night digging through the rubble with the help of flashlights, hoping any cries or sounds would lead to other survivors. As the sun rose the next day, only fifteen survivors had injuries, mostly minor ones. It was the deaths of Dora and Gussie Nell that tore apart the soul of the town. Enid's residents gathered at the church and prayed for the families of the two dead girls.

The only thing that had been left relatively intact in the debris at the gym site was a twelve-horsepower My Jaeger concrete mixer with a Peck Construction logo on its side. The police confiscated the mixer, loaded it into a flatbed trailer, took it down to the station, secured it in the auto pound, and immediately found the contractor who had built the gymnasium, Leland Peck, holed up in his hunting cabin. Peck Construction had been awarded most of the building contracts in town, not because of the quality of its work but because it was the only construction company in the county. Leland was taken into custody and booked under suspicion that his construction malfeasance had caused the tragic deaths. Since the jail had been destroyed by the tornado, he was incarcerated in a makeshift holding pen, a room in the back of the town library. There he awaited a trial date when the circuit court judge for northern

Oklahoma, the Honorable Manuel "Manny" Bonds, would again be in Enid.

Daisy had spent the night in her basement and surveyed the aftereffects of the tornado in the light of dawn. Fortunately, there was minimal damage to the house. The funnel had picked up the tool shed and flung it about thirty yards off its concrete base. Her garden was shredded, but the roof and walls of the main house were still standing. The horror of such recurring spring storms always made Daisy wonder why anyone stayed in Enid.

When Leland hadn't called her, she chalked it up to downed power lines. Finally, after picking up the receiver and hearing a dial tone she called the sheriff's number but quickly hung up. She always had a feeling of gloom when she was about to talk to the sheriff about Leland, something she had done many times before when he hadn't come home on time. She was aware that the sheriff knew Leland stayed out most nights drinking. Just she and the sheriff knew how many times this had happened, as if the sheriff were a priest who kept her confessions secret to honor a code of silence. But why did she feel guilty about Leland's whereabouts, as if she had done something wrong when she hadn't? She stared out the window at the row of downed trees just past what was left of her vegetable garden. Those trees were like a fence, a curtain of protection hiding what went on in her house from the neighbors. Now they were gone. The whole town knew Leland was an absentee papa, the only father missing from Little League games and father-son pancake dinners, which took its toll on Junior. It was a relief that she had decided to send Junior away for the summer. Daisy picked up the phone again, called, and said, "Hello, Sheriff, is everyone accounted for? My husband Leland didn't call this morning."

"No, and he's not going to," replied the sheriff with self-assurance.

"Why? Did he go on another bourbon bender? I don't see how that's a crime," replied Daisy, becoming increasingly concerned.

"Mrs. Peck, your husband is under arrest for suspected murder. He's in the temporary jail awaiting trial," stated the sheriff.

Daisy was so shocked she dropped the receiver. Leland wasn't a bad man, or at least he didn't start out that way. But as his construction business had grown so had his penchant for drink. She was glad she had sent Junior away to summer camp so he wasn't being exposed to his father's shocking and embarrassing behavior. Meanwhile, she struggled to comprehend the chain of events, conditions, and public perceptions about Leland that had led to his arrest and her current plight.

Daisy didn't go see Leland while he was incarcerated. She couldn't bear the thought of going into that courthouse one more time. After all, she had been there at least five times before with Leland when he had been arraigned on variations of disturbing the peace, including drunk and disorderly conduct, inappropriate public behavior, and driving under the influence. At various times the judge had called Leland a reprobate, rapscallion, scalawag, miscreant, and malefactor. Daisy didn't understand what all those names meant, but now he was being branded a murderer. She understood that only too well. Daisy wished all this would just go away like a bad dream.

In the days following the tornado, as she walked into town the stares and the way the townsfolk crossed the street when they saw her coming made her feel as if she were isolated in a prison just like her husband.

Five weeks after the tragedy Leland's trial was scheduled to begin. Daisy didn't plan to go to the trial, but her best friend Mildred insisted she go.

"Leland needs you, Daisy. You go in there with your head held high. Show him support. You need to get your hair done and buy a new dress. You are looking really down in the mouth lately. Besides, I hear he hired Dabney Little as his legal counsel, and that man couldn't find his own rear end with a flashlight," said Mildred, trying to show Daisy support but at the same time realistically assessing the situation.

As a consequence, Daisy relented, and on the first morning of the trial she and Mildred took their places in the viewing alcove, which was packed to the rafters. The courtroom looked the same as the many times Daisy had been there before, but Daisy did not. Even a new hairdo couldn't disguise her downtrodden appearance. She had always dressed smartly with a hat and gloves whenever she left the house, but now she was a bent, scraggly, hollow-eyed image of her former self.

"She looks like warmed-over death," whispered someone seated close to her.

Daisy surveyed the courtroom below to avoid making eye contact with the other people who had come to witness the goings on. The courthouse had been built in 1922 and had a cornerstone plaque that read: "Peck Construction." There wasn't much crime in Enid, so the courthouse was used infrequently. On the main floor, the wooden planks creaked when anyone walked across them. The construction workers had forgotten to attach judge's chambers behind the judge's bench, so any conferences necessary between the attorneys and the judge occurred out in the hall. Just inside the entrance to the main floor was a spittoon, which was moved around as needed. One side of the courtroom had faulty wiring, so the other side was where the floor fans were plugged in, leaving the jury box with little airflow. She and Mildred, however, were seated near the two wooden frame windows, which remained open to relieve the heat and humidity on the hot midsummer day. This alleviated the dead still air somewhat, but a hole in the screen let in a few flies, which were likely to swarm around anyone on the witness stand. Wrists fluttered hand-held fans everywhere in an effort to compensate.

Leland Peck's lawyer, Dabney Little, was about five feet two, portly, dressed in rumpled clothes, and given to hyperbole underscored by the use of wild hand and arm gestures. He stabbed the air, punctuating at least one word in every sentence. He had a florid face and carried two handkerchiefs, one in his vest pocket and one in his trouser pocket, as he perspired heavily and got very excited when delivering what he thought was great legal discourse. As during all of his trials, he carried a stack of three-by-five-inch lined index cards on which were written common legal questions, such as: Were you alone at the time? Was anything out of the ordinary in your opinion? Some of his cards had legal terms written in Latin, which he would routinely refer to when stuck for an idea on how to continue questioning a witness.

The prosecuting attorney, Allan Boone Blount, was, in stark contrast, almost gaunt, had horn-rimmed glasses, and wore a pin-striped suit with a perfect crease in his pants. He carried an air of confidence and superiority. He was a man of few words but words well chosen. Having graduated magna cum laude from the University of Oklahoma, he was considered the thinking man's lawyer, versus the defense lawyer, who behaved as if he might not have even gone to law school.

When the jury filed into the courtroom, Leland was already seated at the defense table. Daisy was glad to have her fan, which she flapped back and forth, as much to hide her face as to get relief from the stagnant air. There was muffled chatter in the room and then silence as the bailiff entered.

"All rise," stated the bailiff.

The Honorable Judge Manuel Bonds entered the courtroom, took his place, raised his gavel, and pounded it several times on the bench.

"Please be seated," instructed the bailiff.

"Thank you, bayless," said Bonds, nodding in his direction.

Oh no, thought Allan Blount. It's not bayless. He knew Bonds wasn't the sharpest knife in the drawer, but a lawyer cannot expose a judge's incompetence without jeopardizing his own practice.

"Go ahead, Blount," said the judge.

"Distinguished members of the jury, you have been selected because you are individuals without bias and with sympathy in measuring the gravity of this crime. In the next few days, the prosecution will prove that the defendant, Leland Peck, exhibited gross negligence of safety in the construction of the Enid High School gymnasium, and was directly and solely responsible for the deaths of two of Enid's finest young women in their prime. His negligence took them away. Took away their future, and he must, in turn, pay with his future as a convicted man. The gymnasium can be restored, the tornado's destruction of our town repaired, but these two lives are gone forever," said Blount.

"Thank you, Counselor Blount. Bayless, ask the jury to nod if they understood his remarks."

"All nod," instructed the bailiff.

They nodded.

"Okay, it's my turn now," shouted the defense attorney, Mr. Little.

"Of course, do go ahead," said the judge.

"Your Honor, ladies and gentlemen of the jury, distinguished guests, person or persons accused, the defense will systematically and beyond a doubt prove that Mr. Leland Peck, seated here to my left, was not complicit in this tragic accident that cut short the lives of two of Enid's finest youngsters." It was on the word *doubt* that Little stabbed the air with a ham-fisted gesture. "Mr. Peck did not, as he is accused, cause the failure of the gymnasium wall. Rather, it is Mother Nature who should be on trial here today," he concluded, foaming at the corners of his mouth like a pot of boiling over cream of wheat.

Leland showed little emotion and perfect posture as he listened to opening remarks. He glanced around the room searching for some sign of support from anyone, and got none. His eyes found Daisy's. He had seen her look of disapproval before, but always when he had a hangover. Now, with him sober and clearheaded after his incarceration, her look of disappointment and disdain made him realize the severity of the situation.

The court reporter noticed that Leland had bags under his eyes, which was not unusual. Everyone knew that Leland could be seen most afternoons in the hardware store wearing a stained denim shirt under red suspenders holding up well-worn corduroy pants with the top of a small flask peeking out of his back pocket. He would be buying nails, attempting to get remnant lumber at the cheapest price, or trying to hire on the cheapest hands, mostly day workers. He wasn't especially tall, but he carried himself like a man of importance, being the most successful, actually the only, contractor in Enid. His glasses had a bent frame, which people thought had resulted from Leland falling down after one too many bourbons. Today he was clean shaven, his hair was slicked back, and he smelled of Wild Root Cream Oil. His lawyer had advised him to look more presentable than with his usual grubby beard and uncombed brown mop, which he did, except for his ill-fitting brown cotton jacket.

"Why, Mr. Peck here is from one of Enid's oldest and finest families," continued Little. "His daddy settled here, working the railroad in the face of threats by savage Indians. He was here when Enid got its name. As you know, the original sign read "DINE," as it was the only stop on the railroad heading west that had a café and served hot meals. But some youngsters from the Indian reservation went on a tirade and were probably drunk and climbed on top of the station platform sign and rearranged the letters. The town attempted to prosecute them, but they were protected under tribal jurisdiction. They've been here since our town was first designated by the governor of our great state as the Wheat Capital of America. Mr. Peck even built the first grain elevator. That ought to tell you how long the Pecks have lived here and the difficult times they have lived through." Little wiped the beads of sweat from his forehead with one of his handkerchiefs and stabbed the air.

His opening remarks were interrupted by the prosecuting attorney, Allan Blount, who stated, "Objection, Your Honor, relevancy."

Judge Bonds blinked a few times, taking the measure of the courtroom, swallowed, and agreed, saying, "Sustained."

Little shot a look of surprise at his competitor as he thought he was on a roll that held the jury in rapt attention. Always, before this particular trial, if he kept talking about just who knew what and anything that came to mind at the time, the jury got really bored, generally went with the absence of logic, and voted to acquit.

"Mr. Blount, call your first witness," instructed Judge Bonds.

Blount first addressed the jury. "Ladies and gentlemen, we all know the history of the Peck family. That is not the purpose of this trial. What we have here is an unimaginable tragedy. It is well beyond misconduct. It is borderline murder. Moral turpitude." Blount called Leland Peck as his first witness.

Leland, feeling bulletproof and ignoring the advice of his lawyer, shuffled over and took the stand.

Blount continued, "Isn't it true that you were awarded the contract for this courthouse, underbidding the competition by at least thirty percent?"

"Objection, Your Honor, relevancy," shouted Little, wiping the foaming spittle from his mouth.

The judge, who was not supposed to have an opinion, already did. In those times, judges were paid only by convictions not acquittals. He had heard that Leland had underbid other contractors routinely and given kickbacks to those letting the contracts. It was common knowledge that Leland would always cut corners on specifications and materials to stick to the awarded budget.

"I'll let that stand. Proceed," said the judge.

Blount recalled case after case of Leland's kickback schemes, to which Little objected each time. That didn't matter, though, because Blount had already painted a picture of Leland in the jurors' minds as unethical and calculating.

The judge, noticing that jurors were starting to perspire and yawn, called a recess for lunch.

Upon their return, the jurors noticed in the corner of the room a large misshapen object, about the size of the back half of a pickup truck, covered with a sheet.

"May I introduce the first piece of evidence, the twelve-horsepower My Jaeger concrete mixer confiscated from the scene, Your Honor?" asked Blount.

"Well, okay, I guess so," replied the judge, quizzically.

The sheriff removed the sheet to reveal the concrete mixer. It was set on a square wooden platform with wheels on each corner. The sheriff began to push the concrete mixer away from the wall, motioning to Johnette, the court reporter, to help him. The object appeared to be fairly heavy.

"Careful, Johnette," cautioned the sheriff. "If we get this thing going too fast, it might just plumb bust out the other side of the courthouse."

"Please place the concrete mixer in front of the jury, sheriff," instructed Blount.

Once it was situated in front of the jury, Blount asked Leland several questions about it. "Mr. Peck, is this your company's concrete mixer?"

"It's got my name on it, duddin' it?" replied Leland.

"Did you perform the required slump test on the tensile strength of the first batch of concrete?" asked Blount.

"No, sir, we did not have a sump pump on the construction site," replied Leland, stifling a burp. His eyebrows knitted together, and his gaze shifted from left to right and back again.

Blount could feel the legal tide turning his way. "Your Honor, I have no further questions of this witness," he said, sitting down as he shook his head in disgust.

Judge Bonds instructed, "You may call your witnesses, Little."

"Your Honor, ladies and gentlemen of the jury, distinguished guests, person or persons accused," started Little, as if he thought he was being paid by the spoken word and not the outcome. "I will now call my first expert witness. The defense calls Kenneth 'Buck' Attaway to the stand."

Judge Bonds inquired, "And what is the nature of Mr. Attaway's involvement?"

Mr. Little simultaneously shuffled his index cards and wiped his brow with one of his handkerchiefs.

Blount wondered if all that sweat over the years might cause the ink on the index cards to run.

"Why, Buck here was on the Peck crew building the gym. Now, Buck, where were you on the afternoon of the tornado?" asked Little.

"Well, I think I was in the basement of my house; of course I was, since it was a tornado, for Pete's sake," replied Buck.

"I see. Any witnesses?" asked Little.

"Yes, my wife and three kids and two dogs were down there with me," answered Buck.

Little was determined to make some relevant point although he couldn't, for the life of him, figure out what that point might be. He shuffled the index cards again. He had done this so often that several of them were now facing different directions, some stacked vertically and some horizontally.

"Did you see anything suspicious?" asked Little.

"Well, now that you ask, before we went down there, some of our chickens started clucking more than usual for that time of day. And they produced twice the number of eggs that morning." replied Buck, scratching his head.

"Objection, relevancy," interrupted Blount.

"Any further witnesses, Mr. Little?" asked the judge.

Little shuffled his deck of index cards and replied, "No, not at this time. The defense reserves the right to call somebody else later if I decide I want to."

"Very well. You may proceed, Mr. Blount," ordered the judge.

"I now introduce the sales receipt from Moraney Hardware that shows Mr. Peck purchased an incorrect mixture of sand and gravel, which produced an inferior grade of concrete," said Blount.

"Objection, Your Honor," shouted Little, now waving his last clean handkerchief in is air. "What does gravel have to do with this?" He concluded with a phrase from one of his index cards, "*Vis to wit*" ("As can be seen").

"Good grief," murmured Blount under his breath. "Your Honor, I believe establishing that Mr. Peck might have cut corners in his sand and gravel mixture would support the idea that the collapse of the gymnasium wall could be attributed to using incorrect materials, a substandard mix of materials bought according to Mr. Peck's personal specifications."

"Sustained. Let's move this along," said the judge.

"No further questions, Your Honor," replied Blount. At this point, Blount had just about given up and was resigned to moving out of this one-horse, two-cow town once he had won this trial. He had never before witnessed such mangled logic or language.

"I'd like to see both of you boys in my chambers, but I don't have any chambers. Please approach the bench," ordered the judge.

As the attorneys walked forward, Judge Bonds said, "Bayless, I'm invocating a habeas corpus to bring forth the victims."

"Your Honor, they are dead," stated the bailiff.

"Well, hellfire and damnation, I had no idea. We've got to put an end to this trial. Bayless, please ask the jury to repair to the room outside but near enough so we can get them back in here when we need to," said Judge Bonds.

The jurors walked in lockstep behind the bailiff, out the main door into the hall outside. These twelve people reflected the makeup of the town—wheat farmers, railroad workers, housewives, and schoolteachers.

"Wait a minute, we haven't had closing arguments," shouted Blount. He murmured, *"Non compos mentis"* ("Not of sound mind"), under his breath.

At the time, Little was making goo-goo eyes at the youngest lady juror, who had a plunging neckline, was wearing high-heeled black patent leather shoes, and was backlit by the fading sunset.

"Oh that's right, bayless, bring them back in. Do continue, Mr. Blount," said Judge Bonds.

Blount paced back and forth in front of the jury members, who were now struggling to stay awake. "What we have here is a clear case of *res ipsa loquitur* (it is as it appears). Mr. Leland Peck designed the gymnasium, specified and bought the lumber and concrete materials, and supervised the crew who built the faulty gymnasium. It collapsed. The girls are dead; he is guilty," concluded Blount.

Gasps from the public viewing area in the balcony were muffled by hand fans rapidly flapping in the muggy air. Covered mouths mumbled about Leland: about the drinking, all the contracts he had been awarded under the table, and the shoddy construction of most of his buildings. But since there was usually at least one tornado every spring that leveled so much property no one knew for sure if shoddy construction was entirely to blame for buildings collapsing; half the time, post-tornado reconstruction was purposely inexpensive because people knew that in a matter of twelve months or so another tornado was likely to rip through town and destroy the property again. However, this was the first instance involving the loss of life. Eyes repeatedly fixed on Daisy. Mildred took Daisy's hand in hers, but the gesture provided little comfort.

"Okay, your turn, Mr. Little," said Judge Bonds.

Addressing the jury, Little stated, "Well, since you have learned the particulars, you will have to agree that Mr. Leland Peck is not at fault. It is Mother Nature on trial here. Simply put, if there hadn't been a tornado, nothing bad would have happened. Quite a rat demonstration." Both of his handkerchiefs were soaked through, and he wrung one out, dripping sweat on the wooden floor in front of the jury.

Little's conclusion made perfect sense to the jurors, who nodded.

Blount made a note on his papers: "*Quod erat demonstrandum*" ("Thus it is proven"). He supposed that was what Little meant.

Judge Bonds bellowed, "I admit I happen to agree with Mr. Blount's position." He stood up and banged the gavel repeatedly on the bench. "I instruct the jurors to acknowledge that there was a tornado and therefore find Mr. Peck guilty."

"*Dementia praecox*" ("Rapid cognitive disintegration"), scribbled Blount on his pad.

Ten minutes later the jury found Leland guilty.

Since the judge had to leave town right away, he held the sentencing at 8:00 the following morning. No one could have anticipated the outcome. Leland Peck was convicted of misuse of public funds resulting in involuntary manslaughter and sentenced to ninety-nine years in prison without parole. Such a harsh sentence had never been given in Enid. Yet the spectators yelled and raised their fists in support of it. Due to shock and despair, Daisy turned as white as the wrist-length gloves she wore, immediately fainted, and was taken straight away to the nearest nervous hospital, in Terrell, Texas, where she remained heavily sedated and unable to come to terms with how this turn of events would impact her standing in the community, her life, and her son Junior's life.

Chapter 2
Weldon (Not So) Christian Camp

 When Daisy had sent Junior away to Weldon Christian Camp, he had just turned seventeen. Ever since he had been a little boy, Daisy had tried to foster a bond between her husband and son, thinking that if Leland would take an interest in Junior's activities, like getting involved in Cub Scouts, that might give him a sense of responsibility to fill the emptiness that led him to drink. Daisy would sometimes ask Leland to take Junior duck hunting. Her worries about gun safety were unfounded because hunting to Leland meant getting outfitted in camouflage gear, putting on waders, tucking his duck call and binoculars into his khaki vest, and climbing up into the duck blind to sip whiskey from his flask until he passed out, after which the honking of a flock of ducks flying overhead would wake him up. No guns were involved.

Two months before the deadly tornado, on the evening of her eighteenth wedding anniversary, Daisy had thumbed through the album containing pictures of her wedding to Leland. She was innocent then, and he had courted her in the sweetest of ways, bringing flowers and candy. Marriage to Leland had seemed her means of getting out of her mother's house. Since her daddy had died in a grain elevator fire, her mother had been alternatively despondent and cruel. Leland wasn't going into the grain business; he had his cap set on construction. Daisy was eager not only to leave home but to have a man who wasn't in the grain business.

Daisy remembered that Leland got completely soused at their wedding. At the time, she had hoped this was just due to nervousness. She had thought Leland would settle down and become responsible once they had children. But she was wrong.

Leland had his Irish daddy's penchant for "the Creature," meaning he stayed drunk every day from about 4:00 pm to whenever he passed out, usually around 1:00 am at home. Sometimes, though, another town drunk would ask Leland to have a nip at the local bar—Carl's Come Drop Inn—and on such occasions Daisy would get furious at him when he would make a fool of himself whooping down Main Street on his way home after midnight, tainting their family reputation in the small town and making Daisy's marriage more difficult.

A year after their wedding, Daisy had given birth to Junior. Over the years, she and Junior had became a sort of team, sticking together during the challenging times when Leland had given them no emotional support or had embarrassed them with his behavior. She constantly struggled with how to protect their only son from the negative influence of Leland's behavior.

Daisy shuddered when she remembered her frequent fights with Leland, always the same scenario. "Leland, goddammit," Daisy would scream, "if you want to get drunk at home, fine. But when you go out acting like a fool in public it hurts our family's good name."

Around the time Daisy planned to send Junior to summer camp to shelter him from Leland's vices, she had pleaded with Leland, "Can't you just please stay sober until I put Junior on the train for summer camp? The next time you throw one on, I'm banishing you from the house, and you're going to have to move out to the hunting cabin, I swear."

But the very next night Leland had tied on another bender. So Daisy confronted him, saying, "In case you haven't noticed, I've got my mother's twelve-inch cast-iron skillet right here. You get out or I'll rearrange your face so's you'll have to walk backward to see where you're going."

That night after Leland passed out, Daisy made a pile of his work clothes and put them in his old Ford truck, banishing him from the house. He left the next morning for the hunting cabin without saying good-bye to Daisy or Junior.

The morning Junior was to board the train for the two-day trip from Enid to Weldon Christian Camp in Kentucky, Daisy had gotten him up early.

"Mama, the train doesn't leave until nine. It's just seven-thirty. Why do we have to get up so early?" Junior had asked.

"Well, son, we need to have a talk before you leave. I want you to understand how important it is for you to leave Enid.

You see, if you stay in the same place you could probably grow up but not out," Daisy had explained.

"What does that mean, Mama?" Junior had asked.

"If you stay here, all you'll ever know is Enid. If you leave, you will see different people, different places, different weather, different food, and all sorts of new things that will make you more experienced. So, for example, if the only place you ever ate at was Jewel's Smokehouse you'd only know how to eat smoked catfish and brisket. Then if you were to go to a fancier place that didn't have smoked catfish and brisket you wouldn't know what to order," Daisy had continued.

"So I'm going away to camp to grow out so's I can know how to order different things for supper?" Junior had queried.

"Yes, that's sort of correct. When you go there, you'll see," Daisy had replied.

Daisy had gone into the kitchen to make a sack lunch with a sandwich and a banana for Junior's train trip. Then she said, "Get your duffel bag, son. I'll start the car."

When they arrived at the station, only five other passengers were waiting to board. One of the men had started a conversation with Daisy after overhearing some remarks she had made to Junior. "I'm off to St. Louis, Mrs. Peck. I lost my job at the mill, so I'm moving on to a city where there's more work. What's that you say? Sure, I'll watch Junior for you, at least till St. Louis. He's headed to camp? Well, that's just fine, young man."

Junior looked around the station. Always before, he had watched the arriving trains with a sense of excitement, wondering what new people might come to Enid. No new people had come in months. Now here he was among a bunch of grown-ups who seemed to know where they were going, although Junior knew nothing about his destination.

"Why didn't Papa come?" Junior asked.

"He had to go away to see about his thumb," Daisy said as she had looked down the track to see if Junior's train was coming.

"His thumb?" Junior asked, perplexed.

"Yes, you know he uses a hammer a lot at work, and he recently hit himself by accident and smashed his thumb," Daisy replied, an explanation that was the best she could think of. She hoped Junior would just accept it.

Then staring at him she added wistfully, "You remind me so much of your papa when we first met. You even sort of look like him, with your sandy brown hair, that dimple in your chin, your greenish hazel eyes twinkly with excitement for each new day, your height and wiry build. Why, he even played music like you do." Daisy recalled the day she had met Leland at the post office. He had been wearing khaki pants and a brown tweed jacket. Now here was Junior on the train platform in khaki pants and a tweed jacket. She hoped and prayed Junior would grow up to look like his papa but have none of the seriously compromised Peck gene pool. "Please, Lord," she prayed, "don't let Junior meet 'the Creature.'"

When Daisy heard the whistle signaling the arrival of Junior's train, she said, "Oh, son, I will miss you something awful," as she handed him the brown bag and a twenty-dollar bill for meals along the way. Since Weldon Christian Camp required all campers to wear a uniform of white cotton T-shirts and navy or white shorts, Junior hadn't needed to take many of his own clothes, just a few pairs of dungarees, underwear, socks, and pajamas. Daisy had also tucked a baseball and glove into Junior's duffel bag.

"Son, when you get there, just remember how good you are in Little League. You've got the best fastball in three counties. They'll have baseball at that camp, and you'll feel right at home," Daisy had said, encouragingly.

"Mama, don't worry. You saw this letter. It says they assigned me a roommate named J. W. Gilmore, who is from Fort Worth. I'm sure they did that on purpose since we are the only two from the Texas area at the camp. All the other boys are from Kentucky, Alabama, and North and South Carolina. I've got my banjo here, and that'll keep me company on the train ride and help me make friends at the camp," Junior replied.

Daisy spoke to the conductor and asked him to look after Junior. The man shook Junior's hand and said, "Just follow me, son, I'll get you settled in. I see you have a day seat."

"What does that mean?" Junior asked.

"No sleeping berth, but the train's not full so you can spread out across the whole seat," the conductor explained.

"Okay. Who are those boys outside the window next to the track?" Junior asked.

"They're not just boys, son. They're both men and boys looking for work. They're called hoboes. It stands for "help our brothers out." They can't afford tickets or food, so they walk along the train tracks, and when we pull into the station they beg for food. The engineer sounds the horn to warn them to clear the tracks and go away, but they have nowhere to go and sometimes hop onto vacant freight cars and ride to the next stop. Since our second stop is St. Louis, a pretty big city, most of the hoboes will hop off there and look for work. Son, you stay away from those hoboes. They can be a bad influence," advised the conductor.

"Yes, sir, I will," Junior promised, trying to understand how not having money could make hoboes so undesirable.

When the train left the station, Junior waved at the hoboes as they ran down the tracks to jump on a freight car, disappearing in the steam from the coal-fired engine. Intrigued by their sense of adventure and clever ways of coping with their lack of resources, Junior thought about going to see the hoboes in the freight car but decided to stay put. He whiled away the time gazing out the window at the unfamiliar scenery, strumming his banjo, and occasionally nodding off. He didn't understand why he had to leave Enid and didn't really want to, but he was better off than those hoboes wandering on the tracks, he reckoned.

When Junior finally arrived at the train station, he was met by the Weldon Christian Camp director, who put Junior's bag in the camp truck and said, "Welcome, my boy."

The man wore a flat straw hat and a bow tie. He was dressed like the ice cream man in Enid, so maybe the camp would be fun, Junior thought.

"We are delighted to have you here with us. I trust your roommate will be to your satisfaction because he is also a southerner—not from the Deep South, mind you, but from Texas—near you people in Oklahoma. I don't believe you people recognize the Confederate flag, do you?" the director said.

"I'm sure that'll be just fine, sir," Junior responded, although he had barely been able to understand the man's slow, sticky molasses drawl and the only flags he knew about were those of Oklahoma and America. Getting into the truck, Junior thought about how far away he was from home. The farthest he had ever been before was thirty miles, at the regional Little League playoffs. Of course his papa hadn't gone, but there had been enough other dads around so he felt safe. As they approached the entrance to the camp, where he saw a white fence marking the perimeter, he realized he had been traveling two full days by train and over an hour by truck and thus was very far from home. Though he was a little apprehensive about the experience, he felt calmer as he saw that the camp was a pretty place and the weather was cooler and more refreshing than at home.

That afternoon Junior met his roommate, J. W. Gilmore, who asked to be called "Dub." He had spent the past two summers at Weldon Christian Camp and knew the ropes.

"Well now, it's mighty nice to meet you. Glad you're here," Dub told Junior. "It's good to have an Okie at Weldon. Most of the other guys are from Alabama, Kentucky, and the Carolinas."

"Thanks," Junior replied, throwing his duffel bag on the empty twin bed he guessed was his.

Sitting on the edge of his bed, dangling his leg over the side, Dub said apologetically, "So I got here a little early, and I'm afraid I took up most of the closet space."

"That's okay. Mama told me we didn't need a lot of extra clothes since we are supposed to wear the same outfits. My stuff will all fit in a drawer just fine," Junior replied.

"I have extra clothes because sometimes my parents come for the weekend and I have to wear khakis and a dress shirt. Gotta be prepared," Dub remarked.

"Oh, I didn't know parents would come visit," Junior said, unpacking.

"Not a lot do, but since I come here every summer and my folks like to get away from the summer heat in Fort Worth they usually come out for a few weeks," Dub explained.

Based on Dub's family pictures hanging on the wall, Junior guessed that his roommate was from one of Fort Worth's most prominent families. There were pictures of his mom and dad next to a fancy car and a group shot of them on a ski slope. There was a third photo, of Dub and his dad holding the horns of a dead deer, with their rifles by their sides. Junior remembered the times his mother had asked his daddy to take him hunting and they just went out to a duck blind and sat around while his daddy sipped whiskey from his flask. Junior had never had any photos of himself with his family. In fact, he and his daddy and mother were seldom in the same room. He could only recall seeing photos of his parents' wedding.

To Junior, Dub seemed sophisticated though very nice. However, Dub wore some peculiar clothes. The camp didn't officially start until the next day, so no one was required to wear the standard camp uniform yet. Dub's shirt had the initials JWG sewn into the fabric, which was very different from the white identification tags that read "Peck," which his mama had sewn onto the back of his shirt collars and waistbands of his pants. Dub was wearing a pink cotton shirt over a green turtleneck T-shirt and a matching striped belt, making Junior wonder why he had on such Eastertime colors. When Dub shook Junior's hand, his grip wasn't especially firm—his hand was soft, and he had a gold ring with lettering on his pinky finger.

Staring at Junior's plaid pearl-snap-button Western shirt, Dub remarked, "Haven't seen one of those in a long time."

"It's new. Mama got me three new ones. Do you like music? I brought my banjo. Do you play the guitar or drums, or something?" Junior said, figuring he needed to get off on the right foot with something that might be familiar to both of them.

"No, I'm tone deaf when it comes to playing anything. Mother made me take piano lessons when I was six, and everyone gave up on me, which was fine with me. Let's hear you play, Junior," Dub replied.

Junior began playing and humming along to "Foggy Mountain Breakdown." Since most of the campers were arriving that day, the doors to all the cabins were all open, and the banjo playing attracted about ten campers moving into cabins adjacent to Junior and Dub's. Junior felt that he was off to a good start. He noticed that many of the boys had gold rings with lettering on their pinky fingers like Dub and wondered if they gave them out at camp.

Junior looked out his window across the common area and said, "Dub, who are all these kids? Why are there so many of them? There were maybe sixteen in my class at home, and there's about two hundred here."

"No, not really. More like eighty. But we're the only Southwest guys. The others are mama's boys from what they call the Deep South," Dub replied.

"Well, I don't know about mama's boys but they sure look different. It's good that we got shirts and shorts all alike because nothing else about me looks like them," Junior remarked.

"You know, Junior, you might let your hair grow out," Dub suggested as he slicked back his hair with some cream from a tube.

"Why?" Junior asked.

"'Cuz you look like you been sick or had lice or something," Dub replied.

"Then I'm wearing that stupid cap from now on," Junior answered, pulling the cap down around his ears.

"Speaking of wearing, what are you gonna wear next Saturday?" Dub asked, trying to imagine what sort of strange getup Junior would have for a social event.

"What's Saturday?" Junior asked.

"Only the most important event of the summer, a mixer with Woodall, our sister camp for girls," Dub explained.

"What's a mixer?" Junior asked.

"You'll see," Dub replied, realizing just how naïve Junior was.

During all this time of Junior's orientation at camp, he had had no inkling of the events transpiring in Enid and the fate of his parents.

When it was time for the mixer at the dance hall on Saturday night, Junior took in the scene. The room was huge. "It's lots bigger than our church meeting room, Dub," commented Junior, trying to adjust to the activities going on. "What are all these girls doing here? They smell good and look good, but why are they here?"

"You're supposed to dance with them," replied Dub, amazed at Junior's lack of sophistication but sympathizing with his need for help.

"What ya mean dance? There's a group of square dancers that come to Enid for the Fall Harvest Festival every year. Those women wear full skirts with stitching on the bottom, and they sort of twirl around with the men while some man stands off to the side telling them what to do next. I don't know how to dance, and there's no man off to the side callin' out the steps. Why do all the guys have on white jackets with black bow ties and all the men carrying around drinks have on white jackets and black bow ties?" said Junior.

"Oh, brother. Just stick beside me, and I'll tell you what to do. First, you need to look at the girls and categorize them, noticing how they are separated into groups based on how they look. The fat ones are the girls whose daddies have all the money. That's the group most of the boys will focus on. But the really skinny ones with no boobs are the best ones to be around. Their daddies don't have money. They are desperate to have someone to dance with. The last group is the blonde girls with big boobs. They are the most popular, but they're not much fun to talk to. Anyway, let's go to the skinny girl group."

"If you say so. In Enid, from behind you can't tell one girl from the next, or even from the front, for that matter. There's only one dress shop in town, so most of the girls wear the same dress, only in different colors and sizes."

Dub, concentrating on the task at hand, told Junior, "Watch me now." Dub approached a mousy-looking girl about five feet two with a nasal drip and said, "Why, hello. You sure have on a nice dress. Do you go to Woodall every summer?"

Having observed Dub's technique, Junior followed suit. He approached a girl with thick glasses and said, "Why, hi. What's your name? I'm Junior."

"Junior what? Junior high," the girl replied, giggling. "When's the last time you had something to eat? And what is wrong with your hair? Were you just in the hospital?" After a while, many of the skinny girls started calling Junior "Ichabod." They were tired of being the most ignored girls at the mixer, and Junior provided an easy target. Nor would any of them dance with him, which might have been a blessing since he didn't know how to dance anyway.

Junior went to the bathroom and looked in the mirror. He thought he looked pretty good in his plaid snap-button Western shirt and bolo tie. He certainly looked as good as he had on the day pictures were taken for his high school annual. So he wondered what was wrong with these Woodall girls. They were mean—not like his friends at home.

Dub watched as Junior continued to be rebuffed by girls through the night. He felt sorry for Junior.

Dub danced with several girls, while Junior stood off to the side hoping to disappear into the woodwork. Nobody was very nice, and each time he tried to talk to a girl she would just giggle.

Finally Junior said, "Dub, we don't have this many girls in Enid, but at least they'll talk to me. These girls are just hateful."

"Come on, Junior. Let's get out of here," replied Dub, deciding he could at least shield Junior from further humiliation.

Since the camp was in Slugville, the heart of baseball country, some of the Weldon campers organized a baseball team to compete with a rival camp some twenty miles away.

"Dub, are you going to the baseball team tryouts?" asked Junior one morning.

"No way. I'm about as athletic as a moose," replied Dub, making Junior laugh. "How about you, Mr. Banjo?"

"I believe I will. I played on a summer team, and I guess I've got a good fastball, or so I'm told," replied Junior.

"Great, I'll come watch," said Dub.

Junior felt confident about the tryouts. After all, he was good at sports, especially baseball. He grabbed his glove and ball, put on his lucky socks, and walked with Dub across the camp commons to the baseball diamond.

After Junior's tryout, the Weldon team captain yelled, "Holy Mother of Christ. Did you see that fastball? I couldn't even see it, it was so fast. Who is that kid?"

"I have no idea. Haven't seen him in any activities or at the dining hall. It's no wonder; if I was that goofy-looking, I'd just hang out in my cabin, too. But if he can throw like that, we ought to give him a chance. Maybe he would look normal, or at least like the rest of us, when he's in uniform," said another team member.

Junior was immediately asked to join the team. After a few weeks of practice, the Weldon Wildcats were scheduled to play their archrivals, the Beavers, from nearby Camp Beaver Lick. The night before the big game, Junior put on the special jersey the team had made for him that said "Banjo" on the back and, feeling happy to belong to the team, fell asleep in it, twitching his throwing arm and dreaming of victory at the big game the next day.

In the morning Junior said, "Wow, Dub. Today's the big day. Gotta find my lucky socks. I bet we can beat those Camp Beaver Lick guys. Practice has been great. I like the coach. He makes me keep a jacket over my pitching shoulder. Kinda special. We even practice game chatter…'Hey, batter, batter, batter.' We practice throwing base to base. Nobody's gonna steal a base off of me."

The game promised to be exciting—there were more spectators than there had been for any other game in years. After Junior took the mound, he struck out the first, second, and third batters. At one point in the second inning, the Weldon Wildcats had two men on base and scored three runs.

As Junior took the mound in the third inning, he noticed some of the skinny Woodall girls from the mixer were in the stands, including, he was sure, the one who had been the most spiteful to him, undermining his self-confidence. He threw a ball that resulted in a center field hit. The crowd booed. An opponent stole a base. They booed again.

"Look at that hayseed Okie," yelled someone from Junior's own dugout. The Beavers scored four hits in the third inning.

When it was Junior's turn at bat, the Beavers' pitcher sized up the situation and exchanged looks with his catcher, arriving at a mutually satisfactory decision on what type of ball to throw. It was a wicked fastball that hit Junior's left elbow so hard he dropped the bat. That got him a walk to first base, which didn't make him feel any better. His arm became swollen and a trickle of blood ran through his fingers. Worst of all, it was his throwing arm.

The fact that nobody seemed to care about Junior's injury, combined with the pain it caused, compromised his pitching ability. Subsequently, he threw his opponents hit after hit, resulting in the Beavers loading the bases inning after inning until they had achieved an 11–3 win over the Weldon Wildcats. The Weldon boys booed loudly, while the girls ridiculed

Junior by chanting, "Ichabod, Ichabod." Junior was humiliated and ran off the field.

Dub clapped Junior on the back and said, "Let's go to our
cabin. I've got some bourbon stashed under my mattress."

As the two walked back to the cabin, Junior felt defeated
and alone, except for Dub. It was as if nobody at the camp
paid attention to him or gave him support unless he had on
his pitcher's glove and threw good fastballs. Feeling invisible,
Junior said, "Dub, I thought I was finally part of a team of
people who appreciated me, and all of a sudden I'm not. My
daddy never played sports, and he sure never played any with
me. But here the others would play sports with me, which
made me happy until today. You have friends and you don't
even play any sports, so what's wrong with me? I'm a good
pitcher; no, I'm a great pitcher, at least most of the time. So
why do you have a bunch of friends and I don't?"

"Simple, really," Dub replied. "I have money. Money from
my daddy's oil wells. My daddy grew up poor, having to
work. He was a golf caddy, manicured the greens, groomed
the clay tennis courts, and whatever else clubs needed. He
was around rich people who treated him like dirt. That is,
until he became a rich man himself by speculating in the oil
business. Then he suddenly had plenty of friends and people
showed him respect."

"But I can't get rich here at Weldon Christian Camp,"
said Junior, feeling a little better at the prospect of perhaps
being able to change his fortune in the future like Dub's dad
had done.

"You can get rich when you get home. We don't need these assholes. We're from the Southwest. We've got oil, and they don't. When I get home, I'm gonna get me some, and you oughta get yourself some oil, too. It's all over Texas and Oklahoma. To hell with them," replied Dub.

When the boys got back to the cabin, Dub put a bandage on Junior's elbow and poured them both three inches of bourbon in paper cups. It warmed Junior and gave him thoughts of belonging and happiness. He wondered what it would be like to have a family that gave him these sorts of feelings.

He picked up the picture of Dub with his dad and the dead deer and remarked, "I used to ask my daddy stuff like: Where do mosquitoes come from? How come all the older ladies don't have husbands? He would never answer. Then one day I made a big list and asked him seven questions in a row. The last one was why dirt dabbers are named that. He just stared at me and left the room. My mama said not to bother him anymore, so I didn't. My daddy never told me anything or made me feel like I belonged or was loved. And now the others here at camp are making me feel the same way."

Dub swirled his bourbon around in his cup, looked out the window, and said, "Junior, someday you'll understand how the types of people who go to this camp have a limited perspective and will live narrow lives. I want you to have a little story about a worm I kept from my high school Latin class. It's here in this envelope. One day you should read it, okay?"

Junior had never felt such a range of emotions. He had gone from hero to leper in just two innings. His mama would not have approved of him having a drink, though the bourbon helped shore up his ego. And she would have beaten the crap out of every one of those girls who had ridiculed him. The events of the day had quickly taught him that admiration from your peers could disappear in an instant and that loyalty and genuine friendships, like the one he had with Dub, are few and far between.

As a result of the events of that day, Junior developed a lifelong hatred of others who thought they had more or were better than him. He had no idea of the challenges that awaited him when he got home to Enid, but he was ready to leave Slugville as soon as he could. His mother had tried to explain the difference between growing up and growing out. It no longer meant anything to him, if it ever had. He just knew he wanted out of that camp. Even if his daddy was the town drunk and his mama was ashamed, at least he had some friends in his school back in Enid.

Then and there he determined that one day he'd show those drawling lily-livered pretty boys, and those stupid skinny girls with no boobs and no money, what he had that they'd never have. He vowed never to feel this low again.

Chapter 3
Wooing Wealth

After the social mixer with Camp Woodall and the disastrous baseball game with the Beavers, Junior was ostracized by everyone at Weldon Christian Camp except Dub, and he wanted to go home. Compounding Junior's feelings of isolation was the fact that he hadn't heard anything from Enid. The first few weeks at camp he had received letters from his mother at mail call, but after that he no longer did. He knew nothing about the so-called "Tornado Trial" that had made his parents outcasts and all but put them out of touch with the world.

At times Dub had tried to ease his mind by suggesting positive reasons for the lack of communication: "Lord, Junior, haven't you been reading the papers?" asked Dub one day. "My folks are too busy to write me about anything except to say that Daddy is making a killing in oil exploration in East Texas. Here's a picture of Daddy with his first well. Hell, Junior, they been finding oil all over the place down there— Oklahoma, Louisiana, Arkansas, just everywhere. The stuff is in people's backyards, water wells...shoot, might even be in the pipes of kitchen sinks. I bet your dad's just been busy building houses for all the new people moving in. Or he's speculating in oil himself. Don't worry, okay? Mother told me to plan a nice trip to Europe or somewhere to celebrate graduation and to ask a friend to go along. How about it?"

"Well, I need to go home to Enid right now. I don't care if I've only been away four weeks. I don't know why, but I think something is going on there, and I have a funny feeling it might not be good," said Junior pensively. Little did he realize how much had been going on in Enid, unaware as he was that his daddy had been given a life sentence and his mother was being held indefinitely in the nervous hospital in Terrell, Texas, making him an orphan, of sorts.

That night Dub had his usual three fingers of bourbon and promptly fell asleep. Junior waited for Dub to snore as he looked out their cabin window for the last time. Then he quietly packed his duffel bag containing his return train ticket, picked up his banjo and the envelope Dub had given him about the worm, and left.

Junior slept in the Slugville Train depot waiting for the train back home. Once he boarded the morning train, he pulled the paper out of the envelope Dub had given him and read:

The Worm Ouroboros

Plato spoke of a self-eating, circular being as the first living thing in the universe. It survived independently of all other creatures. It had the shape of a large serpent or reptile curved in a perfect circle. Its head appeared to be eating its tail. Since it survived on itself, it had no need for eyes because there was nothing outside of it to be seen. No ears, no feet, no hands. Just the serpent who survived by eating itself. No outside food was necessary. Its food was its own waste.

The rest of the words on the paper, which were in Dub's handwriting and appeared to be an excerpt from his diary, read:

Dear Diary,

In the two years I've been here at Weldon, I've learned most of these folks seem like the worm ouroboros. The campers here will stay the same all their lives. They are the sons of men who attended Weldon Christian Camp, as their sons will one day. These guys will all marry women from Woodall, the sister camp, as their fathers did. All the offspring from every generation will go to Weldon or Woodall, and so on and so on. They are stuck in their own circle of life, not needing or wanting other influences. God, these people are awful. This sort of life is the very thing Mother thought I would avoid when she sent me here to Weldon. Why, it's no different from the stupid Junior College in Fort Worth. Everyone there grew up in Rivercrest Heights. The guys all pledged Phi Rho, and the girls were all Tri Kaps. They married each other, bought houses in Rivercrest Heights, and sent their own kids to college to pledge Phi Rho and Tri Kap, round and round year after year after year. What good are they to the outside world? They don't add anything. If and when they get into any kind of trouble, their daddies just bail them out. They're isolated, self-sufficient, self-destructive, self-indulgent, and maybe even morally ignoble.

This made Junior ponder the fact that most folks in Enid also didn't leave when they grew up, and generations of them did the same things. All his friends had grandparents and great-grandparents who were still in Enid. Junior certainly agreed with many of Dub's observations about those at Weldon Christian Camp. Even if he couldn't understand all of his conclusions, it made him feel better to know that Dub didn't think much of the behavior of the Weldon Christian campers, like the ones who had humiliated and ostracized Junior.

As Junior's train approached Enid, he felt a combination of relief and trepidation. He had sent a cable from Slugville and was expecting his mom and dad to meet him. But when he arrived, to his surprise the Baptist preacher was at the depot along with a man in a white coat with blue stitching that spelled "Terrell," the name of the hospital where his mom was being held. The preacher took Junior by the hand and sat him down on a bench. Townspeople hurriedly walked by him with their heads down, as if avoiding him. He was soon to learn that members of his family were now considered pariahs.

"Junior, something terrible has happened. There was an accident. Your daddy had to go to jail. Your mother is in the hospital," explained the preacher.

"What do you mean? Did daddy hurt his thumb again?" asked Junior, naïvely.

"Son, your daddy might get out of jail sometime but not right away. There was a terrible tornado. Two girls were killed, and people thought it was your daddy's fault," said the preacher.

"My daddy can't cause a tornado," objected Junior.

"I know, son, but for now he is in jail. And I'm not sure if you want to go see your mother," replied the preacher.

"Yes, I do," insisted Junior.

The Terrell man drove the three of them across the Texas border and pulled up to a big white building with a security gate. Once in the lobby, the man signed them in then warned Junior, "You might not want to go in there, son. Your mother doesn't feel too good."

"I don't care. I want to see my mama. I didn't hear from her, and I want to know what's going on," insisted Junior.

"Son, she ain't right. Just at the end of the trial when your daddy was convicted and sentenced, right or wrong, your mother fainted, and they brought her here to Terrell. She stayed about a week, and the doctors told her she could leave. When she went home, your daddy wasn't there but in jail, and your mother locked herself in the house for almost a week. She wouldn't answer the door or the phone. People left her food and notes of support, but she all but vanished inside the house," explained the man.

"So, why is she here again?" asked Junior.

"You see, since she didn't have your daddy at home and she didn't have you because she had sent you to summer camp, your mother took to sleeping in the train depot. She went there every night for a week. The conductor talked to her, but she wouldn't respond, only sat on one of those hardwood benches in the waiting area, occasionally looking down the track. We figured she was looking for you, Junior. For her own safety, we brought her back to Terrell," said the man.

"I don't understand. I just left a place with no friends, where I was treated like an outcast. And now you're telling me my papa's in jail and my mama's in some strange hospital. So, I'm alone even though I'm home?" asked Junior.

As Junior took all this in and tried to adjust to his circumstances, he heard moans and screams coming from behind the door marked "Private." The lobby smelled like stuff his mother used to do laundry. He was led to a room. When he walked in, he froze as he looked at the person who was supposed to be his mother. Her hair was a tangled gray mess. She was thin, and her eyes, vacant, looked away at something distant. This frightened Junior, but he knew he had to talk to her to find out what was going on.

"Hello, Mother," Junior said, as he tried to make eye contact with her.

"Hello, Mother," said his mother.

"Why are you here? Why aren't you home? Where's Papa?" asked Junior.

"Why are you here? Why aren't you home? Where's Papa?" she repeated.

"This place is awful. I'm going to take you home," said Junior.

"This place is awful. I'm going to take you home," she repeated.

Just then a man in a white coat with a stethoscope entered the room and said, "Junior, it's time for your mother's nap."

His mother said, "Junior, it's time for your mother's nap."

"Oh my God. This is a crazy place!" Junior screamed. As he ran out of the room, he could hear his mother repeating what he had just said.

The doctor came out and said, "Junior, your mother has acute echolalia."

"What the hell is that?" asked Junior.

"It means that for now she wants to talk but can't figure out what to say, so she says the last thing she heard," explained the doctor.

"When is she gonna stop that?" asked Junior.

"We just don't know. Why don't you run along? These nice men who brought you here can take you home," said the doctor.

"I wanna go home. I don't want to see my daddy right now. Maybe never. I realized when I was away that he was no daddy to me. He was just a useless drunk," replied Junior.

At his house, which was strangely quiet and empty, he saw stacks of papers that looked official. There were bank statements, letters from the courthouse, a bunch of bills marked "Overdue," and a big legal-sized piece of paper that was stamped "Foreclosure" in big red letters. Junior finally climbed into his bed for his last night in the house where he grew up. The only sound was the wind rattling the castor bean tree outside his bedroom window, the noise that used to sound like shaking beads in a baby's rattle, lulling him to sleep. But now the rattling beans sounded foreboding, urging him to leave.

He finally fell asleep and awoke around 10:00 the next morning. He sat at the kitchen table and listened to the grandfather clock marking time. He remembered his mama telling him that staying in Enid meant he would grow up but not out. All he wanted now was to get out of town.

After finally understanding the ramifications of what his daddy had done and realizing the condition his mother was in, Junior knew that the smart thing to do would be to invent a new life for himself. He knew that Dub was right about the potential riches in Texas. There was an incredible amount of money to be made there in the oil business. He opened the ball jar where his mother hid her spare money, counted out forty-three dollars, and put the bills in his pocket. He cabled Dub to decline the trip to Europe, using the excuse that his dad had indeed gotten into the oil game and needed Junior to help out. Then Junior took the train to East Texas and planned to get off at Bullard, near the Louisiana border. There he was sure he could escape the shame of his parents' circumstances and create a respectable life in new environs. Remembering how people in Enid now avoided him and how he had been ostracized and humiliated by the campers at Weldon Christian Camp, he vowed he would become accepted, respected, and admired in this new place. Dub was popular, even though he didn't play sports. He had said the reason everyone liked him was because he had money. "Whatever it takes, I'll have money," Junior muttered to himself.

Junior decided to tell people in Bullard that he was an orphaned only child of a prominent Kentucky family who had lost his parents in a fire and that they had left him just enough money for use as a grubstake to start over. He thought it would be easy and fun to make stuff up in order to influence how others perceived him. He also realized that he had better get some sort of identification related to Kentucky since his driver's license was from Oklahoma.

He remembered the first train trip he had taken when the conductor had told him, "Don't leave your train car, and don't talk to those hoboes." Now he would do and say whatever he wanted since there was no one to contradict or admonish him. He would seek his fortune and self-assurance, as well as the admiration of others, through creating the self-image of a prominent and successful man by whatever means.

When Junior disembarked, he felt like he was in another world. He stepped off the platform onto a wooden sidewalk bustling with people. Along the side street were hundreds of wooden oil derricks evenly spaced every five feet or so, tall, rigid, and straight, as if marching into town. Beyond them, about thirty feet out and looking like a field of iron grasshoppers, were clusters of pump jacks bobbing up and down, sucking out oil from wells. The smell was obnoxious, reminding Junior of rotten eggs, or the time his family had cleaned out the septic tank. The air made his eyes sting. He could see where buildings had been torn down and wood stacked nearby to build more derricks. Wide pine planks had been placed across the main street, stretching from wood-slatted sidewalks on either side, anchored on top of paint cans. This makeshift platform was perched above the impassable, deeply rutted orange oxide clay ooze that had once been Main Street.

The arrival of so many new people bringing wagons and trucks loaded with drilling pipe, bits, and other equipment had torn up the street. The oil equipment suppliers numbered in the hundreds, as did the camp followers. Saloons had sprung up like weeds. There were Model Ts and old Dodge motorcars stuck up to their wheel wells in mud, abandoned, trapped like flies on fly paper. Junior saw two mule-drawn flatbeds loaded with pine planks struggling through the mud and spurred on by the driver's whip, their cargo destined to become more derricks, he guessed.

Junior spotted a sign in front of a two-story building that read: "Arlene Hotel. Rooms for an hour, a day, a night, or longer." He pushed his way into the lobby. Inside, it was like an anthill someone had poked with a stick. Dozens of people were waving their arms in the air, yelling and running around.

Pressing on toward the left of the bar, Junior spotted a handmade sign that read: "Check in." As he approached the desk clerk, he asked, "What's going on? Is it like this every day?"

"Yep. It's been nuts here since that well came in last year," said the clerk. "These people all showed up seems like over-night. We used to have the occasional traveling salesman here, but now the place is thick with strangers. Anybody with an extra bed or cot can make money putting these wildcatters up. Why, they even have to run all the squatters out of the church to disinfect it on Saturday so it can be safe and clean for Sunday services. Look at them. They're exchanging pieces of paper supposed to be legal contracts for acres where they can drill. I actually saw the same acre change hands three times in one hour, and the price just goes up and up. These men are leasing and buying acreage they've never even seen. Why, there's more land traded than even exists."

"So somebody's not telling the truth?" Junior commented.

"Almost no one is. They just come and go. The flashiest, best-dressed ones seem to last the longest, but none of them sticks around for very long. As they say in the animal world, only the strong survive," replied the clerk.

Wow, this is very different from Weldon Christian Camp, thought Junior. None of those kids ever broke out on their own or took a different path. Here everyone breaks out on their own, and who knows if they even have family to support them. Hell, that describes me.

The desk clerk interrupted Junior's thoughts, asking, "How many nights you need here, son?"

"How about a month," replied Junior.

"Sounds good. Give me ten dollars down and the rest at the end of each week," said the clerk.

Junior was parched and needed to get some air even if it did smell bad. But after being outside for ten minutes, he had to escape the stench, so he stepped inside a saloon.

"What'll it be?" said the barkeep.

"Uh, how about three fingers of bourbon?" Junior replied, remembering what Dub drank in his room at Weldon Christian Camp.

"Say, what do you make of all this hubbub?" Junior asked the stranger next to him at the bar.

"Listen, kid, this is the biggest thing since Spindletop in 1901, thirty years ago it was. All them shysters and wildcatters moved twenty-five miles north, up here to Bullard. The place is crawlin' with thieves," said the man.

"What's Spindletop?" asked Junior.

"The first oil well in the whole state. It's in Beaumont, and they found it almost thirty-five years ago. You want the story, go over to the courthouse. There you'll see throngs of folks trying to file papers and nefariously claiming to own mineral rights to our land around here. Son, it's crazy. Watch out. See those gals over there? They're ladies of the night," continued the man.

"But it's the middle of the day," replied Junior, naively.

"Son, watch your wallet," advised the man.

Smells from the ladies' perfume mixed with those of oily sweaty men in overalls and cigarette and cigar smoke. .

"Just how much oil you got here?" Junior asked a big fat man with a cigar in the corner of the room.

"Dunno'. They're finding it too fast to keep count. They're trying to keep up on it over at the courthouse," said the stranger.

Junior paid up and elbowed his way through the outside crowds into the Smith County Courthouse, where the pushing and shoving continued. On the back wall, there was a photograph of a well spewing 150 feet straight up through the derrick into a clear cloudless sky. The inscription read: "Spindletop Well Comes In. January 5, 1901. Beaumont, Texas." Below the photograph was a glass case with bits of pipe, a core sample of the bore hole, and several yellowed newspaper articles. Junior read:

Beaumont Examiner, Voice of East Texas
January 1, 1901
Oil Exploration Sputters Along

According to Mr. James Lucas, the chief wildcatter and foreman on the new speculative oil well play on Spindletop Hill, there's not much time left. "We're operating on a wing and a prayer....We took a flier on a new rotary-type bit—an Acme Sucker Rod. At 250 feet we hit quicksand. With the new bit, we could pump a water-clay mixture in there to keep the bore hole open. The next time we got to 575 feet, 70 feet deeper than the first attempt. We have enough money and pipe for the crew to go maybe to 1,100 feet, and then we're flat broke," he reported.

In another newspaper article, James Lucas, the well foreman, gave his firsthand account:

Beaumont Examiner, Voice of East Texas
January 5, 1901
Finally the Big Gusher

"At 1,000 feet the pipe lodged on some sort of ledge. The men worked it up and down to break it loose.

Just then mud started to bubble up on top of that hole. There came a roar out of the ground, and it began to shake. I yelled, 'Get out, boys, get out!' All them roughnecks ran for their lives. Then six inches of four-inch drilling pipe came shooting up out of the ground. Things got quiet. All you could hear were the crickets in the pine needles. The sulfur smell was overwhelming. Like stinking eggs. Five minutes later more mud spewed out of that hole, then gas come up, creating wavy images near the ground like heat on a tar road. Next the hole spewed a stream of crude oil over 150 feet high. The sound was deafening. It darkened the morning sky. We all screamed, 'Let her rip. Let her rip!'"

The photograph accompanying the article showed the roughnecks and Lucas covered in a thick dark gooey sludge, unable to see even each other. The scene reminded Junior of a photograph in an issue of *National Geographic* featuring natives in Brazil dancing ritualistically around a campfire. But, as he soon discovered, there was a difference: the yield of 90,000 barrels of crude oil per day had made Mr. Lucas and his investors $40 million richer overnight.

Now that he had read some history about the place, Junior went back to the Arlene Hotel for a nap. But sleep was impossible. His sheets were sticky with humidity, and no one had vacuumed the carpet or cleaned the bathroom for a long time. The continuous noise of the clanking chains on exploratory derricks and the pump jacks bobbing, pulsing, and sucking up the oil kept him awake.

At night, makeshift strings of lights wound around the derricks cast a yellow glow so the roughnecks could continually watch the pipe and drill bit and change it out when needed. There were twenty-foot flares in the distance every thirty feet or so, burning off the natural gas seeping up near the bore hole intermittently between the streams of crude oil. The smell was nauseating, and the heat and humidity stifling. It reminded Junior of gasoline fumes from a lawnmower. The entire scene gave the effect of a state fair midway. All that was missing was the bark of the carneys hawking the arcade games, calliope music, a knife thrower, a fat lady, and some midgets to make this place a fairground from hell.

After a fitful night's sleep at the Arlene Hotel, Junior woke up with visions of wealth. He knew he could make a fortune here in oil. His mind flashed back to the stuck-up Weldon Christian Camp boys. He would make those campers look like poor church mice. After all, his own papa had made good money and he was incapacitated most of the time. Seemed like these wildcatters stayed incapacitated, too.

Junior went to the bar every afternoon, ordered bitters and soda, and sat for hours taking in the activity. Regardless of the time of day, the bar was packed. He wondered how the wildcatters made any money since they spent so much time in the bar with one another. They were similar to the Weldon Campers Dub had described who lived in their own world, not knowing or caring what went on outside, self-propagating in their own circle of life like the worm ouroboros. What the hell, thought Junior. I'll create my own circle. I'll find a wife, make a bunch of money, and give it to our kids so they can turn around and give it to their kids.

He began to make a plan. Since all the riches in Bullard were from oil and there was plenty to go around now though maybe not forever, Junior figured he'd also better find something else to do to make money if and when the oil ran out. He wrote out a to-do list on his cocktail napkin:

1. Get new identification
2. Find oil
3. Make money
4. Find a wife and have some kids
5. Find something else to do
6. Make more money
7. Repeat steps 5 and 6

After settling on a plan, Junior slept soundly for the first time since his arrival in Bullard.

At 7:30 the next morning he went down to the lobby for a cup of coffee. The only signs remaining from the hubbub the night before were the stench of cigar smoke and the empty whiskey glasses stuck to the tops of the tables. The only other soul awake was the front desk clerk.

"Say, what was Bullard like before all this excitement?" Junior asked the clerk.

The man shook his head as if to remove the cobwebs and replied, "Before all the oil? It's kinda hard to remember when things weren't turned so upside down. It was a sleepy town of maybe twelve hundred people, with the only trade coming in on the Sabine River docks."

"So who were the most important families?" asked Junior.

"There were really just two. The Teasles, who own the only dry goods store—Pop Teasle, his wife Iota Mae, and the two boys, Talford and Tim. That Talford, he's a different breed of cat," said the clerk.

"And the other family?" prompted Junior.

"Oh, that's the Mullins. I expect they are the richest people here. Mr. Mullin owns the lumberyard. He and his wife have one daughter, Priss. That's all they could have, and that's probably lucky. She ain't no prize," continued the clerk.

Junior's ears pricked up. "Are the Mullins still around?" he asked.

"Yep, but Mr. Mullin don't have much of a lumber business anymore. All his help quit on him to go roughneck, and most of his lumber was bought up for derricks. He still owns the majority of the pine tree forests around here, but there's nobody over there at his mill except Mr. Mullin. He's a good decent man, but people can make more money roughneckin'," explained the clerk.

"You reckon this Mr. Mullin is at the lumberyard now?" asked Junior.

"No, the Mullins are out of town. They went to their cabin at Lake of the Ozarks in Arkansas to get out of the heat, relax, and do a little fishin'. Be back Tuesday," said the clerk.

Armed with a little information, Junior asked about the location of Mr. Mullin's lumberyard and strolled over for a visit. Giant lathe machines sat idle amidst piles of sawdust. With the rate new derricks were going up and the time it took for the metal pipes to arrive by rail, Junior figured lumber planks for derricks would sell at a premium. Junior had the idea that getting in good with Mr. Mullin might help him in the long run since he had not only a solid business that didn't rely solely on oil but also lots of money and a daughter who might be useful in implementing his seven-step plan.

Since the Mullins were out of town, Junior decided to use the time to research the family. He spent days at the newspaper office poring over records. He discovered that Mr. Mullin had inherited his lumber from his father. There was a photo of the two men—shaking hands when the ownership had been transferred—near Mrs. Mullin with a baby girl. The photo caption read: "Next generation of Mullins keeps lumber business flourishing, guarantees economic health of Bullard." Well, if that ain't something, Junior thought. In this family, he saw again a closed circle of life perpetuated through generations and wondered what it would be like to be part of it. He took out the seven-point list from his pocket and read aloud point four—"Find a wife."

At night he would go to the local tavern to mix with the men, who reminded him of his father—absent most of the time, drunk, and useless. Junior continued to order soda water and bitters, making it look like he was drinking as much whiskey as the others, so he could blend in without getting drunk. He figured out that the more the men at the bar drank, the more they talked. Conveniently, the man who drank the most was the newspaper editor, so Junior befriended him.

"You must know an awful lot about Bullard before the oil discoveries and now," said Junior.

"Yes, son. Nobody can trust nobody around here. Even the old-timers aren't safe. Why, everyone was distraught when our oldest citizen, a nice widow lady named Vicey Woolsworth, passed on. Some of those newcomers made up the paperwork and just plain took her land, drilled on it, and hit," reported the editor.

"That's awful," replied Junior, aghast at the fate of the old lady but making a mental note of her name in case it might be useful in the future.

"There's lots more. Just go over to the Records Department at the courthouse and you'll see," said the editor.

Junior continued his research at the newspaper office until he felt he had sufficient information about Mr. Mullin's business. Then he went to the high school and looked up Priss Mullin in the annual. The desk clerk had been right: she was not a pretty sight. She was a member of Future Homemakers of America, United Daughters of the Confederacy, and State Choir. There was only one photo of her besides the class picture: it showed her winning the pie contest at the state fair. Well, at least she can cook, Junior figured. Hmm, an ugly only daughter with a rich daddy. That rings a bell—like one of the groups of girls from Camp Woodall, thought Junior.

Back at the hotel, he asked the desk clerk, "Just how big is the lumber business here?"

"Let's put it this way, since the Mullins own the only lumberyard in a three-county area, they provide all the lumber for any construction that goes on. It's a huge moneymaker, and that's why Mr. Mullin decided not to get into the oil fracas. He's got plenty of money in the bank already."

"I think I'll go see Mr. Mullin. You say he will be back tomorrow?" said Junior.

Unbeknownst to Junior, the hotel clerk was in cahoots with Mr. Mullin and immediately called the lumberyard after Junior left, saying, "Sir, I'm sending over another candidate."

Mr. Mullin had made an arrangement with the hotel clerk because he realized the need to take a proactive stance if he was to ever get his daughter married off. He had instructed the clerk to assess any young man who came looking for a room and find out a little about his background. If the young man passed muster, he was to suggest that the "candidate" go see Mr. Mullin for a job to build a grubstake while waiting for the right opportunity to get in the oil game.

When he left the hotel, Junior took his banjo, figuring that since Priss was in a choir maybe it could come in handy. As he approached Mr. Mullin's lumberyard, it looked deserted except for a man in a suit coat smoking a pipe and staring at a pile of sawdust.

"I'm looking for Mr. Mullin," said Junior.

"I'm Mr. Mullin. What's the nature of your visit here, son?" asked Mr. Mullin.

"Mr. Mullin, I'm Junior Peck. I'm here for work," said Junior.

"Is that right? What makes you think I got any work?" replied Mr. Mullin.

"A successful man like you must have some work. I saw a map one time that showed Bullard in the middle of a pine tree forest with elms and other kinds of trees. People need lumber for all sorts of reasons, and you have the only lumberyard," reasoned Junior.

"What kind of work do you do, young man?" inquired Mr. Mullin.

"May I sit down, Mr. Mullin?" asked Junior.

"Sure. What's wrong?" asked Mr. Mullin.

"I'm just in a bad way. You see, sir, I grew up in Kentucky, and my mama and daddy farmed mostly. Then last month the most horrible thing happened." Junior began to choke up. "There was a huge fire. The Volunteer Fire Department was called out to the Indian Reservation for some sweat lodge problem and couldn't get to our farm in time to save it. It just plumb burned down to the ground. Papa got burned real bad. Mama told me I needed to get a job, but there weren't any. My uncle told us we had a rich aunt named Vicey Woolsworth in Bullard, so I used up all our money and took the train here last week. I can't find anybody named Vicey Woolsworth. I'm in a real pickle. I don't know anything about this oil stuff, and I think I might be too late anyway," said Junior, breaking down and sobbing.

"There, there, son. Miss Woolsworth died eight months ago, and the wildcatters grabbed up all her land. Let me think. Come into my office. I guess I could use some help. Lookie there, my old guard dog likes you. He doesn't usually take to strangers," said Mr. Mullin. The dog sidled up to Junior, who had had the foresight before leaving the hotel to put a piece of cracker in his pocket in case a dog presented a problem.

"I guess you could help me with the sawdust situation," continued Mr. Mullin.

"What's the sawdust situation?" asked Junior, wiping the snot from his nose on his shirt cuff.

"We got piles and piles of sawdust left over from making finished wood products like roof shingles, two-by-fours for fence pickets, and lately a lot of oil derricks. They are a serious fire hazard," explained Mr. Mullin.

"We used to use wood shavings in the stalls in our barn. It soaked up horse pee. Maybe farmers would buy it to soak up pee," suggested Junior.

"Son, that's brilliant. We could sell it to the oil field people to soak up oil spills before they cap off wells. With a mind like that, I'm sure we could figure out some way to use you, Junior," said Mr. Mullin. Of all the possible suitors for his daughter Priss, this Junior kid seemed to have the most promise. He was nice looking, well-mannered, and smart, thought Mr. Mullin. Junior, too, had more than horse pee, oil spills, and sawdust on his mind. He hoped that Mr. Mullin would eventually see in him the son he had never had.

Later Mr. Mullin asked Junior to come home with him for dinner.

"Well, who is this vision?" began Junior when he first saw her sitting on a bench in her hydrangea garden. As he had noticed from her high school photo, Priss wasn't exactly nice looking or trim or stylish. What she was, though, was the only child of a wealthy man and not taken.

Priss had a fondness for her hydrangea garden because it was the custom of the day for suitors to give hydrangeas to their sweethearts to wear as wrist flowers and since she had no suitors her hydrangea garden was a compensation. Once she had thought she had a suitor. At the Sure Save grocery store, before it was turned into a prison, there had been an especially handsome checkout boy named Eric, who had always signed her register tape after she checked out, showing he cared for her, she thought. Sometimes she would forget to buy something on her list on purpose so she could go back through the line and get him to sign again, and she saved all the checkout receipts. But then, after her mama explained that the bag boys had to sign the checkout register tapes in case there was a problem with the order or someone had to return an item such as spoiled milk, Priss retreated back into her hydrangea garden.

Junior took off his cap and looked at Priss. She blushed and asked his name and if he was new in town. Then she asked him a bunch of questions about where he was from. He repeated the tale he had told Mr. Mullin.

After the two talked awhile, Junior realized that Priss was uncommonly smart, though not much of a conversationalist. She then asked him what his favorite books were. The only one he could think of was *Huckleberry Finn*, so he told her and immediately asked her the same question to avoid having to think up the name of another book.

"I just finished rereading *The Black Stallion*," replied Priss. "I love horses, don't you? Oh, and I liked *The Mystery at the Moss-Covered Mansion*. Last weekend I read one of Mother's books. It was a play called *Blithe Spirit* about a man whose first wife came back from the dead to haunt him and his second wife…Are you listening to me, Junior?"

He couldn't get a word in edgewise and figured he needed to find a library to read some of the books Priss was talking about. He then asked, "What's your favorite song?"

"'You Are My Sunshine,'" she replied.

"Oh, let me play that for you," he insisted, picking up his banjo.

At the end of the song, Priss clapped. She told him her mother wanted her to go away to school, that she could go to any of the eastern women's colleges—Smith, Wellesley, or, closer to home, Sophie Newcomb—but she didn't want to. Instead, she wanted to make a home with a husband and have children. She said her daddy was dedicated to fulfilling her wishes, and that he needed a male heir, a grandson to take over his lumber business and other holdings.

Mr. and Mrs. Mullin were delighted that Junior was polite and nice to Priss, thinking he just might eliminate the problem of Priss's potential spinsterhood. Junior was the third "candidate" the clerk had sent over in the last three months and, to date, certainly the most promising.

For his part, Junior reckoned he would make a little money and get established as respectable in Bullard then possibly marry Priss. She would have a substantial amount of money, which alone would make up for her less-than-attractive body. His plan was to flirt a little with her in the beginning, weasel his way into the good graces of her father and mother, and then, if he could stand it, marry her. He thought he had a fair amount of time as she currently didn't have any suitors and probably wouldn't. To Junior, Mr. Mullin seemed like a really nice man with whom he could talk more easily than he could to his own father, and Mrs. Mullin reminded him of his mother, the way she looked after Priss, always complimenting her and supporting her. It was the first time in a long time that Junior had given any thought to belonging to a family.

Junior soon settled into Mr. Mullin's lumber company as a grunt. He oversaw loading the few trucks, swept up and bagged the sawdust to sell to the oil men, and, in general, wasn't challenged at all. He was surrounded by men making huge amounts of money in oil. Many of the newcomers seemed to effortlessly make millions by hitting oil and even more by selling their leases to big oil companies from the East Coast, like Standard Oil. While the Mullin family provided Junior with a sense of belonging and stability, he longed to try for oil riches and be out from under Mr. Mullin's rule. He felt like he was making progress on his goal to "find a wife" but not much on his goals to "find oil" or to "make money." Something had to change.

One Friday Junior waited until the last truck had left the yard, approached Mr. Mullin, and said, "I am so happy to have this job and that you are all so kind to me. Why, I don't know what I'd do without your support. I have so many ideas for helping. You know, it takes an awful long time for metal pipes to come in by rail to make derricks. You could supply wood planks right away and maybe even charge a premium. I'd be happy to drive around and sell wood to the wildcatters."

"Great idea, son," said Mr. Mullin.

"Oh, you called me son. No one's called me son since I left Kentucky. That word is like honeysuckle to my ears. I just wish I could give your daughter more right away. She makes me so happy, and I want to do the same for her. But I'm not in a position to do that, sir. I really need to make more money to provide her with what she deserves. I'm not asking you for a raise or anything, Mr. Mullin. Just a chance to get my feet wet in this oil game." Junior explained that he really wanted to make a significant amount of money, and if Mr. Mullin would just sponsor him in the oil business he would pay him back certainly within a year. Then he remarked, "I see the store windows, and I see the nice dresses some of the women wear around here, especially Mrs. Mullin. Oh, how you keep her spoiled with fine things. I want the chance to do that for

Priss. I want to be worthy of her love and devotion." I want her to stop wearing baggy clothes, too, thought Junior.

Mr. Mullin was aware that with Priss now in her early twenties, time was not her friend. He thought he'd give Junior a chance. The kid was seemingly intelligent, honest, and a hard worker who had just had a run of awful luck. He deserved an opportunity to strike out on his own. He would probably make a great daddy, and it was high time Priss gave him a grandbaby, hopefully a boy. Consequently, Mr. Mullin gave Junior a grubstake of $3,000.

Over the next year, Junior sold and resold prospective oil property using a scam he had learned from hanging out at the local bar night after night. Underneath the land of unsuspecting cotton farmers were huge deposits of oil. Due to the downturn in the economy during the war plus the recent boll weevil infestation, many of these farmers were nearly destitute. When offered good money to sell or lease their acreage to wildcatters to prospect for oil, they were quick to sign, regardless of the reason.

Junior anticipated that the leasing scam would bring easy pickings. He figured the farmers would want to work with him instead of out-of-towners. His papa hadn't told him much, but he had said, "Junior, people want to work with their own kind. You remember that. Look people in the eye, and call them by name. Even a dog likes to be called by his name." All that mattered to his papa was getting contracts, not doing quality construction. He would say, "After you catch a fish, it gets stinky. The fun is in the catching." Junior decided he would concentrate on "catching" farmers and not think about the aftermath, just like his papa.

In preparation for his foray into the leasing venture, Junior got a topographical map and went to the county courthouse to make a list of who owned what property, including the mineral rights. He then drove around the countryside, stopping whenever he saw a farmer working his field as marked on the map. Junior would saunter over to the man and begin his spiel: "I see you have a parcel for sale for fifteen dollars. It's been for sale for about five months, is that right?"

The man would say something like, "Yep. Them oil men have come in here and are finding oil all around my prop-ty. I reckon they don't think my prop-ty has any oil, and we're just about bust on cotton."

Then Junior would respond, "Yes, isn't it a shame? You know farming cotton probably contaminated the underground water table. I reckon you thought you might have oil under there, but maybe you didn't know what cotton farming does to any oil there might have been. It just plain ruins it. However, my company, Mertz Cotton, thinks cotton will come back. We are prepared to lease your acreage for twenty-five dollars."

Finally persuaded, the man would reply, "Stop right now. Gimme the money."

Junior invariably replied, "All right, sir. Sign right here." Junior would lease the property, including the mineral rights to whatever riches lay beneath the unsuspecting cotton farmer's land. He would then turn around and lease the same property to a wildcatter for $100 plus retain a percentage of the profit if the well hit. This soon escalated to leasing property for $200, and re-leasing it for upward of $500 per tract. Eventually, though, as word got out among the farmers, most smartened up and began to deal directly with the big oil companies.

Through swindling the cotton farmers, Junior's confidence in his ability to make money had grown. He regularly visited Priss and was convinced she could be his meal ticket if and when his income from leasing land from cotton farmers dried up. In their courtship conduct, the two were like the blind leading the blind. Junior had never dated anyone and was painfully shy around her, based in part on his experience at Weldon Christian Camp. And since Priss had never had a suitor either, at least neither one could recognize the inadequacies in their courtship ritual.

One day Junior practiced playing "You Are My Sunshine" as he prepared to visit Priss, an activity that calmed him down and built his confidence. Once they were together, Junior said, "Priss, how are you this fine morning? I've brought you a lanyard I made at summer camp. I saved it for the right moment and the right place."

"Junior, how thoughtful. How did you know blue and yellow are my favorite colors?" asked Priss.

"I didn't know, but they are the colors of your pretty hydrangeas," Junior replied.

Again Mrs. Mullin asked Junior to stay for dinner, and he mustered up as much charm as he could, which was a lot.

Noticing Priss had put on some makeup and perfume, he remarked, "Priss, you look so lovely with a little sun on your face, and your flowers never looked better."

Priss's eyes turned downward and then toward her mother as she asked, "Did you see this pretty lanyard Junior made me?"

Junior looked at Priss then at Mr. and Mrs. Mullin, thinking that he was getting a lot of mileage out of those strings of plastic and that makeup helped Priss look better, a little like her mother.

"Oh, I just wish it were made of silver or gold," Junior said, gulping down some sweet tea.

After dinner, Junior asked Priss to go for a walk. As they strolled hand in hand, Junior remarked, "Priss, I'm finally making a little money. Not much compared to your father, mind you, but a little. I do hope you'll be patient with me. I've got to leave town for a while for business. If I can't do better for you, I don't deserve you."

"Oh, of course you do. Mama and Daddy think you're just swell. And me, too. Don't stay away long, promise me," she insisted.

"May I have a kiss to sustain me, Priss?" Junior asked.

"Of course, but don't tell Mama and Daddy," replied Priss as she kissed him. Junior left, walking backward and waving to Priss as she blew him more kisses.

Chapter 4
The Gulf Coast Cares Caper

 Since the cotton farmers now refused to deal with Junior, he had to move beyond Texas. He traveled into Louisiana and pulled the leasing scam again and again. After his rope began to run out in Louisiana, he traveled on to his next target, Alabama. Junior figured that his papa hadn't cared what happened after he finished a construction job, so why should Junior care about stupid cotton farmers?

In mid-July, the hottest and most humid time of year for the Gulf Coast region, Junior holed up in a flimsy fleabag motel in Gulf Shores, Alabama, along with migrant workers up from Mexico to harvest peaches and cotton. He realized the leasing scam wouldn't work as well in Alabama because oil was not as plentiful and that he needed to devise another plan. One morning, after tossing and turning all night listening to a raging rainstorm, Junior was awakened by the night desk clerk coming off his shift, who said, "Say, are you staying long? We just got hit with a really bad hurricane that came ashore about fifteen miles from here, and we need all the rooms we can get for the locals who lost their homes. I already sent the migrants away since there's no peaches or cotton left for them to harvest."

"Yes, I believe I'll stay," answered Junior as he pulled on his blue denim pants and plaid work shirt on his way out to assess the damage, already wondering if there might be a way he could profit from the catastrophe.

When Junior arrived at the site he saw a kind of destruction that was incomprehensible. Buildings and homes had been leveled and were under water. Several of the townspeople gathered on the hill overlooking the area with Junior. Displaced families had been moved into temporary quarters in school classrooms with as many as five children each and their dogs. The people of Gulf Shores would likely never be able to return to their former lives. Looting by the displaced migrants was rampant. The Alabama governor, Bibb Graves, had declared a state of emergency and requested they receive assistance from President Roosevelt. Roosevelt had allocated $100,000 in relief funds. The problem was that no one knew exactly how to go about reclaiming the town of Gulf Shores or how to appropriate the funds.

Since there was money to be made in the confusion and no concrete plan in pace, Junior devised a new scheme. He created a fictitious company, Gulf Coast Cares, then found a plot of land untouched by the hurricane, two fenced-in acres thirty minutes north of Gulf Shores, called the real estate company that listed the two acres, and said, "Sir, I'm prepared to offer you cash to lease that land out there."

"What for?" asked the company representative.

"As long as I got cash, I don't see how it's any of your business. So if you're not interested, just say so," replied Junior.

"No, no. I'm interested, but you can't build a house or anything on that property. It's not zoned residential, so nobody can live there," the representative informed Junior.

"Who the hell would want to live there?" asked Junior in disbelief.

Subsequently, Junior leased the land for one month. This was odd, thought the owner, but since Junior had paid cash up front and nobody had extra cash after the hurricane he didn't care. Junior tied a small hand-lettered sign that read "Gulf Coast Cares" to the fence. Then he leased five big earth-moving trucks from the local Caterpillar dealer, equipment that had been spared damage since it had been in a warehouse on high ground. He explained he was under state contract to provide relief from the hurricane damage. He had dummied up some paperwork on state letterhead he took while making an appointment with Bibb Graves, so the dealer thought nothing of it. Junior then had the earth-moving equipment delivered to the fenced land he had leased.

Next Junior met with Governor Graves. He carried a Bible and asked the governor to pray over the situation with him. "Pray with me now, Governor Graves. Do you have a Bible?" asked Junior.

"Why, yes. Right here by the picture of the missus, Miriam, and our twins Cletus and Yura Mae. Let me hold their picture as we kneel," answered the governor.

The Graves family photograph had been taken in front of a painted backdrop of a shrimp boat and what appeared to be two dolphins leaping in an arc behind it. Bless their hearts, thought Junior. You couldn't tell Yura Mae from Cletus, as they both had severe buck teeth and jug ears. There must be something strange in the Graves's backyard woodpile. This could be another type of ouroboros family as they look a little inbred. Eying the framed documents behind Governor Graves's desk, Junior was amazed to see a familiar-looking emblem.

"Did you go to Weldon Christian Camp?" Junior asked.

"That's right, I did, son, and so did my daddy. And young Cletus here will attend next year," he replied, pointing to the family photo.

"Isn't that somethin'," said Junior. "I did, too. Certain parts of Alabama remind me of Weldon."

"How's that?" asked Governor Graves.

"Everyone's so friendly and honest. You know, just wanting to help each other out, " said Junior, remembering the hypocritical two-faced campers. The fact that Governor Graves had gone to Weldon as well as his family seemed to reflect some of the principles Dub had identified as being like a worm ouroboros in their repetition of behavior through generations made Junior think he might especially enjoy an opportunity to scam the governor.

Junior knelt down in front of Governor Graves's desk and motioned for him to join in.

"I have already prayed over this tragedy," said the governor as he knelt with the family photograph clutched to his heart. "I prayed to the Lord to tell me how this wrath came upon us. What wrought this tragedy? I asked for a sign.

Then this morning on my way to the capital, I noticed that the blue-plate special at the Two Over Easy Café was a bean burrito. That's what told me the cause of this disaster. We never had any kind of burrito here before the migrans started coming here about five years ago. They brought nothing but trouble and odd food like burritos. So that was my answer. Letting all those migrans come in on us caused the hurricane. It's a sign that they must leave."

"I know about foreigners intruding on a life," said Junior. "Some people back home caused problems when they came in with the boll weevil. Let me invoke Saint Genevieve in charge of excessive rain to stop the floods and Saint Leonard of Noblac for danger from robbers to keep the migrans from looting. Say, 'Amen.'"

"Amen," said the governor.

By now Junior was feeling very good about the prospect of screwing over a Weldon man. As they rose, Junior produced a five-page document outlining how he would handle the cleanup. It included references to the cheap, fleabag motels that dotted the coastline where the migrants stayed. His company, Gulf Coast Cares, would clean and upgrade these motels right away, and the locals could stay there for the three months he reckoned it would take to restore Gulf Shores to pre-hurricane conditions.

"Let me take you out to our headquarters, governor, and let's discuss how Gulf Coast Cares can put Gulf Shores right again," said Junior. They drove out to the fenced acreage, and Junior waved a sweeping arm toward the lot with the earth-moving equipment. "That is all of Gulf Coast Cares's equipment," Junior continued. In a way, it was true. "We got some offshore-drilling rig workers coming over from New Orleans tomorrow, and we could start restoration by three in the afternoon." That was not true.

But to Governor Graves everything seemed in order, and he was desperate to show his constituents that he was doing something to provide relief. Every morning about twenty locals marched near the capitol steps carrying signs that implored the governor to take action. The entire fishing industry had come to a standstill, and without that Alabama had no other sizable source of state revenue. He had to do something, and Junior's "company" was the only one that had come forward. Desperate, Governor Graves signed a contract with Junior allocating some $50,000 in government funds for Gulf Coast Cares to begin restoration work. The federal funds were coming in a cashier's check from Washington the next day.

"You know, governor, the rig workers are going to want their pay in cash since none is from here and they won't have any bank accounts. Do you think you could see your way to process the government check so I can pay the workers in cash and get going on the restoration immediately?"

"Well, son, I don't see how that could hurt nobody," replied Governor Graves, who had the idea that he himself could use some of that money in cash without anyone being the wiser.

The next morning, within an hour of collecting the agreed upon half of the money for his contract, Junior boarded a train back to Bullard $25,000 in cash richer. As the train came into the Bullard station, Junior started laughing and singing the Weldon Christian Camp spirit song:

> To Weldon, we pledge our hearts
> Forever to be true.
> The friends we made while camping here
> Will last our whole lives through.
> To Kentucky, where the grass is blue
> We pledge our hearts to you.

Chapter 5
The Mr. Alabama Deception

 Immediately after returning from swindling the state of Alabama, Junior checked back into the Arlene Hotel. Now that he had cash, he needed someplace to put it. There were three or four new banks in town that had been established mostly by local businessmen to capitalize on the influx of income from oil. Only one had been founded by an outsider—the Second National Bank of Upper East Texas. Junior wondered about the name, Second instead of First, but he paid a call to it anyway. He preferred to keep his monetary transactions private, away from the prying eyes of the Bullard locals.

"Hello, I'm Elmer Sugton. Welcome to our little bank. Would you like some coffee?" said Mr. Sugton.

Junior noticed that the tables and chairs looked like they had come from a cafeteria.

"No, sir, I don't need any coffee. I need a bank. I don't want a locally owned one. My business activities extend well beyond Bullard, and I need a bank with a more progressive view on the world and a banker who can grow with me," stated Junior.

"Say, ain't you the fellow who owns Mertz Cotton? I understand you bought up a bunch of acreage from cotton farmers for cents on the dollar," remarked Mr. Sugton.

"Well, I did own Mertz Cotton but not anymore. I sold it to some East Coast fellas who didn't know it was too late to get into the oil game. I've moved on, and my most recent business deal was helping restore Gulf Shores, Alabama, after that horrible hurricane. You know, I was awarded a federal contract, and there's no telling how many displaced people I helped," replied Junior, hoping to impress Mr. Sugton.

"Well now, you sound like an enterprising businessman. It's smart to diversify. This oil thing won't last forever," said Mr. Sugton.

"If I open an account here, what sort of paperwork are we talking about, Mr. Sugton? I told you I don't want a local bank meddling in my affairs, if you get my drift," said Junior.

"Why, of course I do, Mr. Peck. We can proceed with only a handshake if you prefer," said Mr. Sugton.

"Okay, I got some cash here to start with," stated Junior.

Mr. Sugton's eyes grew as wide as a full moon when Junior plunked down the $25,000 he had received from Governor Graves in Alabama. "That's a mighty large amount of cash, Mr. Peck," he remarked.

"I don't want any questions, you understand me, Mr. Sugton?" insisted Junior.

"I got ya. I heard about the Mertz Cotton Company. You seem to have a knack for making money, and I have a knack for taking good care of it, if you catch my drift, Mr. Peck. I bet you we'll have a good partnership," replied Mr. Sugton.

"Perfect. Let's call my new account Mr. Alabama, okay? One other thing. I need you to send a check for three hundred dollars on the first of every month to Daisy Peck, Room 157, Terrell Arms, Terrell, Texas," added Junior, gazing out the bank window and thinking he should go see his mother. But what if she was worse? Or, more daunting, what if she was better and blew his cover, destroying the new life he had so cunningly established? No, better to leave her be, he concluded.

Mr. Sugton, aware that the only housing in Terrell was in the state lunatic asylum, said, "Oh, Terrell? Your sister needed to get away?"

"Never mind why, just do as I say," demanded Junior. The two men shook hands on the deal.

Once Junior had his bank account established under a false name, he sauntered over to the Mullins' house and said to Priss, who was out gardening, "Priss, my darling, oh how time away has made you more beautiful. I'm so happy luck brought us together. At last I've found happiness. Ever since I met those snotty girls when I was away at camp, I just haven't cared for girls at all. They were just so hateful and mean. My roommate at camp was a really nice guy named Dub, from Fort Worth. He tried to help me fit in and get dates, but it didn't work. Then when the fire destroyed my childhood home…well, I lost all faith in finding happiness."

Priss stood up and removed her gardening bonnet, wiped her hands on her apron, and smiled as big as one of her prized hydrangeas. "Oh, Junior, all I have in this world are Mama and Daddy and my hydrangea garden, especially since my dachshund got run over last spring. You make me happier than I ever imagined possible."

Mrs. Mullin watched and listened to this exchange out her kitchen window. She had just put a pot roast on for dinner and was making fresh iced tea. She stepped out onto the porch and said, "Oh, my dear boy, it's so nice to see you. You must be parched. Come here, you two. Junior, sit in the shade and let me pour you a sweet tea."

"Oh, no bother for me, Mrs. Mullin. Just the sight of your beautiful daughter wipes away the rigors of the train trip," said Junior. He had watched Dub in action with the girls in Kentucky and picked up a few pointers. Thank God the combined common sense of Mrs. Mullin and Priss was less than a plant, thought Junior. Nevertheless, he still had work to do to keep to his plan of marrying Priss.

After the pot roast dinner, Junior said, "Mrs. Mullin, let me help you with the dishes. Priss, won't you go out on the porch and get out of this miserable heat. Your pretty face is flushed red as a beet." Once Priss plopped down on the swing, Junior began, "Mrs. Mullin, I'd like to get Priss something nice. What size would I get her?"

Eyes downturned, Mrs. Mullin said, "Why, Junior, just get her a nice accessory, maybe a scarf or a bracelet. That way we'll know it will fit. Her weight fluctuates so in this heat."

Wooing Priss was challenging. Junior made up the courtship ritual as he went along. Although Priss treated him just fine, neither he nor she knew what to do next. To shore up his confidence, Junior took to drinking vodka. He chewed gum and smoked cigars to mask the smell of the vodka and to steady his nerves for this new challenge. No one acknowledged that he was half drunk every time he called on Priss. She and her mother and daddy were all too happy to go along with this deception to get her married off. The two continued courting through the summer.

Unbeknownst to Priss or her parents, Junior had started betting on college football and gambling over at casinos on the Louisiana border. He was losing money faster than he was making it, so he had to seal the deal with Priss sooner rather than later. In an effort to step up the time line on his marriage proposal, one Sunday Junior rented a paddleboat, and he and Priss set out across one of the several lakes surrounding Bullard. Junior had the idea that when they returned to the dock after a romantic afternoon on the lake, perhaps he would propose. But when Junior stepped out in the shallow water, he sank five inches or so in mud. As he struggled to gain his balance, he tumbled headfirst into the gooey mud.

"Oh Lord, Junior, are you all right?" asked Priss, jumping out of the paddleboat and getting stuck in the mud next to Junior. Fortunately, the boat rental attendant had witnessed the fiasco and was able to drag them out using his winch truck. They squished their way back to the Mullins' house, where Mr. Mullin hosed them off from their knees down.

Having had enough of courting, one day that fall Junior simply got down on his knee and proposed. He had taken his mother's wedding ring from the sanitarium, where she was being held indefinitely, and planned to present it to Priss as a wedding ring. He felt a pang for his mama but realized his life with Priss would be better. The Mullins were good people.

Another day Junior said to Priss, "Priss, my darling, I made a fake identification card for you that says you are twenty. In Texas, the legal age for marriage is twenty-one, but in Louisiana it is only eighteen. In less than an hour's time, we can drive across the Louisiana line to Bossier City and get married right away by a justice of the peace."

"Oh, dear Junior, the idea of that makes my heart sing. But shouldn't we talk to Mama and Daddy before we go off and do something this important?" Priss asked.

Junior lied, "I don't think I can wait another minute to hold you in my arms and truly express my love. You're driving me mad with desire. I've already asked your parents for your hand, and they were ecstatic. This way we can save a bunch of money. Who needs all the folderol of a big elaborate expensive wedding ceremony, anyway? I've got a full tank, let's go."

He wanted to elope just in case Mr. Mullin said no or tried to delay the marriage, and he wasn't about to be humiliated by making a big social splash to celebrate marrying possibly the least attractive girl in town. The other advantage of this hurried maneuver was that such a marriage might not actually be legal since Priss's identification card was fake and the cards showing their photographs both had wrong social security numbers and birth dates.

Once they arrived, Priss was enthusiastic about the wedding. "Oh, isn't the chapel lovely?" she remarked. Obviously, the one glass of champagne that the justice of the peace had given her was taking effect. The well-worn wooden altar was badly in need of repainting. The two Bossier City ladies on call to be witnesses wore lavender bridesmaids dresses with plastic lilies of the valley bouquets. The justice of the peace had on what appeared to be a rented judge's robe as it didn't fit. For twenty dollars more, Junior had selected the additional element of live doves released at the end of their vows. Junior placed his mother's wedding band on Priss's ring finger. The deal was done. Priss was now officially Mrs. Junior Peck Jr.

They checked into the ARK/ LA /TEX Motel situated on the border of the three adjoining states. Priss had only been away to her family's cabin at Lake of the Ozarks, so she had no frame of reference for what a nice hotel would be versus this fleabag joint. The Vacancy/No Vacancy neon lights flashed on and off all night depending upon how many rooms were suddenly available for an hour or two.

In their room, Junior put a quarter in the bed, and it began to shake. "Oh my beloved, I have never done this sort of thing before. Mama told me not to," said Priss.

A lost sentiment, thought Junior. "My darling, I'll be gentle. It's the most special thing a man and woman can ever do. There, that feels all right, doesn't it?" asked Junior. His member was entering and exiting some type of opening on the front of Priss's body. He pushed his hand down there only to realize he was humping between the rolls of fat just below her midsection. "Baby, let me try again. I've just never felt such lust. I have to admit this is new for me, too."

Junior tried again. He could tolerate Priss in the dark. Her facial features were fairly nice—high cheekbones, well-formed full lips, and a nice jawline. Her hair was silky, and she smelled just like her garden. Her ankles were rather small, as well, indicating good family stock. However, in between lay the problem. Between her fine jawline and small ankles lay a vast corpulent orb. He stroked her jaw and ankles and then dove again onto the orb. No chance of missing where to place his mighty sword the second time. Somewhere below her ample stomach was the wet spot.

Priss, who had never before experienced passion of the flesh, was grateful and now felt like a complete woman. As for Junior, he imagined she could have been some other girl, any other girl.

They returned home and made the grand announcement of their marriage to Mr. and Mrs. Mullin. Delighted to have Priss finally married off, they offered the newlyweds the empty gardener's cottage in the backyard as a first home.

Chapter 6
Wedded Bliss with Priss?

Nine months after Junior and Priss experienced conjugal bliss at the ARK-LA-TEX Motel, Bobby Leland Peck was born.

"I am so fulfilled, honey. What with making you breakfast, lunch, and dinner and rocking little Bobby, I've just never known such happiness," Priss said as she held her hands over her heart, eyes turned toward the popcorn-textured ceiling of the gardener's cottage.

Junior had some income from percentages of oil wells he had invested in. He traveled a lot and came up with the most excuses heretofore known to mankind as to why he wouldn't be home: Big meeting in Dallas. Well shaft stuck (was it the well's or his?). Hospitalized with recurring gout. New opportunity in Louisiana. When he was home, he usually slept on a bare mattress on the floor with the window open. On the floor, he felt closer to the oil, and he could fall asleep to the rhythm of the pump jacks bringing up the oil through the night, reassuring him that more money would be coming his way soon.

Mr. and Mrs. Mullin, proud first-time grandparents, were especially pleased to have a grandson. They were determined to hold a proper christening celebration to make up for the elopement, which had deprived them of a wedding that would have made a social statement. They vowed that the next time Junior was home they would have the service for Bobby.

At the appointed day and time, the congregants gathered at the First Sabine River Bend Worldwide Baptist Church to witness little five-month-old Bobby's christening. The seating was a little lopsided. Before the service, Tom Bob Croxton, the preacher, had placed a sign in the vestibule that read: "Mullin guests on the left, Junior Peck's guests on the right." The pews on the left side filled up fast, while many on the right remained empty.

"Goddammit, Priss. Why aren't there more people on my side? And why do we have to have sides? This looks ridiculous. Don't you dare take any pictures, you hear me?" Junior whispered in Priss's ear.

"Junior, honey, we've lived here much longer than you have, and we just know more people, that's all," cooed Priss. "And besides, Daddy's paying for everything at the after-party."

"Okay," agreed Junior, experiencing the satisfaction of finally being a member of a wealthy, prominent family.

As he ascended to the pulpit, all eyes were fixed on Reverend Tom Bob Croxton, who wore his baptismal best, a purple vestment with a blue sash designating a boy child.

"Harrumph, harrumph. Welcome, friends," he started, taking the measure of the room and noticing the vast inequality in the numbers of congregants sitting on each side of the aisle. "And acquaintances," he went on, looking at Junior and nodding toward the sparsely populated pews on the right. We are gathered here to celebrate the blessing of our newest worshiper of Jesus and his gateway to eternal life. And to increase—nay, augment—our precious fold."

"Praise the Lord," shouted the congregants. Of course, the left side of the church was much louder than the right. Junior was reminded of how he had felt like an outsider at Weldon Christian Camp compared with the other campers and knew he was also in the minority among these lifelong Bullard families.

"We are present today to share our love and support for the newest Mullin," said Tom Bob.

"Peck," shouted Junior.

"Right, Peck, of course. Let us gather by the baptismal bowl," instructed Tom Bob.

Tom Bob took Bobby from Priss and continued, "We are here to welcome Bobby and surround him with love to carry him through the depths that may await." Tom Bob motioned to the choir director, who commenced playing the organ and singing.

As Tom Bob dipped Bobby's bald head into the bowl, Priss said softly, "Mind his fontanel."

Tom Bob made the sign of the cross and rubbed some olive oil on Bobby's forehead. He spoke loudly, looking up from the baby into the church rafters. "Whomever I dip in this bowl let no one put asunder. Let's meditate on this and the goodness and joy of birth. May this child always be free of misery."

Maybe this little creature would grow into a little boy with whom he could play ball or something. Now he was just a little blob. His mother, on the other hand, was a big blob, thought Junior.

"I say unto you, let this holy water, this precious cleansed water, be the only liquid to pass through his lips. Abstain from—nay, shun—the devil's brew, the poison scourge, the bloody monster that defiles innocence, dethrones reason, literally takes bread from the mouths of families," said Tom Bob. Junior thought about how his father had certainly not shunned the devil's brew and what misery it had caused his family.

Then Tom Bob handed Bobby to Mr. Mullin, saying, "Take our newest Christian soldier and go forth."

Bobby promptly threw up on Mr. Mullin, who abruptly handed him back to Priss. She held him at arm's length facing away from her so she wouldn't have spittle on her clothes at the reception following the ceremony.

Tom Bob closed by saying, "The more love this child receives, the more he will in turn be able to give to others. So your presence at this celebration today is appreciated, as will be your interest and involvement in the years ahead."

"Amen, praise the Lord," shouted the congregants.

After the christening service, the entire group of about thirty people retired to the Rigview Country Club for a celebration. Right off, all the ladies went to the table in a corner set up with a coffee urn, and each took a demitasse. They then proceeded to the Ladies' Card Room to ostensibly powder their noses and freshen up their eye makeup, but once there they made a beeline to Locker #17, where they kept a secret supply of cream sherry. Each filled her demitasse with the sherry and returned to the buffet, figuring everyone would think they were drinking coffee.

All the women looked the same. Their torsos were the shape of marshmallows, rather fluffy and square. Their calves and ankles were quite slim and girlish by contrast, so they each appeared as a marshmallow mounted on two toothpicks. They wore various shades of melon-colored printed silk dresses with thin contrasting reptile-skin belts. As their waistlines grew from twenty inches to twenty-six and on toward thirty inches, the local shoe repairman would simply let out the belts by adding more notches with his hole punch. This wasn't noticeable since the reptile pattern hid the ever-growing number of holes. All wore Playtex girdles, covering them from the bottom of their bosoms to the top of their thighs. When any one of the women was hugged, there was little give to the trussed flesh. Indeed, there was quite a bit of yanking on and rearranging of undergarments when the women were in the Ladies' Card Room. They mostly smelled like baby powder, but occasionally there was a whiff of Jungle Gardenia, reminiscent of overripe camellias.

While the women were in their locker room, Junior, some of his wildcatter men friends, and his banker Mr. Sugton had proceeded to the bar and ordered drinks of double bourbon and branch waters. They then went to the Men's Card Room to place bets on the various college football games already in progress. Betting on intercollegiate sports in Texas was illegal, which explained the presence of a full-time bookie in the Men's Card Room and the need for a secret password. Priss's daddy, Mr. Mullin, and the respectable town leaders didn't know about the illegal betting going on in the Men's Card Room.

Once the women and men were reassembled in the main dining room, Mr. Mullin cleared his throat loudly and, looking at Junior and hoisting a glass of champagne, said, "We are so proud to have you in our family and that you and our precious Priss have blessed us with our first grandchild—Bobby Peck—the first of many, we hope and pray."

"Mr. and Mrs. Mullin, my pleasure," replied Junior, stifling the bile coming up in his throat.

Priss began to cry. Her breasts, swollen with milk, were painful. Her body was sixty pounds heavier from carrying the baby. Her hormones were raging. She had tried on several outfits that morning, and none had fit. The only solution had been to wear a sweater over her dress to conceal the zipper in back that wouldn't close.

Mrs. Mullin had brought baby pictures of Priss and held them next to Bobby. "Look at the resemblance. Can you believe it?" she cooed to the friends assembled.

How could you tell, thought Junior. They both looked like big fat pink balloons with fat pink balloon arms and legs.

"Let's enjoy the buffet," announced Mrs. Mullin.

There were celery sticks stuffed with pimento cheese, catfish with tartar sauce, prime rib, fried chicken, fried pork chops in mushroom gravy, fried okra, French fried potatoes, fried green tomatoes with hollandaise sauce, grits, corn fritters, potato salad, and fresh rolls with butter pats in the shape of little pinwheels, hush puppies, three colors of Jell-O with whipped cream, and several types of cobbler. The pièce de résistance was a new dish Mrs. Mullin had read about in *Life* magazine—shrimp Newburg. It was in a silver-toned serving dish placed on top of a pancake griddle to keep it warm. The shrimp were floating around in what looked like a white cream sauce, and next to it was a big pot of converted white rice. Since Mrs. Mullin was the only one familiar with this dish and was eager to show off her sophistication, she went first. She took a plate, put rice on it, and ladled out some shrimp Newburg on top. Not wanting to appear ignorant, the guests followed suit.

Priss was standing by, still holding little Bobby away from her to avoid his spittle. Her mouth was watering as she waited to indulge in the buffet. She hadn't eaten a thing since blueberry pancakes that morning. "Mother, wouldn't you want to hold your grandbaby now?" she asked. After all, this was in her honor and her daddy was paying for it.

Junior was at the bar, sucking down a vodka martini with extra olives. He watched the television monitor above the bar in horror as the team he had bet on, the University of Southern California, was taking a beating from the underdog, Notre Dame. Oh shit, he thought, there goes another sixty thousand dollars. Got to change my bookie.

"Junior, why don't you come take a plate," urged Mrs. Mullin. "I'm sure you're starving."

"Great, that'd be nice," said Junior, barely concealing his displeasure as he gulped down his third martini. Maybe it'd be better if I don't watch my bet get kicked across the goal-post, he thought.

"Oh, my darling, this is our first special meal with our new son," said Priss, clutching her plate to her chest and tilting her chin toward Junior, ensconced at the bar.

After a long silence, Junior said reluctantly, "Hand me a plate." He wanted nothing more to do with this ridiculous ritual. He only wanted to go through the line and get back to the bar, especially since it was all on his father-in-law's tab. Plus, it was halftime and maybe the Southern California team would rally.

Priss followed along behind Junior with her plate, heaping it so full of rolls, butter, potato salad, and fried chicken that she had to put it down and start another one.

Junior, on the other hand, had passed up everything until reaching the end of the line, when he stopped at the shrimp Newburg and asked, "Priss, what the hell is this?"

"It's something new Mama found. It's shrimp in a cream sauce, and you ladle it out over that rice on your plate, honey," replied Priss.

"Okay, I'll try some," said Junior. He lifted the ladle and began to fill his plate.

"Dear, why are you fishing around with the ladle in that Newburg?" asked Priss, eager to get her serving before the shrimp were all gone.

Junior remembered his mama's talk about growing up in Enid but leaving so you could grow out and learn to eat different food. Well, this was sure different. "Goddammit, I've been fishing around in this Newburg and I don't see more than one or two shrimp. I'm gonna find me six or seven shrimp if I have to blackmail the mayor, you hear me, Priss?" insisted Junior.

The room fell silent.

The melon-colored marshmallows all scurried back to Locker #17 for a demitasse refill. The men all got another round of bourbon and branch waters.

The head chef brought out a bucket of boiled and peeled shrimp and handed Junior some tongs so he could add extra shrimp on top of the rice with the small amount of sauce he had ladled out on his plate.

"That's more like it," he commented.

Priss, following Junior in line, said to the Rigview Country Club chef, "Thank you, Jeeter. I'll have some extra shrimp, too." Things at the celebration settled down after that.

When the cobbler ran out, Mr. and Mrs. Mullin, Priss, Bobby, and Junior went back home. Once inside, Junior knew he had to find a place for his family to live that wasn't thirty feet behind his in-laws. Having fathered Bobby was now his insurance policy for access to the Mullins' fortune, he figured, so it was no longer necessary to live under their thumbs.

Within a week Junior found a suitable three-bedroom, two-bath wood-frame cottage with a small hydrangea garden just two blocks from the Mullins' home, an ideal location that provided a built-in babysitter with Grandma nearby and a hydrangea garden for Priss.

Soon thereafter Junior announced, "Priss, I've got to hit the road again. I lost a bundle on that football game Sunday."

"That's okay, precious; I have some money Daddy keeps for me in a little account over in Marshall," replied Priss. Concern about finances was an unusual concept for Priss as she had grown up not having to worry about money. She knew of families who didn't always get new cars or go on vacations, but not any of her or her parents' friends.

"Priss, you would let us use some of your money? Oh, you are a treasure and a savior. You don't have to tell your daddy, do you?" replied Junior, delighted at Priss's attitude of generosity.

"Heavens, no. What goes on behind our walls is our business, and that's that," answered Priss.

Junior continued to make money by pulling his leasing scam, now in West Texas. The more money he made, the more Priss spent. He showered her with gifts and often kisses, and maybe three or four times a year he climbed on top of her with a condom. She wondered why she didn't have another child, but essentially they both had what they needed—Junior had a wife who would inherit a family fortune, and Priss had a seemingly successful husband and a baby son.

Since Junior was out of town much of the time, Priss didn't feel the need to be at home cooking three meals every day. Besides, she had a maid three times a week to cook and clean. So Priss began to avail herself of activities and indulgences that her social circle offered, participating in Embroidery Club, Knitting Club, Garden Club, and Book Club, and making monthly trips to Dallas to shop with the other young rich Bullard wives. All these women lived within a ten-mile radius in the wealthy part of town known as The Bubble. They shared the same domestic help, yard workers, grocery delivery service, babysitters, and hairdressers. They seldom ventured outside their neighborhood except to occasionally do volunteer work with shut-ins. Another thing that linked their lives was the type and amount of jewelry they wore. No one knew who set the agenda, but each year their husbands would buy them the same new style and design of jewelry— one year new brooches, the next Majorca pearls or gold charm bracelets. They had so much jewelry that their husbands could get away with taking some of it to the local pawn shop, the Pawn O'Plenty, on an as-needed basis during down times. The Pawn O'Plenty continually did a brisk business since Junior and his wildcatter buddies were either flush with money and buying or way down on their luck and selling. They took turns helping each other buy back their wives' jewelry; and the pawn money kept them afloat while they sought new opportunities for drill leases and new investors to fund their exploits.

After five years of making money catch as catch can and making little or no progress financially, Junior became embittered. He felt he had to come up with a new scheme to get a bigger piece of the pie. He needed to differentiate himself somehow from the rest of the men barely hanging on, who were not respected and considered to have "more hat than cows." He determined that his next move had to bring him both a large amount of money and respect.

Chapter 7
The Teasles

 While Junior and his cronies were out drilling for oil, or just acting like it to save face with their wives and satisfy investors by sending fake borehole samples and core reports, the Teasle family was carrying on as they always had, running the only dry goods store in Bullard, Teasleville Dry Goods. The Teasles, like the Mullins, were one of the original families in town. In contrast to Junior, the Teasles were as honest as the day is long. They always allowed customers to buy on credit, and they honored their commitments even when money was tight.

Pop Teasle had grown up in Bullard and inherited his daddy's store. At five feet ten and two hundred pounds, he was a strapping man of twenty-eight who managed all the purchasing, stocking of goods, and inventory records. He had impressive upper-arm strength from dragging thirty-pound bags of flour and sacks of beans from inbound boats off the docks of the Sabine River to his buggy and then unloading them at the store. He wore wire-rimmed glasses and was a bit prematurely gray. At the age of twenty he had met his future bride, Iota Mae Button, a local girl who had shown up one morning with a crate full of canned pickles to sell to Pop for his store.

That day he had been on his ladder rearranging the top shelf to accommodate more boxes of baking soda. The front door had opened, signaled by the ringing of a brass bell mounted on a chain.

"Well now, there's a pretty sight," he had said upon seeing Iota Mae.

"You mean my pickles?" Iota Mae had replied, blushing.

She's a spicy one. Got some gumption, Pop had observed.

After a brief two-month courtship, Pop had asked for Iota Mae's hand in marriage, and she had accepted.

Theirs was a marriage of geography and occupation. Iota Mae was the only eligible young lady in the small town, and she had talent in pickling and could therefore help Pop out with the store, providing a good standard of living for Pop and his family.

At the time, from his small-town perspective Pop never could have imagined what dramatic changes the town of Bullard was in for, or what riches lay ahead for him and at what personal cost.

"Mother," Pop began one muggy hot August morning, "our business has sure changed since those Yankees and Okies came here lookin' for oil." He noticed that Iota Mae had put on weight since their marriage five years earlier. She had never lost the baby weight after giving birth to their two boys, first Talford and, three years later, Timothy.

The older boy, Talford, who had his mother's looks with fine features and a turned-up nose, enjoyed watching caterpillars grow together in their veiled nests. After a month or so, they would hatch and turn from wormlike creatures into beautiful multicolored winged butterflies. Talford kept a sketchbook and routinely drew the butterflies he saw on his walks in the piney woods. He also collected fallen pine cones, painted them, and made wreaths to sell in the dry goods store at Christmastime.

Timothy, called Tim, was built more like a fireplug, as tall as he was wide. He asked for a pony every Christmas, but since he never got one he would spend several hours each week climbing up the maintenance ladders and riding the pump jacks that had sprung up all around the store. When he wasn't riding the pump jacks, he spent time fishing for crawdads with bits of bacon on the end of a string. He loved watching the tadpole eggs hatch in the creek beds. Within days they would crawl out of the slime and up the sides of the creek banks as frogs. He would collect some of the hatchlings and bring them home, depositing them in a bucket with a makeshift ramp up the side and creek water at the bottom. He would watch each day as the tadpoles crawled up the ramp and finally leapt off as frogs. "Mother, I'm growing frogs," Tim would exclaim with sheer delight.

One spring morning Pop looked out the window and saw something other than the frog bucket. "Boys, did you see those two fire ant mounds out back? Yesterday, both were about four feet across, and today they look like they've been blown to smithereens," said Pop, perplexed and suspicious. Both mounds were spread out all over the yard, with parts stuck to the kitchen window like splattered mud, and the hole in the center of one mound a gaping two feet wide instead of the usual width, about the diameter of a pencil.

"No, Pop, I didn't see that," replied Talford as he made his way out for a firsthand look.

"Me neither," said Tim, realizing that his pop had spent a lot more time staring at him than he had at Talford. Finally, Tim admitted, "Okay, Pop, I did see the fire ant mounds. Those things are just vicious. Why, they ate a whole dead bird the other day in just minutes. So I thought I'd try to get rid of them. Some boys found a couple of firecrackers down by the docks, and I decided to blow the mounds up. I thought since the wildcatters are firing off blasting caps at well sites all day around here looking for oil, maybe I'd kill two birds with one stone—get rid of them fire ants and maybe find some oil, too." It was true.

Pop, barely containing his laughter, replied, "Well, son, why don't you let the wildcatters do the blasting and you keep raisin' those frogs of yours, okay?"

The increased demand for items at the dry goods store, owing to Bullard's rapid population growth, had Pop sometimes making three trips to the river docks every week, instead of the usual weekly outing, to keep the shelves stocked. Iota Mae was canning and pickling at four times her usual rate.

"Lordy, Iota Mae, I can hardly keep this place stocked anymore. I counted ten new customers just yesterday. I'm not sure how long these new people will stay, so I don't let them buy on credit. But I did make a deal with some of 'em that, if they hit oil, I'll take a percentage of their oil find in return for beans and other supplies they need from the store," explained Pop.

Before all the new people came to town, Pop had allowed credit to the locals, and everything was done with a handshake. While his new way of dealing with customers could potentially be profitable for him, it was a gamble, he realized.

Iota Mae, concerned about this changing environment with its potentially harmful impact on her boys, took a more jaundiced view. As she considered Pop's arrangement with the newcomers, she wiped her vinegary hands on the flower-printed apron she always wore when putting up pickles. She had frowned upon the men working on the docks. She thought they were worthless drifters with no families, and she tried to shield Talford and Tim from them.

"Pop, these new oil people are strange to me. They're fast talkin'. They've turned our normally quiet Main Street into muddy rutted sludge. After a rain, the red-orange clay turns into a gooey, sticky mess, like melted caramel. The only way to cross the street without getting stuck in the mud is on those wooden boards placed across it. The train brings them in here every Thursday, twice a day. Half of them look like dandies with suits and vests and derby hats, and the other half are just old Oklahoma farmers, dumber than dirt but with strong backs— all of them thinkin' they'll strike it rich quick. I just hope you've got something in writing on your agreements, at least with the men who know how to write," commented Iota Mae.

Pop knew what she was talking about. He had watched the trains pull in every week. However, he had also noticed something that Iota Mae hadn't—painted ladies and assorted other camp followers. The only hotel was overflowing, and each room rented out two or three times every day, probably not just for sleeping. It was best not to point that out, Pop reasoned.

"The boys are in school near here, and I don't want them anywhere near Main Street," Iota Mae made Pop promise. "I know when you've been to town. That red-orange clay ooze is all over your shoes. I'm going to check the boys' shoes every day to make sure they haven't been in town, you hear?" insisted Iota Mae.

"Okay, okay, but I need to go there to keep up relations with the bank. So far, I've traded beans, flour, and corn for a percentage of any oil find. But we may need a small loan to keep enough items stocked until we hit the big one. I am careful about who I barter with. Only the men who are clean-cut, with respectable suits and shined shoes," explained Pop.

"Be careful about appearances," warned Iota Mae. She went into the pantry and brought out a small tin of Underwood deviled ham. "The devil doesn't wander around in a red cape with a pitchfork looking like the little devil on this can, you know." That gave Pop a laugh, but she wasn't kidding.

The next month Pop had the surprise of his life—the discovery of the largest oil gusher in East Texas history located just three miles from the store. Pop had bartered for 8 percent of that exploration. There was no need for any loan now, he mused.

Production at that well, named Caddo Hill, soon swelled to twelve thousand barrels a day. Since no one was keeping accurate records of who owned the mineral rights, everything went up for grabs. Rigs shot up overnight, and it was impossible to determine where parcels of land began and ended, or who owned any of it, except by the use of knives and shotguns. The self-appointed mayor of Bullard realized he needed help, so he contacted the Texas state governor, Coke R. Stevenson. Governor Stevenson paid a visit and, realizing that order was needed immediately, sent in the Texas Rangers. It was like the California Gold Rush, with locals and out-of-towners alike running amok. The Houston newspapers reported that Bullard was like the mayhem surrounding the discovery of Spindletop forty years before. Finally, new federal regulations dictated that contracts be signed by the Bullard county clerk verifying correct land and mineral rights ownership. This settled things down a little bit and drove many of the most corrupt wildcatters away, off to their next nefarious venture among another set of unsuspecting cotton farmers.

This series of events made Pop more cautious about the people he dealt with. Fortunately, his percentage of profits from the Caddo Hill find yielded good money for the Teasles. Iota Mae, in particular, heaved a sigh of relief. Pop now had enough money to invest in wells outright rather than barter goods against the promise of striking oil. Pop continued to invest in oil exploration over the next few years.

By now the boys were seventeen and fourteen, respectively, and it was time to address their future beyond butterflies and tadpoles. Pop and Iota Mae were eager to have their boys get an education and begin to make lives for themselves.

"Boys, we need to have a meeting and talk about what you want to do with your lives. We have enough money to send you to college if that's what you would like," Pop began over coffee one morning. Iota Mae got a little teary but knew the boys were old enough to make decisions and needed to start their own lives.

"Talford, what do you think you'd like to do?" asked Pop, a little apprehensive about his son's reply.

"Well, I sure enjoy it when Mother and I go to the Alley Theater in Houston every Christmas for *The Nutcracker* performance. Maybe I could hire on there. With all my experience working at the store, I bet I could help design sets for plays. Anyway, I'd like to try. I keep up with all the excitement in Hollywood through my movie magazines, and sometimes radio programs come out of KADY in Houston, where they interview actors and actresses from the Alley Theater shows. Last week Mary Martin was on, and she's from around here to begin with. Why, maybe I could be the next Mary Martin—uh, I mean the male version, of course. After all, I was in a couple of church plays and, in the living nativity scene, one of the three wise men, though you couldn't tell it was me on account of the makeup and fake beard. I didn't mind not having a speaking part or the lead role since no one had a speaking part and no one got recognized because we were all in costume," explained Talford.

Pop was less amused by this interest of Talford's than Tim and Iota Mae. Iota Mae had known from an early age that Talford was gifted in the arts. He had showed quite an imagination in producing artwork at school, and he had always decorated the store with symbols of the season, carving pumpkins at Thanksgiving, hanging candy canes at Christmas, and dyeing eggs at Easter. Why, Talford had even been about to redo the shelves in the store and make them look like what she would see in magazines.

Tim's turn was next. "Pop, I really enjoy the adventure of seeing new things, like when ships come in at the river dock and unload, and we buy what we need to stock the store. Or when the trains bring all sorts of new people to town. Except for those times, all I ever do is go to school and come home, and it bores me. There's nothing to do around here unless I make up activities like riding on the pump jacks," he said.

Once again, Iota Mae expressed her dislike and distrust of the out-of-town people who worked on the docks and arrived by train. She wanted Tim to find a good-paying job and associate with a better class of people. Though she tried to understand how he could long for adventure, she worried about this tendency leading him astray and she also knew the value of having a quiet, secure life minding an established store and pickling—like she and Pop had done all these years.

A loud knock at the front door interrupted the family planning meeting.

"Good God," Pop shrieked as he answered the door. "What the hell…is that you, Boggs?" Pop saw the frame of a man with a hard hat covered in blue-black inky oil, with only the whites of his eyes showing.

"Holy shit, Pop, that parcel next to Cherokee Lake came in just now!" screamed the frame now identified as Boggs. Any concerns about the direction of the boys' futures vanished amidst the euphoria of hitting another big well.

As it turned out, the Cherokee Lake well was the largest recorded in Texas history.

Chapter 8
The Cherokee Lake Oil Swindle

 Junior spent most mornings when he was in town at the courthouse reading the daily reports of oil strikes. He read with great interest about the new find at Lake Cherokee. He noted that the Teasle family had the rights, and he figured there should be some way for him to capitalize on this new well. He figured right.

"Would you take a look at this?" Junior said to his buxom secretary, who was filing her nails and snapping Juicy Fruit gum. "Holy crap, Mr. Teasle is on the cover of the *Houston Chronicle*. Damn, that man is on to something," said Junior. "We gotta look into the Cherokee Lake oil field that Teasle family found. We've already leased all the available parcels in Texas and Louisiana and re-leased 'em to the Yankees. I been watching what's going on lately, and I think the next big thing is putting in railroad tracks and laying pipeline to move the oil."

Junior wired the *Houston Chronicle* to get the latest on the Teasle Cherokee Lake well discovery. It seemed oil was all over the place in southeast Texas, about six hundred miles of it stretching from Katy to Nacogdoches. Going for about $10 a barrel, the oil could yield as much as the 1901 oil field discovered at Spindletop. All he needed was a plan, and he had that about figured out.

One day he rented a room at the Arlene Hotel. He didn't want to put the plan into action from his own home because he didn't want either Priss or Mr. Teasle to know what he was up to. To be safe, he also made up a lie about who he was and where he was from. He would be Mr. Alabama, an employee of Gulf Allied Shares, an actual oil exploration conglomerate based in New Jersey with some holdings in Bullard.

In the Arlene lobby you could feel the excitement as all the equipment vendors and oil field supply people hovered around like locusts hoping to make a killing over the new oil field discovery at Cherokee Lake. They were the same hawkers who had been walking over the worn magnolia blossom-themed carpet the past few years waiting for the next big find. They were full of bad scotch, smoked cheap cigars, and hoping to make some kind of deal—on a handshake, if possible.

Junior phoned the Teasle household and said, "It's Mr. Alabama, here at the Arlene Hotel, calling. Is this Mrs. Teasle? I'm real interested in your discovery of that oil field outside of town. We got some extra money from those St. Louis railroad boys and are looking to lay new pipeline to move the oil to market back east. I wanted to talk to Mr. Teasle about his explorations. Is Mr. Teasle home? Well, I see, ma'am. Maybe I could catch him later."

When Pop got home, Iota Mae told him, "Some man from Alabama, I think he said, wants to talk to you about the Lake Cherokee well. Let me tell you one more time, just watch yourself with these out-of-town people."

"Iota Mae, we can't make much more money than we are now unless we get some type of pipeline or train to transport what we're bringing up," Pop explained. "As a matter of fact, we've had to store half our output until we can find a way to get it to market. So I'd better hear this Alabama man out."

"There's the phone again. You go ahead and answer it if you insist on talking about a pipeline or whatever. I'm going out back to throw feed," replied Iota Mae.

"Hello, Pop Teasle here. Yes, Mr. Alabama, I'm aware of the pipeline activities near and around Bullard. I suppose it would be okay to talk about it," said Pop while Iota Mae wagged her finger at him.

Junior managed to set up a dinner with Mr. Teasle the very next night. "Okay, meet me at seven at that catfish place on Central. I hear it's real good," suggested Pop.

Over dinner Junior used a combination of flattery and lies to get Pop more involved, with an even bigger prize than pushing pipeline in mind. "Well, Mr. Teasle, congratulations on that oil find. I understand your family's been in these parts a long time, that your folks helped establish Bullard," said Junior.

"Yes, I suppose that's so. My daddy's daddy founded Teasleville and the Teasleville Dry Goods store that has kept us comfortable all these years. Life's been good," replied Pop with pride.

"Where's the well? Maybe three miles south of here? I'd sure like to see it. You know, I'm working with the railroad people to lay track that will make it easier to transport the oil up north. New pipeline will feed the oil into the railcars.

Maybe I could put in a word for your location—you know, have them consider laying the pipe and track close to your well. I'm only in town a few days, so how about going out there tomorrow afternoon?" suggested Junior.

No harm in that, thought Pop. "Sure, son, we can drive out after breakfast. I'll meet you at the Arlene." Pop was beginning to enjoy the notoriety he was experiencing from hitting the huge well and didn't mind showing it off.

I've got him now, thought Junior. I just gotta line up a couple of strippers from Bossier City. There was nothing on that stretch of road but a string of honky-tonks built in the 1920s outside the Barksdale Military Base, clubs catering to soldiers, oil field trash, and musicians traveling from Dallas to Shreveport to perform on the Louisiana Hayride.

Junior drove immediately to Bossier City and hit the titty bars. He found just what he needed in Becky and Sarah. They looked young and innocent enough to pass for college students. He paid them $100 apiece, drove them back to Bullard, and put them up at the Lariat Lodge, five miles out of town.

"Now, girls, here's how this is going to go down. In the morning we're going to take this man out to an oil well location and shoot some exotic pictures with him. There will be no names involved, not yours nor mine. I'll give you both another hundred dollars each when we're done. You understand? I'll get you back to Bossier City safe and sound tomorrow."

"You mean we don't got to do nothing?" they asked, astonished.

"That's right. And you can leave your clothes on," replied Junior.

The next morning, Mr. Teasle showed up at the Arlene Hotel to meet Mr. Alabama.

"Say, Mr. Teasle, I wonder if it's okay to bring my daughter and her friend along. They're in school in Kilgore and were visiting since I'm in the area, and they'd be awful excited to see the crude oil pump jacks pumping away," said Junior.

"Sure, sure," said Pop, only too happy to show off his well.

"Let's get us some coffee to go," said Junior. "How do you like it, Mr. Teasle?"

"Black, with one sugar," replied Mr. Teasle.

Junior got the coffee, put a horse tranquilizer in it, and drove off. Once they reached the Cherokee Lake pump site, Junior maneuvered the now-woozy Mr. Teasle to a wooded area and laid him down on a carpet of pine needles. At this point, the two strippers changed into their exotic costumes and proceeded to appear to "have their way" with Mr. Teasle. These activities were recorded by Junior in their entirety using a Polaroid camera. He smiled. Blackmailing Mr. Teasle would help him obtain a controlling interest in the Cherokee Lake oil field in East Texas for himself.

When Pop didn't come home at dinnertime, Iota Mae became alarmed. "Hello, get me Police Dispatch right away. My husband, Mr. Teasle, is missing," Iota Mae pleaded with the PBX exchange telephone operator, who only worked until 9:00 pm. She needed to reach police headquarters while she could still get phone service.

"How long has it been?" asked the operator.

"He's always home by six o'clock, and it's nine." Both boys were at a sleepover next door, so she didn't have to worry about them, thank goodness. Finally Iota Mae was connected to the sheriff. "Well, maybe he's just enjoying the newly minted nightlife here and celebrating the Cherokee Lake find at Phipp's Bar?" suggested the sheriff.

"No way. Pop doesn't drink or stay out late...Something's wrong, I'm sure of it," insisted Iota Mae.

Finally convinced that something was indeed wrong, the sheriff sent out two deputies and a junior policeman to search. They checked all the bars in town and found nothing. No one had seen Pop. The deputies then drove out to Lake Cherokee and searched the various boat docks. They stumbled upon a roughneck here and there chained to his cot so as to protect it from other roughnecks with nowhere to sleep, but there was no trace of Pop. The Cherokee Lake oil field was noisily pumping away, so they drove there. In the squad car headlight beams, they saw a man crumpled on pine needles under one of the scrub pines out by the well. It was Pop, looking like he had been in trouble. While putting him in the back of the squad car to drive him home, they noticed that his wallet had not been touched.

When they arrived at the Teasle home, Iota Mae was on the screened-in front porch, pacing back and forth. "Mrs. Teasle, we found your husband. He's not in great shape," said one of the deputies, squinting through the screen door to the porch.

"What is it? Tell me. Is he okay?" asked Iota Mae, with growing concern.

The other deputy removed his cap and said, "Ma'am, we found your husband out near his well. He was passed out under a stand of pine trees. There was no evidence of alcohol or any kind of struggle, but, well . . ."

"Do go on, officer," urged Iota Mae, now extremely upset and nervous.

"Bring him in, Dobbs," the head officer instructed the junior policeman.

"My God, what happened?" exclaimed Iota Mae as she saw Pop's condition.

Pop was disheveled almost beyond recognition. A couple of his suit buttons were torn off, his tie was missing, and his shoes were covered with red-orange clay, indicating he had been either downtown or at the well, or both. He was slurring his words. He still had on his brown felt hat, but it was askew and pulled down low on his forehead. Most disturbing was the lipstick stain on his collar.

"Well, I think this is a matter between you and your husband. There's no evidence of an accident or crime. Maybe he fell under the influence of some of those new wildcatters. They might have tried to cut a deal with him for part of the well," suggested one of the deputies.

"I can assure you there was no inappropriate behavior, officers. Good night. By the way, I would appreciate it if you would forget this happened. I'm sure there's a logical explanation, and it's nobody's business what that might be," stressed Iota Mae, aghast at Pop's appearance.

The officers nodded and said, assuring her, "Yes ma'am, of course."

"I just knew it," mumbled Iota Mae as she watched the squad car pull away. "Those crooked East Coast people, or maybe even those Sabine River dock people, are somehow behind this. They're just plain bad."

Iota Mae had managed to take Pop's limp arm, guide him into the bedroom, remove his rumpled suit and trousers, and position him in the middle of the bed under the covers when she saw something she would never forget. There, in his shirt pocket, were several Polaroid photos of him and two young ladies. The photos were dark, so it was hard to tell exactly what was going on, but the scene looked suggestive. She would take up the matter with Pop in the morning. Iota Mae also noticed a reddish rash on Pop's left thigh. She didn't know what it might be and wasn't at all sure that she wanted to. She got out the unguentine salve she used for welts from fire ant and bug bites and applied a generous layer on the affected area.

Around 10:00 the next morning, Pop awoke to Iota Mae sitting next to him on the bed. "What in tarnation happened?" said Pop, confused.

"You tell me, Mister Teasle," stated Iota Mae, who had been up all night watching his labored breathing and running through various possible scenarios in her mind to explain the events of the night before, none of them acceptable.

"Jesus. I was going to drive out to the well with a man who said he was interested in maybe putting the rail lines close to it. First, we got coffee, and the man's daughter and her roommate from Kilgore Junior College got in the car with us. That's the last thing I remember," said Pop, barely speaking above a whisper since he was still groggy from the horse tranquilizer. "I don't understand the outfits those girls have on in these pictures. They didn't start out dressed that way. I swear nothing happened. We mustn't speak of this to anyone. If I made a mistake, please forgive me," pleaded Pop.

"We've got to get you to the doctor," said Iota Mae. She felt sure the doctor would keep his mouth shut about this incident. They had offered him credit at the store when he was getting started, so he owed them a favor.

The doctor confirmed that Pop had no broken bones, just the rash on his thigh, which he identified as poison ivy, and a major bruise on his right hip, as if he had been thrown up against a tree. The doctor prescribed antiflogistine. Because it smelled like camphor, eucalyptus, and menthol, Iota Mae thought it would benefit a stopped-up nose more than a muscle bruise.

To their dismay, upon returning from the doctor's office they found a handwritten note in an envelope stuck inside the screen door that read: "We have more pictures. You no longer own the Lake Cherokee well. If you speak of this, we will go to the newspaper with the other photographs."

"Pop, I believe you. I don't think you did anything wrong, but whoever these people are, they are to be feared. I warned you about trusting the scalawags coming here for easy money.

They sure got some this time. Have you learned your lesson?" said Iota Mae.

"Yes, dear. I'm a deacon in the church. We have our boys to think of. We cannot afford to dwell on this. I don't want to hear another word about it. Do you promise?" insisted Pop, both angry and embarrassed about somehow having been swindled.

"I do," agreed Iota Mae.

The following morning Junior drew up fake title documents stating that Mr. Joseph Edward Teasle had signed over all rights and ownership of the well to Gulf Allied Shares.

"Take these to the Second National Bank, and ask for Mr. Sugton. Have them notarized, and then file them at the courthouse. Give the court records lady twenty bucks, and she'll take care of it," Junior instructed his secretary. "Oh, and don't let me forget to change the title over to me in about six months."

"Sure thing, Mr. Peck," replied his secretary.

Junior wondered whether, if things kept going the way they were and he could make money this easily, he should go see his mama and try to help her. But once again he decided it was a bad idea since she could blow his cover and destroy the new life of greater wealth and prestige he had attained, even if through questionable means.

A few days later Pop still couldn't figure out what had happened so he went to the courthouse to search for title documents for the Lake Cherokee well. "Holy crap," he said after discovering that the Gulf Allied Shares Company had filed title and ownership papers that very morning, notarized and signed by Mr. Alabama, the man who had driven him out to the well the day before.

When he got home, he broke the news to Iota Mae, saying, "You won't believe who is on file as owning the Cherokee well. It's Gulf Allied Shares. They're the same outfit that wanted to drill on the school grounds. When the town refused, they bought the school, tore it down, and started drilling on what was the playground. There's no way we could win a fight with those people. We've got enough money coming in from the other wells, thank goodness."

Over time, Pop became distant, embarrassed for having allowed this loss to strangers to occur. There was enough money still coming in from the royalty percentages on other wells so that his family didn't have to worry about finances, but the loss of pride and self-esteem that Pop experienced as a result of this incident caused him to fall into a type of zombie routine from which he never escaped. While he used to wear his brown felt hat only outdoors, he now wore it all the time, as if to shield his brain from any further ignominious outside influences. He barely ate, thus losing weight. Even though Iota Mae believed her husband had done no wrong, she didn't want much to do with him anymore, further alienating him. As their parents became more distant, Talford and Tim just went about their lives.

One night after supper Pop was reading the newspaper. His concentration was now so poor he had to read each article twice. Tim tapped him on the shoulder and asked, "Pop, the Walkers next door just got one of them television sets. Are we going to sell them in the store?"

"I got two in yesterday. I reckon we could take one and use it at home. Would you like that, Tim?" replied Pop.

"That'd be super," said Tim.

"Okay, I'll bring it home tomorrow," promised Pop.

It was an Admiral 19-inch black-and-white television set with a four-foot wooden console and Bakelite trim around the screen. Iota Mae put a doily over the top and placed a lime green ceramic panther upon it. The television set would be the family's primary focus from then on, with a particular attraction for each family member, depending on their individual interests and attitudes.

The boys began to notice that Pop became increasingly interested in his TV shows. He would sit on the couch in front of the Admiral and watch *Sky King*, *The Gillette Cavalcade of Sports*, and, when Iota Mae wasn't there, *The Debby Drake Exercise Show*. Tim would watch the sports shows with his father. At the end of the broadcasting day, at around 10:00 pm, the big chief Indian test pattern would come on, which Pop would watch until signoff.

Increasingly, Iota Mae, who had lost interest in Pop, her marriage, the store, and nearly everything else, retreated into

TV programs. She enjoyed *Arthur Godfrey's Talent Scouts, The Admiral Broadway Review,* and *In the Kelvinator Kitchen.* Watching *In the Kelvinator Kitchen* replaced most of the time spent in her own kitchen. She then began a journal of how long it took her to make dinner, and kept it going until cooking no longer seemed worth it to her.

"Pop, do you know how much time I spent making dinner every night last week?" she asked one day.

"No, Mother, I don't have any idea," replied Pop.

"I wrote it down. Take a look. It took about an hour to make fresh snap peas, meat loaf with spicy tomato puree, boiled potatoes, apple cobbler, and fresh pan loaf bread from scratch; twenty-five minutes for all of you to eat it; and forty minutes to clean up. That's over two hours. Then everyone went over to the damned television set. I'm not wasting that kind of time cooking. No more, I tell you," insisted Iota Mae. This information was greeted with a blank stare.

From watching *In the Kelvinator Kitchen,* Iota Mae learned there was a new kind of food available now. She called it automatic food. She now prepared dinners from canned goods, each of which took only about thirty minutes to make and hardly any time to clean up because she had started using paper plates and napkins. Occasionally she would heat up a Swanson TV dinner, which she would transfer to a real plate and claim she made it from scratch—usually

Salisbury steak with mashed potatoes that appeared to be mostly air when you put a fork in them. Her main goal was to save time for watching her TV shows. Nobody seemed to care about the change in dinners since family members seldom communicated with one another anymore except, perhaps, to remark on some aspect of a TV show, a comment that never sparked discussion. Now they lived in their own separate worlds.

Chapter 9
A Teasle Goes Offshore

 Pop continued to deteriorate. Soon he was a shadow of his former self, not even going to the store anymore. He rarely paid attention to the boys, so it was left to Iota Mae to encourage Talford and Tim to plan their futures.

"Remember when you were in the living nativity?" she asked Talford one day. "Didn't you work on building the scene, making the backdrop look like a real manger with hay and all?"

"Yes, ma'am. That was really fun. And we had real hay from the feedstore," said Talford. "I liked doing the scenery and also being in the scene, especially since I didn't have a speaking part, which would have made me nervous."

Tim said he wanted to strike out on his own, still fascinated by the men working independently on the docks. He got a newspaper and began researching the types of adventurous jobs that might be available for someone with only a high school diploma.

By the end of the 1940s, things had simmered down in Bullard. Tim had read that most leases for oil exploration on land had been bought up. The majority of underhanded and illegal business dealings regarding the discovery of oil on land had subsided. Seismic surveys, however, had indicated that oil reserves might exist in the Gulf of Mexico, off the shores of Morgan City, Louisiana. So Tim went to talk to the high school counselor about working in oil offshore.

"You say your name is Teasle? Are you one of Pop Teasle's boys?" asked the counselor.

"Yes, sir, I am," replied Tim.

"I'd be happy to tell you what I know. But first, why don't you tell me about the chickens at the Fall Farm Harvest Festival—that is, if you're the young man who hypnotized them," said the counselor.

Tim replied: "Yep, that's me. I was at the fair looking at the FFA display and watching the boys show off their livestock. There were lots of vendors from around the area. Mr. Elio Bouchene ran the turkey shoot. I spent three dollars trying to shoot a BB gun at little pictures of turkeys on a fence about twenty feet away. If you shot one of the pictures, you got a frozen turkey. Mr. Bouchene sold turkey jerky in little brown paper bags in a booth with a banner that read: 'Turkey Jerky—It's Gobblin' Good.' I bought some jerky and walked around looking for something to do. Then I snuck in the back of the Poultry Exhibition Hall and hypnotized about fifteen chickens. The process is simple: you get down in front of a chicken's face, stare into its eyes, put your index finger on the top front of its head, and draw a line to the tip of its beak then down to the ground and out to a point about two feet in front of the chicken. As a result of hypnotizing them, none of those chickens laid eggs and all were disqualified from the egg-laying competition."

"I see. Maybe you should go offshore. Just might be a safer place for you—and us," said the counselor, amused. "Let me tell you what I know about this offshore business. After the war, sailors who had learned marine skills such as at-sea communications, underwater diving maneuvers, and sea navigation were in demand for the new offshore industry. There were surplus navy vehicles and equipment aplenty. At first, drilling in the Gulf of Mexico took place at the end of extremely long piers off Galveston and New Orleans. In 1947, the first 'out of sight of land' well was drilled by Kerr-McGee eighteen miles south of New Orleans. Workers came by shrimp boats and lived for one month at a time on the rig with another month off. The actual rig was somewhat limited in depth capacity, and the oil deposits closer to land came up dry after a year or so, leaving lots of platforms abandoned," explained the counselor.

Tim was now very interested in this combination of being at sea among men who had traveled the world, like those who worked the docks on the Sabine River. He began to plot. He couldn't get into college and had never had much of an attention span, so he thought such a job might keep him interested. "Sir, I'm just sure this is the kind of job for me," claimed Tim.

"Then pursue it. There are several companies that have set up card tables in the post office looking for help in offshore, Tim," advised the counselor.

Tim went home, changed his shirt and pants, shaved, slicked back his hair, and went down to the post office. That afternoon he hired on as a contract employee with Kerr-Mc-Gee at their new offshore drilling rig near the coast of Saint Mary's Parish in South Louisiana. He rushed home with the paperwork to tell his dad, proud that he had gotten such a decent job on his own.

"Pop, it's the best payin' job around. A dollar fifty an hour. That's more than the thirteen dollars a week you can pay me for workin' in our dry goods store. Kinda excitin', too. Lots of people involved from all over the United States, and it's easier than roughneckin' on the ground. Why, it's the future of this area, and I'm getting in early," said Tim, excitedly.

"I don't blame you for wanting to strike out on your own. I know I haven't been much of a father just lying around. I'm proud of you, and you get to come home every other month and take it easy," Pop said, tears welling up in his eyes.

Tim's first week on the rig was rough. The men running the show had just returned home from the war and behaved like they were still running a platoon. As the workers disembarked from the ferry onto the rig the first day, the men began barking orders.

"Mr. Teasle, you are assigned to the roustabout crew," ordered the head man.

"Okay, what's that?" asked Tim.

"You'll be sanding off the carbuncles and painting the rig at low tide. Crap, those things will just take over if you let them. Make sure you got some gloves. At high tide you got to unload the new pipe and mostly throw the old pipe overboard. The sections are fifteen feet long and eight inches wide, so buddy up or you'll throw your back out," instructed the head man.

"Yes, sir," replied Tim.

Roommates were assigned. Tim's, a young man named Gibson who had been a shrimper in New Orleans, was also assigned the job of a roustabout. The galley accommodated shifts of rig workers who were given three meals a day, and work was round the clock. On the month off, there was always a big party back on land sponsored by oil well equipment vendors, with plenty of floozy women.

One month in, Tim had seen more than he'd ever imagined—and not all of it was good.

"Let me have Gibson, Wilson, Waterman, and all you men in the back row. You boys are going to raise and lower the joint of the pipe in and out of the hole and change drill bits when necessary," ordered the head man.

After about three weeks of drill-bit duty, there was a huge storm, and Gibson almost drowned. Recuperating in the rig's infirmary and green around the gills, Gibson said, "Shit, Tim, did you see what happened? Man, I was in the bucket on the cable connecting the uptake oil valve to the holding tender bound back to Morgan City, and a big wave came up and tossed me in the ocean. And then, I swear to God another wave came up and tossed me back on the rig. It was foggy and all. I guess that's what it feels like to be in a tornado."

"Thank God I didn't see that," said Tim, his eyes as big as saucers. "Hell, man, the captain told us to get inside the galley and just hang on for dear life until the storm blew over. And I thought roughneckin' on the ground was hard. At least there the land under you don't move."

"They're gonna take me outta here this morning," Gibson mumbled, affected by pain drugs. "They think I mighta broke a leg. I'm goin' out on one of them war PBY seaplanes—back to New Orleans. I guess you'll get a new roommate; maybe he won't snore."

Tim insisted, "I'll come back to this rig over my dead body."

Fortunately, it was Tim's time to go back to land, so he rode in the seaplane with Gibson. On the dock in New Orleans, there was quite a stir among the locals. They were making a movie, and there were Hollywood types running all over. Tim had to catch the train back to East Texas, though, so he asked Gibson to write him a letter and let him know how he was doing and what was happening back on shore with the movie people. He thought Talford would be interested in that. It had never before occurred to him that there were real jobs in moviemaking. Maybe Talford could find something in that line of work after all.

Back home Tim reported in to his parents, who were glad to see him. They hoped Tim had found his calling in the off-shore rig business.

"Well, Pop, I'm not so keen on working that rig. Most of those boys aren't even from around here. Why, some came down to work as shrimpers and were hired on after their catch got contaminated by sulfur from the well-drilling. Besides that, I get kind of queasy like I'm gonna vomit, and it makes me dizzy, too."

"Son, that's seasickness. Ain't no cure for it, insofar as I know." Pop noticed that Tim had built a good deal of upper-arm strength but, at the same time, looked awfully thin. His nails were filthy and bitten down, likely from anxiety.

"Plus, Pop," Tim continued, sensing his dad wasn't too upset that he was back home and not really wanting to return to the rig, "the government has stepped in now, and they are feudin' with the state of Louisiana over who owns the oil. So Kerr-McGee has cut back the crew. Of course, why should they drill if the government's gonna take it over? I think the state can keep the oil if it's close to shore and they can't if it's not."

"Well, son, what are you thinkin' about doin'? Comin' back to the dry goods store?" asked Pop.

"No, Pop. They got a new kind of job now called a land-man. First, a team that has seismic equipment figures out where there might be some oil underground. Companies pay them to go around and figure out where to drill and where not to bother drilling. Then a landman goes to check courthouse and county records, figure out who owns the land and the mineral rights, and report that back to the company hiring them. After that, we're done. The job don't involve much. You just wait for the seismic stuff and then go to the courthouse. Anyway, there's some kind of school for it. I'm just real tired of getting seasick and vomiting."

Working on the rig had cured Tim of any desire to work on a ship or near the docks. But he did want to leave Bullard and see a little more of the world. As a landman, at least he would be on firm ground. Tim figured he would start by working again at the dry goods store to earn money for landman school.

The next week, Tim received a letter from his offshore rig roommate Gibson, who was recuperating in New Orleans from his leg injury. It contained news about the Hollywood people they had encountered who were making the movie. With trepidation, he decided to show it to his older brother, Talford.

Ever since they were little, Tim and Talford had shared a bathroom. Sometimes Tim would absently open the door without knocking first and see Talford looking in the mirror while holding up his toothbrush like a microphone and singing, as if in some kind of performance. Talford listened to the radio constantly, especially the latest music out of KADY in Houston. When he sang, it was usually something by Keely Smith, like "Ain't It a Shame about Mame." Occasionally he would reenact the gangplank scene from *Peter Pan*.

This time, Tim knocked loudly on the door of Talford's bedroom twice before pushing it open, in case his brother was doing something Tim didn't especially want to see.

"Talford, I think you might want to read this," said Tim as he peered into the room. He seldom went in there because he wasn't sure about what he might find. Now Tim noticed stacks of *Screen Gem* and *Movie Star* magazines, as well as lots of posters on the wall of Lana Turner and Errol Flynn. These reminded him of the trips to Houston that Talford took with Iota Mae to see performances at the new Alley Theater.

"I met one guy I liked on the rig, and he got in with those Hollywood folks in New Orleans on account of what he knew about the offshore business. According to this letter, my friend got in on the movie. I mean, he helped them out a little. The letter says he met some of the actors. I thought you might be interested," said Tim.

Talford couldn't believe this firsthand news about Hollywood. "Wow, Tim, you actually know this Gibson man?" Talford asked as he breathlessly read Gibson's letter over and over.

"Yep, I do," boasted Tim, glad to finally have something sort of in common with his older brother.

According to the letter, the movie being made was called *Thunder Bay* and was about shrimpers after the war getting into fights with offshore oil-rig operators, starring Jimmy Stewart, Dan Duryea, and Joanne Dru. All the actors had stayed in the same hotel—the Roosevelt—and ate at the same restaurant—Geraldine's Originals. The deputy sheriff had taped up newspapers and put white shoe polish on all the windows to keep the locals from ogling at them. Gibson's job had been to find equipment they needed in the movie, such as automobiles and boats. He also bought special cuts of meat from restaurants in New Orleans because Morgan City didn't have much fresh meat, only seafood, and the actors preferred steak since they were sick of the smell of shrimp after filming near shrimp boats all day. Gibson's letter went on to say, "When the maids went in to clean the rooms of those actor people, I would go in with them and just look around. The actors seemed like normal people, with toothbrushes and pajamas, and everything."

Wow, thought Talford. His own brother actually knew somebody who had worked in the movies. "I wonder if I could talk to this Gibson man, Tim. I never get to read about anything but actor interviews in my magazines. I don't know if I could ever have a speaking role, but maybe I could be some kind of background actor or something," said Talford.

"Well, okay, if I get another letter I'll let you know," said Tim, quickly backing out of his brother's room.

Chapter 10
The Grand Petroleum Shannon Hotel

The newest fortunes in oil exploration continued shifting to offshore rigs in the Gulf of Mexico. Junior was aware of this opportunity, but having enough income from his oil wells so he found no need to dabble in other ventures for the time being.

The other major shift was toward businesses catering to the oil patch. It was like the California Gold Rush, where the suppliers to the gold prospectors were guaranteed a more steady income than the men actually panning for gold. The wildcatters needed supplies, equipment, and a place to stay whether they hit oil or not.

The first families to capitalize on catering to the wildcatters were German immigrants from New Braunfels, about thirty miles from Bullard. Among the original settlers was Flym Slootweghoogen, who, having brought with him old family recipes for stout beer and bratwurst, had started the first of many biergartens in that area. Flym made succulent bratwurst using the finest pork raised locally and brewed the most pungent strong dark beer available. Flym soon married another German immigrant, and they had a son, Wim, who came to be called Sloots. Sloots grew up in the shadow of his father's business and learned it as his trade.

Once Sloots turned eighteen he had had enough of toiling in the back rooms cutting up various pork meats and filling the casings to make bratwurst as well as overseeing the long, dreary distillation involved in turning out kegs of dark German beer. So he decided he would rather sell the beer and bratwurst than produce it. With his father's blessing, Sloots began traveling to East Texas to make sales calls at the various hotels that had sprung up to house the influx of oil wildcatters. These hotels were nothing more than large farmhouses with family kitchens hastily reconfigured to accommodate six to ten itinerant men. The German beer and bratwurst were a welcome taste sensation on a menu normally consisting of fried chicken, grits, and iced tea.

Along with the Slootweghoogens, another family who had settled in New Braunfels was the McArdles, of Irish descent. Their only son was John Harlan McArdle, called John Jack. Like Sloots, John Jack yearned to leave New Braunfels and strike out on his own. Deciding to take advantage of the large influx of wildcatters and roughnecks and the lack of decent temporary housing, he got a loan from his daddy, bought a forty-room run-down hotel in Beaumont, and put in new plumbing and carpeting. Business was brisk, with some rooms renting out more than once a day. The lingering smell of perfume and lipstick stains on the pillowcases indicated that oil wasn't the only thing the wildcatters were drilling. This was the first and only hotel John Jack would outright purchase.

Ultimately John Jack's aspirations went far beyond the hotel business. First, he bought five acres of basically swampland bordering the bay in Port Arthur for $10. The Beaumont real estate agent who sold it to him told him it was a worthless frog pond, mistaking John Jack for an ignorant immigrant, but when the land yielded an enormous oil find the real estate agent had to eat his words.

Within two years, John Jack had amassed a fortune by parlaying the money he had made from the swamp into purchasing a hundred more oil-rich acres along the Texas Gulf Coast, becoming known as the Swamp King. He didn't mind the name at all. Let the locals laugh and call him crazy, he thought. He knew he was crazy like a fox.

The first Irish transatlantic airport had opened in 1942 in Shannon, so in homage to his heritage John Jack began taking his parents on trips to Ireland. The lodging in Ireland, like at home, was very basic and sorely lacking in amenities. Never a small thinker, John Jack had the wildly ambitious idea to build a new type of hotel back in oil country, one with full amenities. He felt that hotels offering more than just a bed in a room for the night would appeal to the growing number of wealthy wildcatters whose tastes were becoming more sophisticated. He believed such a hotel would put him on the world stage of developers and get him the respect he felt he deserved.

In 1946, he broke ground on the new type of hotel he had been thinking about. It had to be located near the lucrative oil boom towns, so he decided on Galveston Bay. He named it The Grand Petroleum Shannon Hotel. With 1,100 rooms, it was the largest hotel in the United States—eighteen stories tall with ballrooms and dining rooms on the first three levels; having restaurants inside a hotel was unheard of before that time. It featured a 170-by-200-foot Olympic-size swimming pool that could accommodate a ski boat. John Jack also put in a 30-by-50-foot lake next to the pool and stocked it with bass, crappie, and catfish. Once again the locals called him crazy. Once again he knew he was crazy like a fox.

For about a year, Sloots had been calling on restaurants in southeast Texas to sell the bratwurst and beer made by his father in New Braunfels. Since there were three restaurants inside The Grand Petroleum Shannon Hotel, which had not yet opened for business, Sloots wanted to be its main food purveyor. He knew he could make as much money selling his goods there with one sales call as selling them to three independent restaurants.

After spending an exhausting day in Houston selling bratwurst and beer, Sloots checked into a small "room-for-the-night-or-an-hour" motel near the Houston Airport. The next morning he called John Jack at The Grand Petroleum Shannon Hotel's main office.

"Mr. McArdle, I'm Wim Slootweghoogen. Our daddies knew each other in New Braunfels," said Sloots.

"Say, aren't you that guy who sells bratwurst?" asked John Jack.

"That's right, Mr. McArdle," replied Sloots.

"What's this about? I'm very busy," said John Jack.

"Why don't you call me Sloots? Everybody does. I've been selling beer and bratwurst all over East Texas, and I have an idea you might like for your new hotel," replied Sloots, trying to appeal to John Jack's ever-growing ego resulting from the fact that he would soon open the biggest, most luxurious hotel in Texas, if not the whole country.

"Tell me more, but make it quick. I've got to plan The Grand Petroleum Shannon Hotel's grand opening," said John Jack. "Nobody will have seen anything like it before."

"Okay, well, I've been traveling to New Orleans to buy fresh seafood, which nobody has around here. I drive straight back through the night with my purchases sitting on big blocks of ice, and by the time I arrive in East Texas the ice has all but melted. I'm the only man around who can get you fresh shrimp and oysters. They have a new concept in the French Quarter called an oyster bar. I think that would be a fine, almost international addition you could offer your guests. I get oysters for one dollar a dozen right off the docks. You can sell 'em for five dollars. One other thing, John Jack," continued Sloots, "I listen to the radio while I do all this driving through Texas and Louisiana. If you listen enough, you'll come to the conclusion that German polka music, Mexican music, and Cajun zydeco music is basically all the same, just played at different speeds."

"And your point?" John Jack asked, starting to fidget with his bow tie.

"Well, if you've got restaurants you could get more than just the people staying at the hotel to eat at your restaurants by offering some live entertainment—like a bar with a band or something. You could probably hire one band and have three different costumes for them, and then you'd have three different types of entertainment. Like Thursday could be German night, with the band dressed in lederhosen; and you could sell beer and bratwurst. Friday could be Mexican night, with the band wearing serapes; and you'd serve margaritas. Maybe Saturday you could do Cajun night at an oyster bar; I don't know what the band would wear for that, maybe pirate outfits. Then the locals could come in. If they drink enough, they might stay for dinner. Anyway, just a thought."

"Hmm…Well, Sloots, I think you are on to something here. Meet with my architect, and see what we can do about putting in an oyster bar. Would you mind bringing me some examples of how German, Mexican, and Cajun music is basically the same?"

As John Jack dashed away to the planning meeting for the grand opening, he turned his attention to drawing up the guest list. He had met Howard Hughes, a Houston man, at a social event about the same time he had broken ground. He was drawn to the glamour of Hughes and his Hollywood friends. John Jack figured if he could get Hughes and some starlets to come to the grand opening it would lend special cachet to the place. More and more people were going to the movies, and since the end of the war people yearned for more lighthearted, upscale entertainment. He figured he could probably get the Houston papers to cover it.

John Jack put in a call to Hollywood's RKO Studios that Hughes owned, and asked, "Say, Howard, how'd ya like to come to the biggest party in Texas?"

"What did you have in mind, John Jack?" asked Hughes.

"I've built me a hell of a hotel. Biggest one in the United States. It's lots fancier than the Bel Air out your way. We're throwin' a big grand opening party, and all the Texas politicians will be there. We're planning a giant fireworks display, bathtubs full of gin, prime rib, champagne, and an oyster bar, just like in New Orleans. It's got a swimming pool big enough for a ski boat or two. I've hired five of the Cypress Gardens girls. They're gonna be The Grand Petroleum Shannon Ski Show Girls." Going in for the big close, John Jack said, "I'd like you to be the main speaker and welcome all the radio and newspaper people." John Jack heard him shuffle some papers on the other end of the line.

"Well, my fee is one hundred dollars an hour. That's door to door. From the minute I leave LA to when I return," said Hughes.

"I'll have to think about that, Howard. I'll call you back," replied John Jack.

"Who the hell does he think he is?" John Jack said out loud to himself. "One hundred dollars an hour for a fee. Let's see, what would I charge for a fee? Hah! I'm worth five times that kind of money. All he'll do is just get old and washed

up while I make more money every day than the day before."
However, John Jack finally reluctantly agreed to the fee
because knew he needed a big-name draw at the party, and
Howard was not only a big star but, in fact, the only star John
Jack knew.

Never one to do anything halfway, Howard Hughes
immediately called his agent and said, "Get me Hedda Hopper,
get me Ginger Rogers, and get me Errol Flynn. We got us a
party to go to."

On the day of the grand opening Howard Hughes flew
everybody who was anybody, as well as a full complement of
Hollywood reporters, on his Boeing 307 Stratoliner into the
Houston Hobby Airport. There limos were waiting to take
the movie people to the pops of camera flashes illuminating
the grand opening of The Grand Petroleum Shannon Hotel.

Surpassing all estimates, the party was attended by at least
60,000 people, including 350 Hollywood people and another
25,000 dignitaries. They came in by private planes and chartered cars on the Santa Fe Super Chief. It was hard to keep
track of all the arrivals. The mayor ended up closing the airport to all commercial flights, and, to make up for any outbound cancellations, he asked the people holding outbound
tickets to just come to the party and stay the night.

The festivities finally got underway with klieg lights shin-
ing through green cellophane bearing shamrock motifs. Since
green was the official color of Ireland, John Jack wore a custom green tuxedo, and all the waitstaff were dressed like lep-
rechauns. Howard Hughes announced over the PA system,

"The sky's the limit. If you people saw *Giant*, well, this is it, and you're all playing your own starring role. Enjoy."

When the fireworks started, thunderous applause broke out. It was a brilliant display, rivaling that of the Giacometti brothers at the World's Fair. John Jack was holding court with starlets on the balcony overlooking the Grand Ballroom. The three types of music Sloots had suggested—German, Mexican, and Cajun—were being played alternately by the same band. Occasionally the band members did not all have time to change fully from the lederhosen to serapes to pirate outfits, so their costumes were sometimes a hodge-podge, but nobody seemed to notice or care. Then the headliner, Xavier Cougat's orchestra, took to the stage.

To escape the din, Sloots wandered through the landscaped grounds and suddenly heard a scream. There in the stocked lake was the state attorney general, who had fallen in. Sloots helped him out and gave him a towel, whereupon the attorney promptly disappeared into a pool cabana before sneaking back into his room. Once back inside, Sloots noticed a woman's sparkly red stiletto heel sticking out from under the buffet table. It was the shoe of Ruthanne Louise, a starlet nominated several times for an Academy Award. Sloots dove under the table and covered her with a sheet, folded her up, loaded her onto the bottom shelf of a serving cart at the end of the buffet, and rolled her into the linen closet. Then he had to coerce the mayor of Houston to stop driving the ski boat in the pool. Two of the ski show girls were riding in the bow of the boat topless, and the *Houston Chronicle* photographer was snapping away. Sloots grabbed the photographer's camera, yanked out the film, and threw the camera into the bushes, hitting Louis B. Mayer in the head during an interview with an emerging starlet. Such activities went on into the night.

The morning after the big party, John Jack and Sloots met in the lobby around 10:00 and congratulated each other on the wildly successful evening. None of the Hollywood stars were awake yet, so Sloots suggested setting a Danish pastry and coffee on a little tray outside each of their rooms, an idea that John Jack implemented immediately.

Later that day John Jack, in recognition of Sloot's entrepreneurial talent and discretion, hired him to be the new general manager at The Grand Petroleum Shannon Hotel. Wait until Mommy and Daddy hear about this, thought Sloots. Little Texas Valley Boy makes good. Too bad New Braunfels doesn't have a newspaper.

Hours later John Jack, gratified at the successful outcome of the grand opening of his impressive hotel, walked slowly down the long corridor toward his office, pausing at each of the eighteen gilded mirrors along the way, one hung every six feet or so, confirming his opinion that his visage shone as brightly as that of any of the Hollywood people who had attended the event, maybe even as brightly as all of them put together, Howard Hughes be damned.

Chapter 11
Talford and Sloots Go Hollywood

 At age eighteen, Talford Teasle was eager to leave home, as his brother, Tim, had done when he went offshore. Like Tim, he wanted to get away from the small-town atmosphere of Bullard. He especially hoped to realize his dreams of being in the entertainment industry.

Talford had been accepted as a summer intern at the Alley Theater in Houston, where he had designed and built sets, taken tickets, ushered patrons, and worked in concessions. He had come to know the booking agent and had watched actors audition. He had also designed some of the posters promoting new plays; the Alley Theater management had told him they were as good, if not better, than the posters they could design. Saving all the Alley Theater posters he produced, he added them to the vast collection of movie posters in his room at home in Bullard. The other promising result from having worked at the Alley Theater was that he had had the opportunity to meet celebrities, such as Mary Martin and Dana Andrews, who had starred in *South Pacific*. They were both from Texas originally and had taken a liking to Talford. They even wrote him letters on occasion, which he had saved in an old shoebox.

The Alley Theater had allowed Talford to experience many facets of the entertainment business. He had done well in all his assignments and had been well liked, but he was still unclear about what he did best. In any case, despite his success working at the Alley Theater there was no point in Talford applying for a full-time position there because the theater would only hire people who had worked in New York or Los Angeles. So after his summer internship, Talford returned to Bullard to figure out what to do next.

Upon his return home, Iota Mae had a great idea for him. "Son, there's a big new hotel about forty-five miles from here. They've been hiring staff. The man who runs it is from New Braunfels, and he has some interesting ideas about how to attract customers by adding live entertainment. He wants to have a restaurant in the hotel and a bar and maybe a band. Why don't you go talk to him, son; you know how the Alley Theater works and what people want in entertainment," she urged.

Little did Iota Mae know that The Grand Petroleum Shannon Hotel was a fabulously successful new lodging concept, although Talford knew this because he had read about the Hollywood stars who had come in droves by private plane to the hotel's grand opening party. It was like nothing ever before seen outside of Hollywood. Talford thought his mother's idea could lead to the opportunity he was looking for.

"When you think about it, working at a hotel like that would be a new adventure, Mother. I might be able to figure out what avenue is best for me by being around all those Hollywood stars," Talford concluded. After another week in Bullard, he was bored stiff, so he set up an interview at the new hotel.

The need for staff at the Grand Petroleum Shannon Hotel had increased exponentially by the time Talford arrived for his interview with the general manager, Mr. Sloots.

"Mr. Sloots, my name is Talford Teasle, and I have been working at the Alley Theater in Houston. I grew up working in my daddy's store, Teasleville Dry Goods, in Bullard," Talford began. Before Talford could reach in his satchel to show Sloots the movie posters he had designed and his letter of recommendation from the Alley Theater, Sloots, compensating for his lack of qualified workers and realizing that Talford was nice looking, personable, and seemingly intelligent, hired him immediately. Without a lot of money available for Talford's salary, Sloots let him have one of the smaller rooms as part of his compensation. Talford was thrilled at this new opportunity to work amidst entertainment and stars.

Subsequently, Talford redesigned the menus, redecorated the lobby, helped plan the menu, and, in short order, became a right-hand man to Sloots. On occasion they would have a nightcap after the Saturday night entertainers had finished their shows. One such evening Talford asked Sloots, "Why do you use the picture of Howard Hughes on your wall as a dartboard?" On the wall behind Sloots's desk hung a newspaper photo of Howard Hughes with Rita Hayworth at the opening of The Grand Petroleum Shannon Hotel, riddled with dart holes.

"Well, Talford, that son of a bitch never earned anything. He just rode on his daddy's coattails at Hughes Tool. He was good-looking and rich, and the women really liked him. Hell,

I'm better looking than him, and I bet I could get some Hollywood ladies interested in me, but I'm stuck here and they're out in California. Some of the ladies here are pretty but not like in Hollywood," replied Sloots.

Talford's mind began to percolate. He had seen articles in *Screen* magazine about how Howard Hughes had bought and sold RKO Studios. He knew the history of all the stars who had come to the grand opening of The Grand Petroleum Shannon Hotel and had even listened to the live ABC radio broadcasts, *Sundays at the Shannon*, from the hotel's ballroom. He had met some of the stars, such as Mary Martin and Dana Andrews, on several occasions. His enthusiasm and youthful naïvete caused him to say, "Well, Mr. Sloots, you are just as good-looking as Howard Hughes, and I'm sure those California actress ladies would like you as much as him, maybe even more. I bet he's kinda uppity. I've got an idea. Why, I bet if those Hollywood ladies knew about you could get a date with one. I can just imagine you with Rita Hayworth on your arm."

"Son, what the hell are you talking about?" interrupted Sloots, who was suddenly very interested in this odd young man's babbling.

"If you were to go to Hollywood, you'd just be one in a thousand handsome men out there. But if you could get some of those Hollywood ladies to come here, well, you'd really stand out. And you're the manager of the Grand, for Pete's sake," Talford explained.

"Why the hell would Rita Hayworth come to Houston, Texas?" mumbled Sloots, skeptical but intrigued. "I'm just a beer and bratwurst peddler who got lucky. None of those starlets would care for me—although some of those Hollywood ladies did go for common thugs."

"I bet Rita Hayworth would come if we had another party as spectacular as the evening the hotel opened. You know as well as I do that the opening about a year ago attracted more attention than any old movie opening ever has. Our newspaper doesn't take pictures of anything but oil rigs, lumber trucks, and the occasional cat stuck up a tree. But photographers were all over that hotel opening like fleas on a stray dog," Talford went on.

This whetted Sloots's whistle. "But we already had that opening, son," he said.

"Put on your thinkin' cap, Mr. Sloots. We got some pretty famous people from around here," said Talford with authority. "There's Miss Mary Martin, who didn't come to the original opening. Why, she's never even been here. She performed at the Alley Theater more than once, and she's always in *Screen* magazine. She'd come, I'm sure of it. I know her." He had gone out on a limb by saying this.

Still skeptical, Sloots asked, "Why would she come? For what reason?"

"Texas pride. You know I know her from the Alley Theater. And let me assure you Mary Martin hates Howard Hughes more than you do," Talford said.

"What do you mean?" asked Sloots.

"She's from here. And Howard Hughes fired her from RKO Studios, so she hates him. Howard Hughes made her come to Hollywood to audition for the part of Nurse Nellie Forbush in *South Pacific*. How absurd." Talford threw his head back and brushed his hand over his forehead. "Miss Martin created that role and starred in it on Broadway, but she was not hired to play the role in the movie adaptation. Instead, he cast Mitzie Gaynor for the role—how insulting. His casting couch was mighty busy, I'm sure of it. It's a dog-eat-dog world out there."

Sloots was impressed with Talford's knowledge about Mary Martin and Howard Hughes.

"Listen to me, Mr. Sloots. Here's an idea I've had since my brother, Timothy, worked on an offshore drilling rig some eight years ago. They started makin' movies around here about that time. When he was on the rig, they were making *Thunder Bay* outside New Orleans. Then most every Christmas I would go to the Alley Theater, with my mama as chaperone for our school theater group, which gave me that internship last summer. All this gets me to thinkin', and I know it might sound crazy, but what if we had a theater on an offshore drilling rig? I mean, why not? There's about forty of those huge rigs sealed off, idle and abandoned. Since the San Jacinto Monument opened, commemorating the men who died during the Texas Revolution, they have run ferries from Galveston Bay out to the gulf to re-create the mission. They have about one hundred people every day on those ferries. Then they serve a lunch at the San Jacinto Monument Café near the bay. Lots of folks take those tours on calm days. Also, the ferries take men out who want to deep-sea fish. They opened the abandoned galleys on some of the rigs so the fishermen can store their catch in refrigerators and then bring it back home," said Talford.

He continued without missing a beat, unaware that Mr. Sloots was sure he had a lunatic in his presence: "Plus, the Hollywood people must like this area since they made the *Thunder Bay* movie. Lots of people go to the Alley Theater— that's live theater. Plus, the Majestic and the Metropolitan movie theaters have live shows now on their stages. I got to thinkin' that nobody needs another theater in town, so why not have a live theater in a more unusual setting, like an old offshore drilling rig?"

"That's the craziest thing I've ever heard," said Sloots, staring at the photograph of Howard Hughes with Rita Hayward and throwing another dart at it. "Let me cogitate on that. You really think we could get some of them Hollywood ladies out here so I could meet them?" Sloots considered the ideas Talford had proposed. He figured if his scheme could get Hollywood ladies out here, why not?

"Sir, I'm sure this would work," said Talford, confidently. He thought his stream-of-consciousness proposal might have just won over someone who could make his dream of working in some aspect entertainment come true. Talford had spent quite a lot of time trying to figure out what he might do in the movies. He was still a little afraid of having a speaking part, but had considered the idea of being in a movie in which the characters wore costumes that disguised them, like *It Came from Beneath the Sea* or *Godzilla*. He'd be happy to start out with such an anonymous role as long as it led to better parts. And he figured an opportunity to mix with any Hollywood types might get him one step closer to a movie role.

Chapter 12
Casa Mer Offshore Dinner Theater

 Highly motivated by the idea of having Hollywood ladies come to Houston, especially Rita Hayworth, Sloots placed a call to John Jack, who was busy with his latest oil patch venture in Ardmore, Oklahoma.

"Yes, what is it, Sloots?" asked John Jack.

"Well, sir, I've been reviewing the various improvements and unusual ideas we've put to use successfully here at the hotel, like bringing Danish and coffee to VIP guests' rooms in the morning. We're also the only hotel to offer live entertainment, even saving money by using the same band with different costumes. And we are still the only oyster bar in town," said Sloots.

"Yeah, that was a good idea. And your point, Sloots?" asked John Jack, becoming impatient.

"Okay, John Jack, I have a new idea. Since we already have a band in place on Saturday night and you know we broadcast live from the ballroom on radio station WKDY, why couldn't we have musical productions on Sundays, like around two in the afternoon?" suggested Sloots.

"Where are you going with this? How would that work?" asked John Jack.

"I'm not sure yet, but you told me to keep trying innovative ideas at the Grand. You must admit, so far, so good. With your permission, I'll iron all this out, write up a proposal, and get it to you next week, okay?" said Sloots.

"Well, no harm in looking into it," said John Jack. "I've got to go. God, these people in Ardmore are idiots. I have to watch over everything those drilling lease people do. Why, just yesterday they used a stencil to indicate where the letters on the derrick sign would go, and it spelled out JOJAK."

Sloots had heard all he needed to hear, that John Jack had agreed to look at a new proposal for innovative entertainment at the hotel. Of course, Sloots and John Jack had totally different ideas about what the new type of entertainment might be. Sloots authorized Talford to investigate how an offshore dinner theater might work. It was worth a try if the Hollywood actress ladies could be persuaded to get involved. If the offshore theater didn't work, maybe a Sunday matinee would, he thought.

Talford needed a big-name singer for the proposed Sunday matinee. He figured if he could get Mary Martin to agree to the Sunday performances she could be convinced that the offshore dinner theater was a super idea. He had recently seen her perform a duet with Ethel Merman on television and wanted her to know how familiar he was with her work and that he was a huge fan. He hoped Mary Martin would, in turn, remember him from when she played at the Alley Theater while he was an intern. Toward this end, he drafted a letter to her on The Grand Petroleum Shannon Hotel letterhead.

Dear Miss Mary Martin:

No doubt you remember me from when you and Dana Andrews starred in *South Pacific* at the Alley Theater in Houston. You have such a huge following in Texas, myself included. We, here at The Grand Petroleum Shannon Hotel, pride ourselves on figuring out new concepts in entertainment, and we are thinking of offering Sunday matinee musicals in our ballroom. I'm sure you are well aware of our luxury appointments, world-class service, and unique entertainment. You would be instrumental in helping us realize our latest innovation—Sunday matinees. We thought we'd start with *South Pacific* since you already know the part of Nellie Forbush, and you can have it outright—no need to audition. We can offer you $150 per week plus all expenses paid in the hotel, including your complimentary stay in the luxurious Wildcatter Suite.

May I expect your prompt and positive response by post right away?

Sincerely yours,
Talford Teasle, Entertainment Director

After posting the letter to Mary Martin, Talford made a plan for the offshore dinner theater itself. With Sloots's approval, he named it Casa Mer. He was sure Mary Martin would think his offshore dinner theater was simply one more example of the brilliance of bringing musicals to people in unexpected ways. Sloots agreed with his strategy.

Next, Talford did some research and learned that the people who ran the ferries on the Texas Revolution/Battleship Texas Commemorative Galveston Bay tours and took the deep-sea fishermen out to an offshore rig were one and the same, a company called Folgier's Fantasy, Float and Fish, whose president was Sterling Folgier.

Talford called Mr. Folgier and stated, "Mr. Folgier, this is Talford Teasle, entertainment director of The Grand Petroleum Shannon Hotel. I'd like to meet with you about a proposal that would help you make some more money."

"Why, that'd be fine. Always interested in that sort of thing," replied Mr. Folgier.

Talford worked all night drafting a chart that showed the days and times the Texas Revolution/Battleship Texas tours and the deep-sea fishermen went out and came back. He was more than ready for his meeting with Mr. Folgier.

At their meeting, Talford showed his knowledge of the logistics, saying, "Sir, your last ferry docks at four o'clock, is that right?

"Yes, son, that is correct," replied Mr. Folgier.

"Well, what if you could run two more ferries every day? At ten dollars per person and thirty people per ferry, that would work out to six hundred dollars per day, if my math is correct," said Talford.

"Are you nuts? It's pitch black out there after six o'clock. Who'd want to go out and come back in total darkness, and why?" questioned Mr. Folgier, skeptically.

"Well, sir, that's why I'm here. As a representative of The Grand Petroleum Shannon Hotel, I am entrusted to let you in on a new entertainment idea—in all confidence, of course. Can I trust you, Mr. Folgier?" said Talford, making Mr. Folgier feel like he had a special opportunity.

"Why, you bet," Mr. Folgier said as he placed his right hand over his heart and got out his adding machine, mint green accounting ledger paper, and retractable lead pencil.

"We have a unique idea to provide dinner and musical performances on top of the offshore drilling rig. We will contract with the owner of it."

"Son, that would be me," interrupted Mr. Folgier.

This will be easier than I imagined, thought Talford. "Well, sir, the idea is that the dinner theater would be open for business on the offshore rig maybe two times a week. You'd have to ferry out the actresses, actors, and audience as well as the chefs and cleanup crew on those two days. The rest of the time we'd need you to ferry the actors and actresses out for rehearsals. Now, none of this would disrupt your existing operations, Mr. Folgier, as it would be done after your normal ferry runs during the day. So it would result in extra money. Are you with me so far?" said Talford.

Mr. Folgier was way ahead of Talford. He was pounding the keys on his adding machine so rapidly that the white printout tape was spooling out at an alarming rate, and writing down numbers in his mint green ledger with his lead pencil so furiously that the lead kept breaking off, forcing him to reload it. "Whee doggie, my son, when can we start?" exclaimed Mr. Folgier.

"Now hold on, Mr. Folgier. I've got almost all the actors and actresses lined up. I still have to figure out food and sets and stuff. Can you take me out to the rig so I can see what's needed to turn it into a dinner theater?" asked Talford.

"How about this afternoon?" asked Mr. Folgier, eager to set the plan in motion.

When they went out to the rig, Talford saw that it was a rusted-out mess. But, undeterred, he got Mr. Folgier to agree to sandblast it and coat the first and second levels with white marine paint, which was at least a start.

Over the next few weeks, Talford got a lot done. He contacted a WPA artist Xavier Gonzales, who had painted the Kilgore, Texas, Post Office mural titled *Youth, Pioneer Saga and Drilling for Oil—1941*, to design and decorate what was to be the lobby inside the oil rig.

Meanwhile, Talford kept checking the hotel mail for a letter from Mary Martin. He hadn't heard anything in over two weeks and was getting a little concerned.

One day he asked, "Mr. Sloots, has today's mail come?"

"Yes, here it is," said Sloots, pointing to a stack of letters.

"Just trying to follow up on Miss Martin," explained Talford. "I'll bet we'll hear from her any day now. She's probably involved in an awards show or charity function. Plus, her agent most likely screens her letters. I think we could start rehearsals without her. I could play her part to begin with as long as I don't have to say anything."

Despite not having heard from Mary Martin, Talford set himself a stringent schedule, working toward an opening night in three months. He arranged various meetings with potential business partners. He met with the owner of the company that catered the luncheons at the San Jacinto Monument Café, which were included in the price of the Texas Revolution/Battleship Texas tours—namely, Quality Coastal Gulf Vittles Food Service run, since 1947, by Harry and Blanche Peppers. One Sunday Talford went to the San Jacinto Monument Café for lunch. He asked the waiter if the owners were there, and as it turned out they lived in the top of the monument, in what was known as "the eye."

"Mr. and Mrs. Peppers, may I have a moment of your time this fine day? I represent The Grand Petroleum Shannon Hotel," Talford said, handing them his card. "We are mighty impressed with your food and service," he continued.

Who is this nut case? thought Mr. Peppers. "Son, all we serve is chicken fried steak, fried catfish, French fries, sweet tea, and once in a while, coleslaw. Don't you run one of the few four-star restaurants in the Bay Area?"

"Yes, sir, we do. Thank you for recognizing that honor. But it has nothing to do with why I'm here. You cater the Texas Revolution/Battleship Texas ferry tour luncheons, don't you?" asked Talford.

"Yes, we have since they began in 1947, we're proud to say. So what do you want with us?" asked Mr. Peppers.

"Mr. and Mrs. Peppers, I have an idea that could make you some money. We are starting a new entertainment venue, and I'd like you to provide the food," Talford continued.

"Go on," said Mr. Peppers, as he glanced sideways toward his wife.

"Starting in two months we will be taking people out to the offshore rig owned by Mr. Folgier for a dinner theater experience. Since you've already got the recipes, the food sources, the hot buffet warmers, the waiters, the busboys, and everything else involved in serving visitors a hot lunch at noon, how about doubling up what you already do and serving people on the rig at night?" After going over more details of the proposal, Mr. and Mrs. Peppers agreed to provide the food for the Casa Mer Offshore Dinner Theater patrons.

Another month passed without word from Mary Martin. Talford had left umpteen messages for her agent about Casa Mer, with no response.

One day he stuck his head in Sloots's office and said, "Mr. Sloots, I think we ought to go with *Peter Pan* for the dinner theater opening instead of *South Pacific*."

"Why is that? By the way, have you heard from Mary Martin?" asked Sloots.

"Well, no, not yet. But I'm sure I will. She acted like she liked me a lot when she was starring at the Alley Theater while I was an intern there."

"What did you expect, son? She's an actress. They act. That's what they do," replied Sloots.

"Anyway, *Peter Pan* has fewer parts, and the costumes are pretty simple. There's not much music, mostly one or two people singing, so we might not need a full band. It'd be a whole lot cheaper and easier to put on. Miss Martin has done fifty-three productions of *Peter Pan*, including one on NBC television, so she knows the part pretty good by now. She even won a Tony for it on Broadway. I could play the part of the crocodile—you know, wear the crocodile suit."

"Whatever you think," said Sloots, gnawing on his pencil eraser. "Say, how about flip-flopping the Thursday and Friday themes in the bar during Lent, making Friday night Cajun night instead of German night since people want fish on the Fridays leading up to Easter?" suggested Sloots, always trying to improve on events at the hotel.

Talford remained convinced that Mary Martin would be in touch any day, so he continued planning and searched for the other cast members. He found the three little Darling family kids at the Alley Theater's Young Thespian Summer Program.

He figured his own dog could play Nana since he used to reenact the gangplank scene as a young boy.

Talford asked the Alley Theater set director, who had befriended him during his time as an intern, if he could use certain props and materials to minimize the work needed to produce the set and finance the production. "Listen, since I am using some of your young thespians, do you think we could borrow a few items now that you're in your off season. We just need two things—well, three. We're gonna do a stylistic set for *Peter Pan*, and Mary Martin will star, of course. First, we need a big scrim. I'm gonna have a large hook made out of Styrofoam to represent Captain Hook and a crocodile made out of foam, or I could play the crocodile. We'll just move things up and down behind the scrim when each part comes along. We can use a flashlight for Tinkerbelle," explained Talford.

"Mary Martin? You're kidding," said the set director, skeptically.

"No, it's exciting, isn't it? So we're also gonna need some big particle boards to paint as a backdrop for the children's bedroom and the pirate ship. And that pulley setup for when the children fly out the window with Peter Pan; we'll hook them up with wire, fly them out using the pulley, and then drop them into a safety net on the third floor of the rig. We need that pulley setup for when Captain Hook goes down the gangplank, too. Now that I think of it, we'll need another piece of particle board—for the plank. The foam Hook can go down the plank, then the pulleys can take it out of the live stage area. We can move it off the stage and drop it into the safety net too, while the clock continues to tick inside the foam crocodile," continued Talford.

"Well, I guess that would be okay. Can you get us six tickets and backstage…uh…back rig passes? That'd make my boss happy, and he'll never miss any of the stuff you have asked for."

Quickly agreeing to the terms, Talford felt relieved that he had arranged for most of the props and materials needed for the production.

With one month to go on Talford's schedule, rehearsals started. Everything was running smoothly, although the cast hadn't yet tried performing on the offshore rig. Talford had used a stand-in for Mary Martin's part in rehearsals, but now he was starting to panic since they had to advertise and print tickets and posters in the next ten days and he needed assurance that Mary Martin would be in the production.

"Mr. Sloots, I don't know what to do," said Talford.

"What do you mean? You told me rehearsals were coming along fine except for Miss Martin," replied Sloots.

"It'll probably be okay. I've got a backup for Mary Martin who's been the stand-in all along. Her name is Miss Identity, and she has been performing at the Cockpit Lounge near the Houston Hobby Airport for months as Mary Martin. People say she looks and sounds just like Miss Martin."

"What? Are you nuts? We can't have a drag queen as the main attraction on that offshore rig or anywhere else, do you hear me?" admonished Sloots.

Talford started to cry.

"Oh, for Christ's sake, snap out of it. I'll call John Jack. He's got connections in Hollywood," suggested Sloots, reaching for his phone.

"John Jack, Sloots here. We have hit a little snag with this Mary Martin production," said Sloots.

"What do you mean?" asked John Jack.

"We don't have a commitment from Mary Martin," confessed Sloots.

"Holy mother of God. I knew we shouldn't trust that little poofter. Huhhh. I'll take care of it," answered John Jack.

Moments later, John Jack made a call to the Beverly Hills Hotel. "This is Mr. McArdle. Put me through to Mr. Hughes's suite," said John Jack.

"Right away, Mr. McArdle," said the receptionist.

"Howard, John Jack here. How well do you know Mary Martin?" asked John Jack.

"Fairly well. She's out in one of the cabanas now, as a matter of fact," said Hughes.

"Who's her agent?" asked John Jack.

"Ralph Biggs. Fine man he is," said Hughes.

"Gimme his number," demanded John Jack.

Then John Jack made a call to Ralph Biggs. "Mr. Biggs, this is Mr. McArdle," said John Jack.

"Yes, say, congratulations on your Grand Petroleum Shannon Hotel. That grand opening must have really been something," said Mr. Biggs.

"Well, that's sort of why I'm calling, Mr. Biggs," replied John Jack.

"Please, call me Ralph," insisted Mr. Biggs.

"You represent Mary Martin, is that right?" asked John Jack.

"Yes, that's right," said Mr. Biggs.

"We're planning another big event at the Grand. I've got several actors and actresses lined up, and since she's from Texas I wondered if she might want to be a part of it," continued John Jack.

"What did you have in mind?" asked Biggs, smelling a percentage.

"We're starting a new concept. On Sundays when it's not football season, we're gonna have afternoon musical performances in the ballroom. They'll be open to the public and broadcast on WKDY radio out of Houston," explained John Jack.

"You know, McArdle, thanks to the unions, our talent gets paid when they perform on the radio, same as live," said Mr. Biggs.

The goddamn unions again, thought John Jack, "No, I didn't, but whatever you say," said John Jack into the receiver, lifting his middle finger toward nothing in particular. "We have another idea, too. We call it the Casa Mer Offshore Dinner Theater."

"Really, I had no idea you were behind Casa Mer. I keep getting high-pitched frantic phone calls from someone about

Casa Mer. I've ignored them. Why didn't you call in the first place?" asked Mr. Biggs.

"I should have, but I'm too busy on the road and I have to delegate stuff now. Anyway, what's it gonna cost me to get Mary Martin for two weeks? She can have full access to all our amenities, including the Wildcatter's Suite on top of that," asked John Jack.

"What's in it for me, McArdle?" asked Mr. Biggs.

"Jesus Christ, do you people ever let up?" said John Jack.

"No, sir, we don't," replied Mr. Biggs.

In the end, to get Mary Martin, John Jack had to triple the $150-a-week offer that Talford had extended in his original letter. If this matinee and offshore dinner theater don't work, Sloots and Talford are history, thought John Jack.

Once her agent had negotiated the final contract, Mary Martin flew to Houston and was driven to Galveston in the hotel courtesy van to check in to The Grand Petroleum Shannon Hotel. Sloots was on hand to greet the star and get her situated in the Wildcatter's Suite.

Talford was out on the offshore rig for a final rehearsal. "Places, people, places. Remember, nobody in this play ever grows up. In act one, the biggest number is 'I Gotta Crow.' Wendy, that's when you and the lost boys need to already be in your harnesses. I'm going backstage to get the crocodile sound synced up with the ticking clock, so carry on," he said.

No one splashed into the gulf, so Talford was satisfied that the final dress rehearsal was a success. He even thought it might be a good idea to have a swinging harness set up at The Grand Petroleum Shannon Hotel, maybe in the bar.

The next morning Talford excitedly went to pick up Mary Martin and brief her on the production. "We've simplified the set and gotten it down to three stage changes. First will be where you fly into the window and interact with the Darling children, after which you and the kids will fly out the window and down to the third level of the rig. Oh, and we have a net in case anyone falls from the rigging cable," explained Talford.

Mary Martin gave Talford an incredulous stare, but since she had agreed to the contract and knew this part like the back of her hand, she listened.

"At intermission, we'll change the set to become the pirate ship. You and the kids will drop in on the ship, and we start to hear the crocodile clock ticking. I might play the crocodile, just so you know, or I might not. Anyway, the next scene is down the gangplank, and the closing scene is back in the living room. Got it?" said Talford.

"Okay, kid, let's head out to the theater—I mean, rig. It's ten, so we have several hours for me to check out the sets, familiarize myself with the harness setup, and run a check with the background music sound track," Miss Martin said to Talford. After spending a little time going over her lyrics, she felt ready for the performance. And she thought the sets looked pretty good for such a cockamamie idea.

Talford had already ferried out the rest of the cast and arranged for the props to be ready. Around 7:00 pm the audience began to arrive and take their seats. The sound guy started the introductory music, and the actors took their places on the darkened set. The lights rose to reveal the Darlings' living room. The audience gasped.

The production went off without a hitch until one of the Darling kids fell off the rigging and into the safety net. Talford cued the sound effects man to blare out music that sounded like thunder and flick the lights up and down to make it seem like a storm instead of a mistake.

Miss Martin flew onto the pirate ship, knocking over the foam crocodile prop for the part Talford had decided not to play. The sound effects man blared out music suggesting another storm and blinked the lights. Then Mary Martin, sensing a disastrous review, belted out a medley of show tunes and ended with a rousing rendition of "I'm Flying" as she soared over the audience.

At first the audience looked perplexed. Couples eyed each other, and people in adjacent seats looked askance at their neighbors. Then they realized the production likely was a farce and started to giggle, culminating in uproarious laughter. There followed a five-minute standing ovation. Then Talford ushered the cast out to the first ferry headed back to shore. The audience milled around comparing notes on which part had been the most outrageous, and then filed slowly onto the second ferry.

That night Talford, along with the cast and crew, anxiously awaited the reviews.

The next day the papers ran surprisingly positive reviews. "Spectacular," "History Making," "Sensational," "Unheard of Entertainment Venue" proclaimed the headlines of the *Houston Post. Variety* had sent a correspondent who wrote: "Not since Van Cliburn ended the Cold War have audiences raved so much."

Both Talford and Sloots had a lot riding on the new concept of the Casa Mer Offshore Dinner Theater and the Sunday matinees and continued to publicize them. In the ensuing weeks, weather interrupted most of the planned performances at Casa Mer; but Miss Martin continued to perform her most famous numbers from *Peter Pan* in her little green pixie outfit and feathered cap for the Sunday matinee.

John Jack continued to expand his entrepreneurial efforts in Oklahoma and Missouri. But as oil deposits became harder to find and his expenses kept mounting, all the expansion caused him to take a hard look at his bottom line. It didn't help that the occupancy rate at The Grand Petroleum Shannon Hotel was down by 22 percent.

Two months after the Casa Mer opening, he scheduled a meeting with Sloots to assess the situation. "Sloots, I have some hard decisions to make," began John Jack.

"Oh ya, what's that?" asked Sloots.

"While you are doing an exceptional job managing things, I'm afraid we are going to need to cut back on expenses and improve the bottom line. I can't be here in Galveston more than a few weeks out of the year, so I'm putting you in charge of the fiscal health of the hotel. Do whatever it takes to bring expenses down at least eleven percent. I've got no choice. To keep funding expansion, I've got to rein in costs."

"That'll be tough, sir. We are known for luxury and amenities no other hotel offers. I guess we could cut services like free dry cleaning and shuttle transport to and from the airport, but that won't help the bottom line as much as is needed," reported Sloots.

"Then I suggest you take a hard look at what we offer that has high overhead, such as entertainment, Sloots," said John Jack.

"Oh no, John Jack. You don't mean eliminating the Sunday matinees and maybe even Casa Mer, do you?" Sloots replied, disappointed.

"Specifically, Casa Mer. Sloots, that thing is hemorrhaging money, and you know it. Maybe we could continue the Sunday matinees in the ballroom but only once a month," suggested John Jack.

"I'll have a detailed recommendation on your desk in two days, sir. I'm going to try to cut corners other than entertainment, if that's okay," replied Sloots.

"As long as you can meet the eleven percent budget reduction goal, I don't care how you do it," replied John Jack.

After John Jack left, Sloots took down all the Casa Mer promotional posters and threw them in the trash. He stared out the window at Talford, who was overseeing the landscape crew, and shook his head, wondering how he would tell Talford that Casa Mer had to close and how Talford might react.

Chapter 13
A Teasle Comes Onshore

 Through Iota Mae, Pop knew about Talford's initial success with the Casa Mer Offshore Dinner Theater. He supposed she had been right to have allowed Talford to follow his dreams, no matter how peculiar they seemed. Ever since losing the Cherokee Lake oil well, Pop had concentrated on collecting the royalties coming to him from the percentages of wells he still owned. He had no need and certainly no desire to pursue more oil ventures. He did, however, intend to speak with Tim, who, in the three years since he had returned home from the offshore rig, hadn't done much except work in the family store. But although Pop meant to talk to Tim, he never seemed to have the time or inclination. He just wanted to watch his TV shows.

Then one rainy evening while Pop and Tim were watching *Sky King* on TV, Tim waited for a commercial and said, "Pop, I've saved up two hundred dollars, so now I can go to landman school. There's a new set of classes starting in two weeks at the high school auditorium. A man named Peck, who married into the Mullin family, is giving out scholarships for the school. "

"Son, we don't take aid from anyone, least of all one of those Johnny-come-latelies who, more than likely, are crooks.

Here's a check if you need it," offered Pop. "What exactly will the landman school cover?" he asked absent-mindedly.

"It's a two-week course teaching about how, after geologists discover a place they think might have oil, a landman finds the owners and negotiates with them for the mineral rights to drill. It sounds like a good job for me since I'd travel around, stay in hotels, go to county courthouses, and talk to landowners. I would have to draw up contracts allowing the wildcatters to drill and figure out who gets what if the well hits—that part might be complicated. Most of the big oil companies have their own landmen, but I don't want to do that. I want to go around by myself, get the rights, and sell them to independent wildcatters. There's plenty of oil around in smaller deposits that the big oil people don't care about but the smaller wildcatters sure do. After being on that rig in Louisiana, I don't want to work for some corporation again with everybody telling me what to do. I'd rather be on my own and work at my own pace," explained Tim.

"That's nice," said Pop, distracted by the heavy spring downpour, which would turn their basement into red-orange clay sludge that he would have to spend all morning pumping out. He then turned his attention back to the episode of *Sky King* he was watching, where Penny, the heroine, was about to go on her first solo flight.

During the next commercial, Pop turned to Tim and asked, "Did you say the big oil companies have landmen? Son, I promised your mother we wouldn't have anything to do with those big outfits."

"No, Pop, like I said, I want to strike out on my own," stressed Tim.

On the first day of landman class the teacher, Mr. Cravet, made a drawing on the blackboard that showed layers of rocks, sand, dirt, and salt underneath the topsoil, which he illustrated in different colors of chalk. He turned down the lights and, with a flashlight, pointed to each layer as he talked about it. His voice was a quiet monotone, which didn't help hold Tim's attention, with the lights turned down and the room hot. Occasionally a fly would penetrate the dust in the flashlight beam.

As Mr. Cravet pointed to the salt layer, he said: "Now the salt layer comes from seawater or salty lakes buried underground. When the saltwater dries out, the horizontal beds contain the salt residue. In some cases, deformation in the geological makeup of the area where salt is found causes the horizontal beds to buckle and jut upward, creating salt 'domes' or caverns. Oil is usually found in cavities in the salt dome cap rock or trapped beneath the horizontal layers because salt is impervious to oil."

Up went Tim's hand. "What do you mean impervious?" he asked.

"Well, you see, son, it's the same as water in a bucket—it doesn't seep or leak out. But if you put water in a cardboard box it'll leak out."

Tim then asked, "If I pour a bunch of salt in the ground, would the oil show up?"

"Not exactly, son," replied Mr. Cravet before launching into a reiteration of the geological process involved.

On and on went the classes for two weeks. Tim learned how to research land titles, draw up royalty contracts, and divide the profits from any oil discovery between the owner of the mineral rights and the drillers. He also did some practice negotiating to learn what the owners might ask for.

One aspect he knew nothing about was obtaining highway construction rights, so he asked, "Mr. Cravet, you're telling us that we can also get paid for talking to landowners about letting highways come through?"

"That's right, Tim," acknowledged Mr. Cravet, who then explained the procedure to the class.

Wow, thought Tim. I don't even have to know where there's salt. This can't be too hard.

After graduation, Tim, continued to explore the idea that oil should be somewhere near salt. He reproduced several maps of the Spindletop oil find and the Caddo and Lake Cherokee wells and, sure enough, there was salt in those spots. Plus, there were lines of salt deposits running up the west side of Louisiana, the east side of Texas, and westward just underneath Dallas. His maps showed that the salt deposits continued intermittently through Waxahachie and on through the southern tip of Fort Worth.

At first, Tim needed money to do some traveling, so he took a full-time job with the Texas Railroad Commission, which worked with the Texas Department of Highways to map out where roads would go. He got to ride freight trains between little towns where highways were planned. He went to the county courthouses of these towns and figured out who owned the land proposed for the highways. Then he negotiated with the landowners for rights to construct the highways. Since there were no connections between little towns, the landowners were all too happy to make some money allowing the state to build highways. In his ample spare time, Tim researched topographical maps he found in the town courthouses and began a list of landowners in towns with salt domes, and therefore possibly oil deposits.

After two years with the Texas Railroad Commission, Tim had saved enough money to start traveling across Texas follow-ing the old maps that showed where salt existed. His first stop was Grand Saline, some forty-five miles due east from Dallas, where he checked into the Trailer Hitch Hotel. He figured there was bound to be some salt in a town with that name.

The next morning he went to the county courthouse to look up mineral rights records. To get to the second floor, where the records were located, he walked up a stairwell that had a greenish brown tint from the overhead fluorescent lights, one of which was burnt out and emitted an intermit-tent buzzing sound. After entering a room through a door marked "Records," Tim said to the clerk, "Ma'am, I'm Tim Teasle, and I'm a landman."

The lady, about sixty years old with silver gray hair tied up in a bun, was sitting in an old wooden chair. At first he thought she might be asleep since her glasses were perched on the end of her nose and her eyes were squinting. Finally, after he coughed she peered up over her glasses at him. Her beady brown eyes blinked, and after a moment, she asked, "Yes, what do you need?" seemingly annoyed. Her body was so still it seemed to be attached to the chair, which exactly matched the color of her gray-brown shapeless smocked dress. To Tim, she looked like she had been sitting in the old wooden chair most of her life, and maybe even been born in it.

Showing her his employee identification, Tim said, "Well, ma'am, I've been working on the Texas Railroad Commission. And I'm just starting out now as a landman, which means…"

"Hellfire, young man, I know what a landman is," said the lady, getting increasingly agitated.

"Ma'am, I'm from Teasleville and worked in my daddy's dry goods store in Bullard and then on the Kerr-McGee off-shore rig in Louisiana. I sold salt in the dry goods store and spent one year on the rig lookin' for oil, so I feel like I'm more qualified than most to look for oil near salty places, like here in Grand Saline. Mr. Cravet showed us a chalkboard drawing of how salt domes are formed and used a flashlight…" Tim continued, chattering away.

"Teasle, say, are you related to the Teasles from Bullard who had that huge oil find at Cherokee Lake around 1940 or so?" asked the lady.

"Well, I guess so," Tim replied. Having been seven years old at the time, he had little or no recollection of the event. "I remember a man on the back porch who came over covered in oil one day and Pop opening a bottle of wine. Right after that day Pop seemed to get sick, and my mother and brother Talford started watching *In the Kelvinator Kitchen* on TV, and our food didn't taste so good anymore."

After a while, the old lady took a shine to him. "Well, son, I suppose you ought to know my name. It's Bessie Rainwater. I've been here almost forty years, since before people found any oil around here. Then there was such a rush it almost did me in. Landmen everywhere, camped out in tents and spending all day in this little room. Why, I had to just sit home for a spell, but I survived," Miss Rainwater explained.

Tim heard a slight sucking sound as she got off the wooden chair and motioned for him to walk with her to the bookshelves housing all the mineral rights records. Rows and rows of shelves with fat navy blue binders covered with dust contained the documents of land ownership and mineral rights. Some people owned both the land and the mineral rights, while others owned just one or the other. The binders were arranged by date. The first row showed binders from 1905 to 1922. Then there was a gap before they continued with the year 1928.

"Just one minute, young man," the lady said as she blew off the dust and removed one of the big blue binders from 1942. "Did you know anyone with the last name of Peck in Bullard?"

"No, Miss Rainwater, I don't recall that name. But there were an awful lot of new folks moving in then," replied Tim, who then asked about the gap in the records.

"There was a fire in the courthouse years ago, and some records were destroyed, so no one really knows who owns most of the land thought to have oil in the years between 1923 and 1927," explained Miss Rainwater.

Then she began reading aloud from the blue binder marked 1942: "'On this twelfth day of December in 1942, be it known that a Mr. Leland Peck Jr., from Bullard, Texas, submitted false documents in the matter of a transfer of ownership of the Cherokee Lake oil field in Bullard, in Gregg County, Texas. These documents are not recognized and not allowed.' I remember this incident. Tim, we might be on to some history-making information," Miss Rainwater said, barely above a whisper. "I thought I remembered something fishy having to do with the Cherokee Lake find—and I don't mean striped bass. My sister Bernice worked in the Records Department of the Gregg County Courthouse at the time of the Cherokee Lake discovery. It made all the papers. There was a picture of your daddy in the newspaper with the caption 'Local Man Becomes Next Millionaire.' Bernice told me that she hadn't gotten any paperwork right away on the Cherokee Lake find, which was highly unusual. Then about a week later she got documents from a man named Peck, stating that Mr. Edward James Teasle had signed over the rights to the Cherokee Lake oil well to some company named Gulf Allied Systems, and a month after that the well was signed over to that man named Peck."

Tim said: "I guess that would have been around the time Pop got sick. He kind of stopped talking to me and my brother Talford, so we didn't hear anything about it. Wow, I wonder what could have happened to cause him to do something so drastic as to sign over those rights." Then, shifting his focus, Tim asked, "What is known about who owned what during the dates of the missing books?"

"The only way to get answers is to find some of the original landowners in Grand Saline and see if they still have their deeds of ownership and mineral rights. None of the big oil companies bothered to do that since they found enough owners on file in the courthouse records that remained intact from the years before and after the fire," replied Miss Rainwater.

"Well, Miss Rainwater, how many possible owners would that amount to? A few or a bunch?" he asked.

"I reckon maybe five. You know, Tim, I'm getting on in age, and no one comes in the courthouse anymore for things. If you want, maybe we can go out and look for these owners, see what we can find out. You'll have to drive because I can't anymore," said Miss Rainwater.

"Wow, that would be a big help. You know, right from the get-go I didn't want to work for any big oil company—I already did that. So I was hopin' to find smaller parcels, like the ones around here that are owned by local folks, with the potential for oil and sell those rights to small wildcatters. Mama hated those wildcatter men and said they were not to be trusted. She hated the dockworkers, too. Come to think of it, she hated anybody who wasn't from Bullard." Tim sensed that Miss Rainwater understood, and had sympathy for small-town politics and perspectives.

The next day Miss Rainwater and Tim set out to find landowners who might fill in information missing from the records. After a few minutes on a dusty oyster-shell road, they crossed a cattle guard and continued down a driveway to a little house, where Tim saw a sign that looked familiar: "Turkey Jerky—It's Gobblin' Good."

"Good grief, that's old man Bouchene's business," Tim exclaimed. He remembered that Mr. Bouchene had operated the turkey shoot concession at the Bullard Fall Farm Harvest Festival each autumn.

"You know Elio?" asked Miss Rainwater.

"No, ma'am, but he might remember me from a hypnotized chicken incident," said Tim.

"What are you taking about, young man?" asked Miss Rainwater.

"Never mind," said Tim, hoping to change the subject. "Do you know Mr. Bouchene?"

Blushing, Miss Rainwater replied, "Why, yes, we used to court a little."

As a man emerged from the house, Tim got out of the car and said, "Mr. Bouchene, I'm Tim Teasle from the Teasleville Dry Goods store in Bullard." Tim stuck out his hand toward Mr. Bouchene, who didn't respond. Tim noticed he was wearing a hard hat and there were maybe twenty golf balls scattered haphazardly in the front yard. Wishing to make conversation, Tim added, "Mr. Bouchene, have you taken up playing golf?"

"Oh no," said Miss Rainwater, "that's from the hawks that pick up balls out at the driving range near here. They think they're mice or something. Then, when they figure out they're not food, they drop them. It pays to wear a hard hat, especially in the afternoon." Just then a couple of golf balls dropped near Tim's foot.

"Elio, my dear, this young man graduated from landman school, and he is hoping to find who has the mineral rights to property around here that might have oil deposits. You remember when the fire wiped out six years records of mineral right owners?" said Miss Rainwater.

As it turned out, Elio Bouchene still had his original land ownership documents, and he legally owned the rights to several small parcels of land running south of Dallas and through Fort Worth.

"Mr. Bouchene, I'd be mighty beholden to you if you would talk to me about your mineral rights," said Tim.

"Well, okay," said Mr. Bouchene. Miss Rainwater had just winked at him, and he thought there was no harm in talking. "Son, I have turned down several offers for a hundred dollars an acre to let oil people drill here, plus eight percent of the net take if they find oil." Mr. Bouchene removed his hard hat and put his arm around Miss Rainwater, who blushed crimson. "But if Bessie Rainwater here agrees to have dinner with me on Saturday I'll give you the same deal I turned down—one hundred dollars an acre plus eight percent of the net," offered Mr. Bouchene.

Miss Rainwater nodded in approval.

"Fair is fair, Mr. Bouchene," said Tim. "I'll give you ten percent of the net. I don't have any wildcatters lined up to drill, but believe you me I'll find some, and then we'll be in business."

The two men shook on it, and Miss Rainwater grinned ear to ear.

As Tim and Miss Rainwater drove back to town, Tim asked, "May I buy you an ice cream cone to thank you for helping me with Mr. Bouchene?"

"No, honey, no need. I have a date with Elio Saturday, thanks to you, young man," she replied.

Tim slept well through the night at the Trailer Hitch Hotel. The next morning, he left promising Miss Rainwater he'd keep in touch. He couldn't remember having been so excited, and felt he was finally on his way. Mr. Bouchene's land was at least a hundred miles long and stretched more than that wide. Even if half that land had oil, it would sure make him a good living, he figured.

Chapter 14
Wildcatter Speakeasy

Junior kept to his morning routine of reading several area newspapers with an eye toward learning about businesses or individuals he might be able to exploit in the future. He had followed The Grand Petroleum Shannon Hotel goings on and admired that ambitious undertaking. Another new business Junior read about was something called a landman. At the moment, though, Junior figured the landman vocation was new so he would just sit back and see if that line of work would produce any real income. His new motto was "Why pioneer when you can poach."

Junior was making $18,000 per month from the Cherokee Lake well he had stolen from Pop Teasle. He had made a name for himself among the wildcatters, the men with whom he drank on occasion. They frequented the Gentlemen's Club in La Grange, thirty miles away, at least his buddies did. Junior would drive the men over to La Grange in his Cadillac sedan, let them out, and tell them he was going to park the car. Once inside, the other wildcatters would immediately select an "escort" then proceed with her to a private room to enjoy whatever "menu item" they chose, ranging from chitchat to pleasures of the flesh. Rather than go into the club, Junior would visit an all-night breakfast place for an hour or so, then return to get his buddies, who thought he had been inside all that time like them.

Abstaining from mingling with the escorts was Junior's little secret. He had to maintain a delicate balancing act. Priss would shoot him if she thought he had had anything to do with the La Grange girls, but the wildcatters would think he was some kind of lightweight pansy if they thought he didn't. Junior felt morally superior to the other men and yearned to climb up in the social strata, but he needed to befriend these men to get information on activities in the oil patch.

One night Junior sat back in his easy chair and took a long drink of bourbon to celebrate his stolen profile as Bullard's richest man and reflect on how to further improve his social status. While increasing his wealth, he had figured that respect would follow, as Dub had indicated, but it hadn't. He had thought marrying Priss would give him the social status he craved, but it hadn't. Although a member of one of the wealthiest old-line Bullard families, she was socially shy; her inability to instantly elevate Junior to his desired standing in the community by marriage had confounded him. Other means he had taken to improve his social status included lobbying to get elected to the board at Rigview Country Club, but he was rejected, along with most of the other wildcatters considered nouveau riche—worth millions but perceived as crude and common, if not outright thugs. It was as if he were radioactive or tubercular. Such rejection had been a hard pill to swallow. But the biggest challenge for Junior had been their indifference. To him, indifference was the worst of foes, reminding him of how he had been ostracized at Weldon Christian Camp. This kind of indifference was like pitching a ball to someone who purposely doesn't catch it—nothing much to work with.

To gain more status, he finally decided to throw one of his drinking and gambling parties, a sort of wildcatter speakeasy previously known only to a few of his buddies. Junior made a list of men to invite, including the bank president, the Rigview Country Club chairman, and a few deacons from the church. Then he remembered that those people didn't like him, so he decided to just ask the usual guys, all of whom were shunned by Bullard society. Junior knew this group would turn out for his party like they always had before. They would come to pay tribute to the most successful of them all—Junior Peck. In fact, they were honored to be included in the party as long as nobody else knew about it, especially their wives.

He telephoned several buddies, asking, "Say, you interested in coming out to my Cherokee Lake house tonight from around ten until we run out of hooch and the ladies?"

The standard reply was, "Does a bear shit in the woods?"

Several area residents kept second houses on Cherokee Lake, mostly so their kids could water ski in the summer. Junior had gotten his house in a barter deal, and Priss knew nothing about it or about the parties Junior had been holding there.

Now Junior needed to hire the "ladies." There was a honky-tonk nightclub just outside of town called The Reo Palm Isle, which had opened in 1935 and was owned by Zelma Middlebury. Its cavernous dance hall featured local talent at the beginning of their careers; Ray Price and his

Cherokee Cowboys had gotten their start there. It also show-cased various musicians traveling from Dallas to Shreveport to play on the Louisiana Hayride live broadcasts carried on radio station KWKH. Nationally known talent played there, too, like Jimmy and Tommy Dorsey and Woody Herman.

Nice-looking girls worked at The Reo Palm Isle. They were known as "dime a dance girls" because men could buy a dance with them for a dime. They were also known as "taxi cab girls" due to the fact that the girls had to arrive and leave by taxi and were forbidden from fraternizing with the men on the way to or from the club. The girls followed a strict dress code: white short-sleeved shirts with scarves knotted at their necks and either pencil-slim calf-length skirts or fuller skirts with wide belts in contrasting colors.

As more and more wildcatters, roughnecks, and oil field trash moved into the area, the nights at The Reo Palm Isle got so rowdy that Zelma hired Cabbie Wells as a bouncer. Cabbie's name dated back to his years of living in New York and screwing women in the backseats of cabs.

The Reo Palm Isle was located in Gregg County, the only wet county in Texas. Traveling salesmen working their territory would arrange to stay in one of the seedy motels near The Reo Palm Isle on Thursdays. These were known as pressure cooker Thursdays because the wives in the surrounding counties would put dinner on in pressure cookers and go to The Reo Palm Isle for a little afternoon dancing. By the time they got home, dinner would be ready and they would be wearing smiles, but not much else, when their husbands came home from work.

Junior made a call to The Reo Palm Isle. "Cabbie? How's about askin' some of your early shift girls to come over to my lake place. Say, around ten? Sure, same deal. You get a cut, the girls get some spending money, and everybody has a good time," said Junior, his voice carrying excitement.

"Done," said Cabbie as he began making a list of the afternoon shift ladies. "Let's see, how about Thelma, Wanda, Patsy, Belinda, June Mae, and Lottie. These are our top hoochy-koochy ladies, if you know what I mean," replied Cabbie.

"Yep, sounds fine to me. Just don't send Lula Jean. She's got great knockers, but Jesus, she is living proof that cousins mate. There's not enough gin, and it would never get dark enough for any of the guys to want to be with her, bless her heart. Get the best booze—don't skimp on that," admonished Junior. He knew that Cabbie was a dirty, smelly, lousy dresser with cigar spittle on his shirt and probably couldn't be trusted, but he could supply girls and booze when needed to make a party memorable.

"How am I supposed to get paid?" asked Cabbie.

"Hell, Cabbie, we've been through this before. You know I can't be caught dead at The Reo. I'll send the money back with Patsy—she's such a doll," replied Junior.

Around 11:00 pm, with the party in full swing, Junior took the measure of the place. He could have filled an anatomical dictionary with the range of appearances of the men and ladies in attendance. The men, collectively, were potbellied,

fat, gangly, tall or short, bearded, and balding. The ladies were busty or flat-chested, peroxided or natural-colored, slender or curvy, youngish, and eager. The air was filled with the smell of cheap cologne, aftershave lotion, cigarette and cigar smoke, and gin and beer. The hi-fi was blaring the latest hits, ranging from Blind Wayne singing "Wake Up, Little Willie" to Rusty Warren's latest hit "Knockers Up." Several party games were underway simultaneously. In the corner by the bar, there was a raucous dart game, with the target constantly altered to feature various female body parts. The ladies were playing boxers or briefs, guessing which men wore what, their correct guesses being rewarded with shots of whiskey. The most popular game was a version of spin the bottle in which each of the ladies had worn a different-colored neck scarf that had been removed and placed in a ten-gallon hat in the center of a circle of men. The bottle, an empty gallon of Jack Daniel's bourbon, was spun around until it stopped at a wildcatter, who then got to pick out a scarf and disappear with its owner to the boathouse for a game of find the gusher.

Everyone staggered out around 3:00 am. The girls might have been in violation of the rule not to fraternize with the men, but no one would ever know. As with the La Grange visits, Junior hadn't partaken of any of the party games, opting instead to sit out on the boat dock and nurse a bourbon or two. He abided by the old saying "Why buy a cow when you can get the milk for free?" and was quite content to take comfort at home in the arms of Priss.

Chapter 15
The Sermon of Shame

On the Sunday morning following Junior's Cherokee Lake booze-and-broads blowout, portions of Bullard attended the service at the Sabine River Bend Worldwide Baptist Church. The congregation typically consisted of wives since most men, aware that oil didn't stop flowing on Sunday, were out checking their rigs—worshiping their religion while the women worshiped in church. Other men didn't attend church because Sunday was a good day to sleep in after a late Saturday night.

On this mid-March morning the congregation was a bright tapestry, with the colors of the dresses worn by the women matching the colors of the flowers blooming outside: yellow jonquils, red and lime-green caladiums, red poppies, and blue irises. Luckily the fan circulated the mixture of heavy perfume away from the altar, down the aisles, and out the front door.

The preacher, Tom Bob, who had officiated at Bobby's christening, entered the pulpit after the processional "Nearer My God to Thee." His double chin shook as he cleared his throat. No one really knew where he had come from except he claimed to have been in Tulsa and studied under the great Pastor Phipps, who had kept his flock on the straight and narrow during Tulsa's heyday of oil discovery. So the flock accepted him as the right choice to lead them away from the sins of what lay underneath their own land. In truth, he had been the only choice as no one else had applied. Tom Bob had insisted on adding the word *worldwide* to the name of the church as he had aspirations to broadcast his sermons live over the radio.

Tom Bob commenced to preach: "It has come to my attention, brethren, that we need to, nay, must revisit Matthew 12:43–45," he began, emphasizing the second syllable of *Matthew* as if it had two syllables of its own, making for a total of three syllables. "For in our very midst the devil walks. He walks in the guise of a man seeking respite from hard labor, from unfulfilled dreams following much sacrifice and investment to no avail. It is necessary for a man to try and, though he may fail time and time again, keep up the effort as it is in the effort that we can be saved, not in the celebration of the failure or as a respite from the toils."

"Amen," mumbled the front row consisting of the most pious in the flock.

"As Matthew 12:43–45 says," Tom Bob went on after a quick drink of water at the pulpit for he was getting all worked up now and his flaccid face had turned as crimson as his vestments, making him appear like some version of the devil. He coughed, gagging at the thick perfume, and then continued, reading: "When the unclean spirit is gone out of a man, he walketh through dry places seeking rest, and finding none. Then, he saith, I will return into my house from whence I came out; and when he is come, he findeth it empty, swept and garnished. Then goeth he, and taketh with himself seven other spirits more wicked than himself and they enter and dwell there and the last state of that man is worse than the first."

He looked up from his Bible and delivered the next portion of the service extemporaneously: "If any of you doubt that the devil walks amongst our community, peer into the souls of those fortunate enough in our community to own a lake house out on Cherokee Lake and ask yourselves why would someone be out at the lake at night and not during the day when people water ski and fish, except to entertain the devil under the cover of darkness?" The congregation hadn't really thought about this but nodded in agreement that there was no reason to be at the lake during the night.

Tom Bob, sensing he had almost made his point, finished at the top of his lungs, "Even so shall it be also unto this wicked generation."

The congregation mumbled with lowered heads and eyes, each looking at the person seated next to them and wondering what the preacher was talking about.

After waiting a few minutes to let this sink in, Tom Bob said, "Verily, I say unto you as Matthew spoke, someone in our community has consorted with the devil in their lake house. Ask yourselves who, among our townsfolk, is not present today. That is your answer. Shun this evil man and his unholy ways, and shun his family," commanded Tom Bob, banging his right fist on the lectern and nodding to the town gossip, who lived in the lake house next to Junior's and just happened to have relayed the news of the party to the preacher earlier that morning.

At this point, the grape juice was passed out row by row along with the collection plate. All the while, everyone in the church was mentally assessing who was there and who was not.

"Oh my God," said Marion Wilson, under her breath. "It's the Pecks." She knew she had to activate the prayer circle the minute she got home. Her mind moved quickly during the "Onward Christian Soldiers" recessional.

Immediately following the service, several women gathered outside the entrance and began whispering about the sad plight of Priss in her marriage to Junior, an outcast among the socially acceptable townsfolk, and how their son Bobby might turn out just like his daddy. What a shame, they thought.

After the party at his lake house, Junior had crept into his home knowing he would to have to deal with something much worse than a hangover if he awakened Priss.

She hadn't slept well that Saturday night, heard the door, and had confronted Junior. "I swear, you've been crazier than a run-over dog since you hit that well. I don't know why you're not more grateful to the Lord for these gifts and helpin' at the new mission for those less fortunate. Most wildcatters don't hit gushers like you did," she declared. Priss didn't know that Junior hadn't hit the Cherokee Lake gusher but had stolen it.

"I know, I know," said Junior. "I was just out tryin' to console ole Jabby, who keeps comin' up dry. You know, I'm a God-fearin' Christian, so I thought by buying him a few drinks it would ease his misery. Well, one thing led to another and…"

Since Junior didn't often stay out late, he almost always got away with such behavior. In the summer months, he would come home and sleep outside in a little pup tent near a castor bean tree. "It makes me so happy and gives me great comfort sleeping on top of all the money that's underground beneath these trees" was how he explained this behavior to Priss. In the winter months, like this particular night, he would sleep on the couch and get up before Priss, putting on the coffee and making her think he had slept through the night in the house. But his trick didn't work after Saturday night's lake house party: Priss launched into a tirade.

Junior, attempting to change the subject and appease Priss, interrupted her, saying, "Oh, I found a way to tithe more to the church."

Without replying, Priss stormed off to the guest bedroom and took a sleeping powder to help her doze off.

As a result of the sleeping powder, Priss overslept and missed the church service. When she finally woke up, she dressed hurriedly in her Sunday best and, to keep up appearances, managed to show up at Rigview Country Club for the weekly Sunday brunch after church usually attended by the wives of the successful wildcatters.

When she arrived, she said to a group of women, "Why, good mornin', Bernice, Paula, Sylvia. You all look so pretty this fine mornin'."

The ladies eyed her up and down.

Priss sensed that something was different. Occasionally, the Sunday brunch ladies would turn a microscopic eye on one of their own should she show up in a brand-new outfit. They all dressed to look their best at church, reflecting their husbands' success. But some of these women went overboard, now having enough money to buy clothes at Neiman Marcus or Harold's in Dallas, and were considered to be "showing out" which was thought to be distasteful. On this particular Sunday, Priss was the object of their inspection, but it wasn't because of her clothes. They were being just plain hateful.

They grouped around each other like a bunch of green, blue, red, and yellow hens glistening while speaking in hushed tones amongst themselves, the feathers in their hats bobbing emphatically, punctuating their intense discussion.

"Well, my dear. How odd to see you here today," said Priss's best friend, Marion, motioning her away from the gossipy group. That took guts, but she thought Priss should know what was going on.

"Priss, let's go into the Ladies' Card Room," said Marion.

"What is happening?" Priss pleaded, as they walked away.

"Priss, I know you have your hands full at home with Junior. He is a good provider and the father of your son, but…," began Marion behind Locker #17.

"What about it?" asked Priss.

"Well, he can sometimes be a real stinker," said Marion as she reached inside the locker for a little nip of cream sherry.

"Marion, you'd better tell me what you're tryin' to say. Is he runnin' around on me? What is it?" Priss asked as she yanked the sherry away from Marion.

"Well, do you know what sometimes happens out at Cherokee Lake at night?" Marion asked as she took the cream sherry away from Priss.

"What do you mean?" asked Priss.

Marion bent over close to Priss's ear. "Junior's been having some wild-ass parties out there with booze and girls from The Reo Palm Isle."

Jesus, Mary, Mother of Christ, thought Priss.

Marion went on to say that Junior's most recent lake party had been the topic of the sermon delivered that very morning by Reverend Tom Bob.

Priss, shaking, ran out of the Ladies' Card Room and tried to collect herself in front of the women gathered next to the prime rib carving station. Then she ran back into the Ladies' Card Room and threw up. She returned to the assembled group with her hand covering her mouth and made feeble excuses to leave that fell on deaf ears. So upset was Priss that she could hardly see well enough to drive home.

Priss found Junior asleep, wrapped up in a sheet and holding fast to the pillow. She then fetched her cast-iron skillet from the kitchen and confronted him, pounding him with the skillet as he squirmed under the sheet, trying to get free.

"My God, Junior," yelled Priss as she administered the beating. "Reverend Tom Bob talked about your little lake party all morning at church. Have you no shame? If you're going to consort with the devil, don't drag our name into it. Go out of town."

He was horrified that his attempt to gain more respect and social status had caused him to lose respect and social status by being publically humiliated by the preacher in church. Then there was the problem of Priss finding out from the local gossip about the house he owned at Cherokee Lake and never told her about. Junior knew he had to put a stop to any more such sermons and any accompanying gossip, and he knew just how to do it. He had no use for that sorry excuse for a preacher man—that short, balding, fat forty-year-old man whose vestigial tab notch on his starched white collar could barely be seen for all the chins. Plus, Junior was sure he had seen the cross that Tom Bob wore in the window of McCarkeys' Jewelry Store the week before Easter last year. Why, he was probably no more a preacher man than his hunting dog, thought Junior.

Chapter 16
The Our Lady of Guadalupe Scheme

 The lake house sermon eventually faded in the memory of the townspeople, replaced by almost daily news of a substantial new gusher. But the sermon still stuck in Junior's craw, and he vowed to take revenge on Tom Bob.

It had been fifteen years since Junior had stolen the Cherokee Lake oil well. Being an astute student of how to make money using other people's money, after studying contracts Junior came up with another scheme, one that he envisioned as a means of seeking revenge on Tom Bob and the church.

Phoning William Fleigh, of Fleigh & Fleigh Attorneys at Law, who specialized in the oil business, Junior said, "Willy, I need to see you at your offices first thing."

"Yes, sir, Mr. Peck. We here at Fleigh & Fleigh are always ready to help you out." Willy pushed the intercom button and said to his boss, "That crazy man is coming in tomorrow."

The next morning Junior put on his newest suit and slicked back his hair. At the law firm, Junior explained excitedly, "There's no sense in me paying rent for any oil rig equipment pumpin' in millions for me every day. Why, I could own the damn stuff outright and buy some other used rigs from dry well operators, and then I could get in the rig leasin' business as a sideline."

"That's a fine idea, Mr. Peck. How can we help you?" asked Willy.

"Well, I'd like to set up a different company altogether from the one I have now. I've even got a name for it—OLG. How should it be set up?" inquired Junior.

"Well, sir, first, what does OLG stand for?" asked Willy.

"Oil Leland Junior Gas. Since I pump the oil that some other company turns into gas, that puts me in the middle, get it?" explained Junior.

"Oh yes, how clever," replied Willy.

"Well, it's even more clever than you think," boasted Junior, lowering his head and eyeing Willy with a knowing stare. "It also stands for Our Lady of Guadalupe," replied Junior.

"What the....," replied Willy, confused.

Junior calmly explained from his self-perceived catbird seat, tilting his chair back so it was resting on the two rear legs, "You know we got a lot of churchifyin' people here, and most of 'em feel bad about getting rich so fast, so if we tell 'em we're gonna tithe three percent of the lease price they pay monthly, they'll feel better about it all. Plus, it will enable me personally to tithe more to the church. Most of the men don't go to church, so this is a way for them to participate in service to the Lord." Junior knew most of the men wouldn't go to church if they were paid and that it was the women who went—primarily to see what everyone was wearing.

Impressed by Junior's cleverness, Willy said, "If you put it that way, we'll set up a regular OLG limited partnership under Oil Leland Junior Gas and a second sort of dummy company representing Our Lady of Guadalupe, and you can print up two sets of stationery depending on what you might need at the time."

"Well now, that's just fine," Junior said, knowing he would never need the original OLG stationery, just the Our Lady of Guadalupe materials.

As he was leaving, Junior added, "Listen, Willy. Since I trust you, I'd like to offer you a chance to get in early on this deal. We'll have only a handful of investors, maybe ten. I can get you in for five thousand dollars. Reverend Croxton is interested. He knows how much it'll help the church." Although Junior hadn't talked to the reverend at the church, he knew he could get him in.

Willy made Junior promise not to tell the other lawyers at Fleigh & Fleigh and signed on as a partner.

Junior registered his new company, Our Lady of Guadalupe, with the county and the next morning called the Reverend Tom Bob, saying, "Tom Bob, could you and I have a private meeting? I'm feelin' like I can help the church more since I have had some good fortune lately."

Tom Bob bit, but he also thought he might be able to get more dirt for his sermons. "Sure, how about ten tomorrow morning in the private rector's lounge," he said.

The next morning, while the two men had coffee, Junior remarked, "You know, Tom Bob, I've recently come into a lot of cash. I got to thinkin', isn't your compensation tied to the income of the church?"

"Yes, I suppose it is," replied Tom Bob.

Now I've got that sanctimonious self-aggrandizing son of a bitch, figured Junior. Even he responds to money, especially easy money.

"Let me explain. You see, I've set up a new corporation, and I have only a limited number of investors. The idea is I'll buy some used rigs, and we'll turn around and lease them. My new corporation will make a bunch of money. I thought I'd tithe five percent of the income from this little operation to the church. That way we would be different from the other rig-leasing companies and maybe more likely to get business. You know, some people feel guilty about making so much money off of oil. I know I do. They'd maybe feel less guilty if they knew some money was going for the church. Whata ya think?" said Junior.

"Hmm, that's mighty interesting," said Tom Bob, cautiously. "Go on."

"Well, the other thing is I'm only lookin' for a handful of investors…and well, I know the church doesn't afford you and the wife a luxurious living, certainly not to the standard of your parishioners. But if you were responsible for an increase in the overall amount of money being tithed, it might give you a raise. Oh, and now that I think of it, maybe you would want to come in on this deal yourself?" continued Junior.

"Oh my heavens, Junior, I don't have that kind of money," replied Tom Bob.

"Well, here's a proposition for you, Tom Bob. If you could see your way to limiting your sermons to stuff in the Bible and not so much about anybody in particular here in town, well, I might be inclined to let you in for half the price the other guys are investing," said Junior.

Tom Bob decided to come in as a "discount partner."

I bet that asshole has a lot of money in the bank and lives for free in the rectory. I just knew he would go for an idea on making money without doing anything for it. What a mooch, thought Junior. He later spread the news that the church was fully behind his new venture and that it was called Our Lady of Guadalupe.

Now that Junior was armed with the ability to say the church was fully in support of his new venture, he sold thirty or forty partnerships, telling each investor that there were only five investors total. The prospective new investors were skeptical at first, but when Junior played the Our Lady of Guadalupe card, promising to tithe part of the money to the church, they signed up. This way the investors could reduce or eliminate their personal tithes and just tithe money out of their business income.

Subsequently, Junior purposely didn't lease many rigs and, as a result, was able to claim bankruptcy. He then bought the company back from bankruptcy for cents on the dollar and emerged as the sole owner. Since none of the investors had put in more than $5,000, it would have cost each of them more money to sue Junior to get their money back than they could recover. Aside from the investors, the other big loser was the church. Since nobody made any money, 5 percent of nothing was tithed. That ought to teach the preacher man not to mess with my reputation, thought Junior.

Once again, without much effort Junior's sinister, under-handed business dealings had resulted in a large monetary gain—in this case, almost $250,000.

Chapter 17
Social Rejection Revisited

Junior and Priss had a daily routine, of sorts. Junior went to his office in the morning to check his holdings, had lunch at the Rigview Country Club with some buddies, and had one drink when he got home. Priss busied herself with various women's clubs and worked in her hydrangea garden. Bobby, about to turn eighteen, was average in every way, including his grades, athletic ability, height, and weight. Even his personality was average. Some said it was because his daddy was larger than life that Bobby had not tried to excel or apply himself, feeling that he couldn't top his daddy's success.

At the last game of the football season for the Bullard Buzzards, Junior and Priss were settled in their season seats, row three on the fifty-yard line. Bobby wasn't athletic enough to play, but he was a yell leader, having been the first male to try out for cheerleader. At half time, a float paraded around the stadium carrying Lometa Goldwaithe, the young lady who in her senior year had been elected Miss Flame by the Bullard Fire Department. She had also been voted Miss Future Farmer's wife by the Future Farmers of America and, in an unprecedented triple-crown sweep, Miss Bunsen Burner by the Science Club. Lometa had to run out under the bleachers into the girls' locker room and change three times to be carried on three different floats in her honor that night. It just so happened that Lometa's parents had been given special seats next to Junior and Priss.

"Say, Mr. Goldwaithe, that's a fine-looking daughter you got there. Does she date anyone now?" asked Junior. He then whispered into Priss's ear, "If we're ever going to get Bobby out of the house, we'll have to intervene. Don't you think it's peculiar he doesn't date or have a girlfriend?"

"Junior, I didn't date anyone until I met you and you didn't date anyone either until you met me. You might remember that those girls at your summer camp were mean to you. Maybe some of the girls in Bobby's class are mean to him, I don't know. What's the big deal about dating?" replied Priss.

Mr. Goldwaithe shot back, "No, our daughter doesn't date. She has such a bright future we don't allow her to go out with local boys. Why do you ask?"

"Our boy Bobby—see him out there in the middle of the field—he is mighty handsome and very fun to be with, and I was just wondering if..." said Junior.

"Stop right there. Didn't you hear what I said?" Mr. Goldwaithe interrupted. "Lometa has a fine future ahead of her, and I will not let some local yokel sidetrack her. She has a scholarship to Gladewater Junior College to study home economics and is on the waiting list to be a Gusherette."

To add insult to injury, the Buzzards lost in the last two seconds to the opponent's field goal. After the game, Junior took Priss's hand, and they made their way out to the parking lot then drove home. Even after giving money to the Bullard

Reconstruction Fund, they still didn't seem to have much respect in the community. Everybody thought they were common, Junior figured, recalling how his daddy hadn't been respected in their hometown, with his mother having to constantly sweep family secrets under the rug, and how he himself hadn't been respected at Weldon Christian Camp despite his ability to throw fastballs and play banjo. He realized that maybe Priss was like his mother. Priss didn't complain about their lack of social status; she was apparently happy just to be married and have an average son. But Junior craved the respect he felt he deserved after so much success in the oil business.

The next day Junior decided to have a really nice party to celebrate Bobby's graduation from high school. "Honey, what do you think about making a high school graduation party for our Bobby? We could have it at the Rigview Country Club and rent golf carts and have a miniature golf contest on the putting green and maybe bring in some ponies or something," said Junior.

"Oh, Junior, that'd be fine. But I don't think kids that age like ponies. Maybe a band, and we could serve Shirley Temples. The mothers could have sherry in the card room, and the men could just stay in the bar. I think that's a grand idea," replied Priss.

"Priss, I'm gonna need some help with the guest list. I don't think I can get too many townspeople to come. You heard what Lometa's daddy said. He doesn't think our son's worthy of his daughter, and somehow I always think that's how people here feel about us."

"Junior, that's not true. People do like you. How many people do you employ at your wells?" replied Priss.

"Oh, maybe fifteen or so, I guess," answered Junior.

"Those fifteen people have wives and families, and they need you and they need the work you give them. Then there's the bankers who have jobs because you keep our money in their banks. And the oil rig supply people. Why, there's probably close to a hundred people who depend on you for their livelihood," said Priss.

"Wow, Priss, I never considered that," said Junior.

"Then there's me and Bobby, my darling. What would we do without you?" added Priss.

"Oh, Priss, what would I do without you? Let's just have our own graduation party for Bobby. How about a trip to Dallas and we'll stay in the Adolphus?" suggested Junior.

"That would be just great. I could shop at Neiman's while we're there, and you and Bobby could go to the movies or something," replied Priss.

"Maybe the Dallas Cowboys training camp? Bobby's a yell leader. I guess he knows something about football. Let's just have us a bourbon and turn in early," said Junior.

As Junior put on his pajamas, he said to himself in the bathroom mirror: "What the hell do I have to do? I married the wealthiest girl in town, we had a son, and he's not in any trouble. Well, really he's not in anything. So what if I started out with a drunk papa who cut corners in his business and is now in prison. I didn't make him drink or have anything to do with putting him in jail or with Mama going crazy. I even gave up carousing, not that I ever did much in the first place. Lord, maybe it's even worse for me in this town than it was at Weldon. There Dub was popular because he had money. Now I have money, and it doesn't seem to matter here. I could buy and sell this town, but still people don't pay any attention to me. I need to find a way to finally get the respect I deserve."

Chapter 18
A Little Respect

 Junior took comfort in knowing that even if he lacked respect he was just fine financially. He still had the original Gulf Coast Cares caper money stolen from the state of Alabama hidden in a separate bank account. He had successfully robbed Pop Teasle of the Cherokee Lake oil find without repercussion, and then he had made another $100,000 in the recent Our Lady of Guadalupe scheme, which he had repeated in West Texas and Oklahoma to the tune of another $85,000. Lastly, his original venture of leasing and re-leasing drilling property had provided him a steady revenue stream of several hundred thousand dollars annually. After so many years of attaining easy money, it wasn't much of a challenge for him anymore.

Bobby had been attending Bullard Junior College, making average grades, and was about to graduate in the music program, which was perhaps due to the large endowment Junior had made, but he didn't care. The junior college had used a good bit of the endowment to build a new football stadium, a facility that had been named The Leland Peck Junior, Bullard Junior College Stadium. In addition, a bust of Junior was commissioned to be installed behind the home team end zone. To further recognize Junior for his generosity, the school decided to honor him with a special half-time show during homecoming weekend. The committee planning the event had resolved to have a reenactment of the original 1901 Spindletop oil field find in Beaumont, Texas, since exactly fifty years had passed since that discovery and it seemed like a natural theme for the homecoming celebration.

For the half-time celebration, one of the college art teachers, Mr. Wutherspoon, made a cardboard and plywood oil derrick, painted it black, and had it mounted on the back of a flatbed truck. Mr. Wutherspoon then cut out about thirty long strips of black construction paper and used thumbtacks to mount them inside the top of the derrick. An air compressor, fitted underneath the derrick, blew the black strips straight up in the air so it looked like a gusher. The truck was to drive around the stadium while the band marched in the shape of a derrick, with the twirlers throwing up their batons, representing the gusher. A special song was commissioned to accompany the festivities. The lyrics, sung to the tune of the Western song "Rawhide," were to be performed over the PA system by Mrs. Anthal Bivins, the chair of the music department:

> Drillin' drillin' drillin'
> Keep those pump jacks drillin'
> All the men are willin'
> Black Gold!
>
> Drillin' drillin' drillin'
> We're gonna make a killin'
> Keep the champagne chillin'
> Black Gold!

Drillin' drillin' drillin'
Coke and Jack we're swillin'
Those bankers, they are willin'
Black Gold!

The rival team at homecoming was the Port La Vaca Sand Crabs. Since the Sand Crabs' band director had just been murdered, they hadn't had time to work up a new routine, so the Sand Crabs Marching Band couldn't march. Nevertheless, they decided to reenact the famous Dalton Gang bank robbery that had occurred at the First National Bank in Longview, Texas, in 1895. Their art teacher made a little jail out of an old horse trailer with just railing on the sides, which was then hooked up to a pickup truck. There was a competition at the school to select four students to act as the Dalton Gang and four to be deputy sheriffs. The Dalton Gang would go out on the field with big cowboy hats and bandannas over their noses, and fake guns. The four students playing deputy sheriffs, who had borrowed real sheriff outfits, would come out and chase the Dalton gang, capture, handcuff them, and put them in the horse trailer "jail." The local sheriff would provide a squad car with a siren to heighten the drama. Ultimately, all the planning paid off as the halftime show exceeded expectations and made Junior feel that at last the local people were paying tribute to him, even if it was due to his endowment.

That same weekend, as part of the fiftieth anniversary of Spindletop, the Rigview Country Club planned a spectacular evening, and Junior seized the opportunity to gain credit for it and thus more social status, he thought, by paying for some members of the Shreveport Symphony to play in Bullard, which had no symphony. He had obtained the right to use the official commemorative anniversary music composed by Maestro Joseph Carlucci from the Beaumont Symphony Orchestra, with lyrics by Violet Newton. Mrs. Anthal Bivins stepped up to the microphone in the Rigview Country Club ballroom and, in front of fifteen of Bullard's finest families, accompanied the symphony in a choral rendering by Violet Newton, poet laureate of Texas:

Gusher! Gusher!

You may sing your rip-roaring ballads
Of sweet decks that are stacked to win
But the liveliest night we ever knew
Was the night that well blew in.

And the moon rose tall, and the air was tense
There came such an ominous sound
Where, all hell bent, came a wild intent
From the bowels of the churning ground.

And that slick black muck gave a roaring boom
As it shot up the Texas sky!
With a gushing roar, it spewed out a stream,
Shot the moon in her good right eye!

This was another proud moment for Junior and Priss. There was a different mixture of people from the usual Bullard crowd since visitors from neighboring counties had come to hear the symphony.

Junior remarked to Priss, "Isn't everyone polite? Maybe we need to make sure we are around new people more often." To be singled out and appreciated by people in Bullard and beyond, and to see his social stock rise, was a new and welcome experience for Junior.

After these events that gave Junior and Priss new social status and a broader outlook, they began to engage in activities that expanded their perspectives beyond the confines of East Texas. Priss, accustomed to reading three books a week, expanded her literary interests from picture cookbooks and *Peyton Place* to more serious fare like *A Certain Smile* and *The Last Hurrah*. She also subscribed to several fashion magazines of the day and yearned to be photographed in the rarefied air of the runway shows Neiman Marcus hosted to introduce the latest fashions to the select few who could afford them.

In addition, Priss and Junior traveled regularly to Dallas on chartered church buses to take in cultural events, like the Summer Music Season at Fair Park. They attended the Dallas Symphony and stayed at the Adolphus Hotel every time the Dorsey Orchestra performed there. Increasingly, Priss found life in small-town East Texas stifling.

Then there was the matter of Bobby. Junior and Priss had to figure out what to do with him after his graduation. Bobby, bless his heart, hadn't inherited his daddy's knack for making money. In Junior's estimation, his son couldn't make a dime if someone handed him two nickels. Junior remained puzzled about why Bobby seemed so dumb. He remembered that when Bobby was six, his smallpox vaccination hadn't taken. Perhaps that was it. Or maybe it was the result of riding his bike in the fog of fumes spraying DDT behind the mosquito abatement truck each summer. Or maybe it was just a case of idiopathy. His eyes had been tested, and didn't need corrective lenses. Whatever the cause, Bobby, having repeated fifth and tenth grades twice, almost didn't graduate from high school.

Nevertheless, Junior knew that Bobby had to make his own life soon. "Bobby, what is it you want to do now? Try as I might, none of the four-year colleges around here seem to be able to find a place for you," Junior remarked one day. Junior and Priss both knew Bobby wasn't mature enough to go to a four-year college away from home and that he probably would flunk out anyway.

"Well, Daddy, I think I'd like to get into a band. I was real good on tuba," replied Bobby.

"Oh, for Christ's sake," fumed Junior. "No self-respecting son of mine is gonna be in some dumb band. Go get a job. I don't care what you do, just get a job. Music didn't get me anywhere, son. I was a good banjo player. Everybody enjoyed my songs and liked me at first when I went to summer camp, but later they didn't. You can't rely on a musical instrument to define your future."

The next morning Bobby went on a job hunt. First, through some firemen friends he got a job driving around and moving the arrow on the half-moon fire danger signs, indicating whether or not it was safe to burn refuse and yard waste. That only took an hour or so. Bobby then got a job as the afternoon cashier at the Tastee Freeze Queen.

Great, thought Priss. Here's just another place where the gold diggers can get at him. She saw it as her responsibility to stave off the local girls who saw Bobby as a potential meal ticket. It didn't help the situation when Priss enrolled Bobby in the Alicia Cogswell School of Dancing and Decorum. She thought he would meet a nice wealthy girl whose daddy could afford the six-week course. But Bobby was asked to leave after two weeks because he had no rhythm and the girls refused to dance with him for fear of getting stepped on. Although Bobby was rather good-looking, when he opened his mouth and spoke the girls realized he was about as useless as tits on a bull.

"You know, Priss, after we gave all that money to Bullard Junior College when Bobby graduated, you saw how we were suddenly respected. So maybe there's a way I could spend a little more money for Bobby's future, maybe buy him a small business to run," said Junior, thinking this might make Bobby look respectful and keep Junior's social status from eroding.

Skeptical, Priss replied, "Junior, what business is there to buy in Bullard? We'd have to look elsewhere for an opportunity." Realizing the wisdom of this, Junior decided to keep his eyes open for such a possibility.

Chapter 19
Gambling on Gushing Oil

Junior met with his banker, Mr. Sugton, about once a month. He continued to hold the fake account under the assumed name Mr. Alabama. Of course, he kept some money in his and Priss's joint account in the unlikely event Priss would want to review their finances. Junior wasn't sure how much money Priss had. Actually, he wasn't sure how much money *he* had. But between the two of them there seemed to be plenty to cover bills and household expenses. The house was paid off, and they didn't live extravagantly.

One day in early spring, Junior asked Mr. Sugton, "How are we doin'?"

"Mr. Peck, sir, I'm afraid I have some unsettling news. Your earnings are heading in the wrong direction. They're flat as a pancake, and you have set up payments to your mother in Terrell of three hundred per month. At the rate you're going, you'll be dead broke in about three years. And since you're not even fifty years old something's gotta change," replied Mr. Sugton.

"Well, damnation, Sugton. That simply can't happen. You know, ever since that West Texas crude oil price leveled off, my investments have been flat as a board. I knew I should've gotten in the pipeline end of things," said Junior.

"Yes, sir. If it's any consolation, I know you aren't the only oil man out there sitting on no go," answered Mr. Sugton.

Junior nodded and said, "Dammit Sugton, you can't buy groceries with consolation. What we need is something to jump-start the oil prices again. Those damn Ruskies are wreaking havoc on petroleum pricing. I am also beginning to think that stockbroker of mine is a crook. It takes him forever to make a trade, which is limp by the time he executes it. Hell, Sugton, I don't have a reason to get more money from Priss right now. I might just have to revisit that racehorse opportunity that was offered to me a while back."

Junior headed for the Arlene Hotel, where the men traveling through Bullard stayed, and found a familiar washed-up–looking cowboy with horse shit on his boots. "Oh good, there you are. Let's get us a drink, and you tell me again about that horse of yours. I know I turned you down a while ago, but things change," said Junior.

"We got us a group out of Oklahoma and have formed a syndicate to buy a thoroughbred. Guaranteed winner, that horse. His name is Gushing Oil, out of a sire named Easy Money. We got Jay Jansen to train. And the jockey is Ted Atkinson, who had the winningest record in 1951. So we figure for the 1952 Kentucky Derby we can't lose. Mr. Peck, such opportunities don't come along every day," insisted the cowboy.

Junior decided he should go in since he had no other investments on the horizon and he needed to make some money.

"I'm gonna have to see if owner percentages are still available," replied the cowboy.

"You do that. To help you along, let me sweeten the pot," said Junior, putting down $15,000 to represent 25 percent of the ownership of the horse and another $8,000 for Gushing Oil to show at four-to-one odds. He figured this was a sure bet since the horse was supposed to finish first or second, according to the bookies.

On the Friday afternoon before the Kentucky Derby, Junior and all the other syndicate investors gathered at Churchill Downs to watch Gushing Oil during his workout. "Look at him go—best time I've ever clocked him," said the trainer. "You boys will be real happy tomorrow." The syndicate investors held an early celebration that night in the VIP clubhouse, with steaks, prime rib, and bourbon all around.

The next morning they each had one mint julep and took their places in the owners' boxes. The men watched the tote board numbers roll and spin, still confirming Gushing Oil as the odds on favorite. The trumpeter played "My Old Kentucky Home," and the field of horses entered the starting gate. Then as quickly as it started it was over. Gushing Oil lost big time in less than five minutes, coming in fifth. To add insult to injury, the Kentucky Derby was nationally televised—for the first time ever.

The morning after the Kentucky Derby disaster, Junior went back to the bank to strategize on how to turn his finances around. "Mr. Sugton, once again I have screwed the pooch. I just lost right about twenty-three thousand dollars on that hay burner Gushing Oil. Nobody will run him again since he just about killed his jockey loading into the starting gate. And he's not likely to go out to stud," confessed Junior.

"That's not all your woes, Junior," said Mr. Sugton.

"What the hell do you mean? How could things be worse?" replied Junior.

"Reverend Tom Bob Croxton came by yesterday saying something about a tithe you supposedly guaranteed the church," said Mr. Sugton.

"Oh, crap. That's the OLG money," answered Junior. "About a year ago I formed a company called OLG—Oil Leland Junior Gas. Clever, huh?"

"Clever, yes. But what's that got to do with Reverend Croxton?" asked Mr. Sugton.

"Oh, that fool put some money in. I was gonna start an oil equipment leasing company. I'd lease out some rigs and drilling equipment then turn around and re-lease them for more money. Anyway, I got several investors in at eight thousand dollars apiece. I told Tom Bob I'd tithe a percentage of my profits to the church. Trouble was, I never intended to lease any equipment so there was never any money to tithe. And the other investors didn't come after me since it would have cost them more in legal fees to recover their initial investment than the investment to begin with," explained Junior.

"He's madder than a hornet in a light fixture. He put in a line item in his church budget, and now the congregation expects the tithe money," said Mr. Sugton.

"How much does he think he should get?" asked Junior.

"A total of eighteen thousand dollars. That's fifteen hundred dollars a month," reported Mr. Sugton.

"You're shittin' me. I gotta figure out somethin' real fast," replied Junior.

"It better be fast, Mr. Peck. The reverend is threatening to preach about it if he doesn't get his tithe money," warned Mr. Sugton.

"Goddammit, that last sermon on my lake house party really put me in Dutch with Priss. That old fart masquerading as a preacher has way too much influence in this town, especially among the womenfolk. I'll tell you what," said Junior squirming in his chair, "go tell Tom Bob he can expect his money starting next month, then just start paying that little shit to get him off my back. Now I'd better go and get me some more money. What is the name of that hotel in Galveston everybody raves about?"

"I believe it is The Grand Petroleum Shannon Hotel," replied Mr. Sugton.

"Yep that's it. I know the man who built it, John Jack McArdle. That's a great name for John Jack's operation, that Irish son of a bitch. Fine man he is. We used to see each other around town in the early days, right after Priss and I got hitched. He dabbled in lumber for a while and knew Priss's dad, Mr. Mullin. He came for dinner a time or two. Then he just up and moved to Houston. He said there was more money there and more people, more wildcatters, more oil. He must have done something right because he built that hotel. Tell you what. Let's go pay him a call. Maybe, just maybe we could get him interested in one of our investment opportunities," said Junior.

"What do you mean? You don't have any investment opportunities, just a couple of old wells that are about to peter out," replied Mr. Sugton.

"Yes, but John Jack doesn't know that. Surely he's smart enough to know there's still money left in laying pipeline," said Junior.

"Pipeline? You're not in the pipeline business, as far as I know," answered Mr. Sugton.

"No, but he doesn't know it either. That's how I started out—acting like I was in the pipeline business. Maybe you don't remember but...now that I think of it, you don't need to remember," said Junior, catching himself before admitting he had tricked Pop out of the Cherokee Lake well by promising he had enough influence to get pipeline laid near it, something nobody here knew about. Since he'd pulled the scam off once, it should be easier the second time around, Junior thought.

"So, Sugton, let's go to Galveston tomorrow and see John Jack. Call and get us the best suite they got. Use my name," suggested Junior.

Junior and Mr. Sugton arrived at The Grand Petroleum Shannon Hotel around noon.

"Woo wee, this place is some kind of fancy," said Junior as they entered the lobby and headed toward the registration desk.

"I'm sorry, Mr. Peck, we don't show a reservation for you or Mr. Sugton," said the desk clerk in response to Junior's inquiry.

"What do you mean? We're supposed to have a suite," said Junior, giving the front desk clerk and then Sugton a look of disgust. "There must be some mistake. Didn't you call, Sugton?"

"Yes, sir, and I told them you were very close friends with Mr. McArdle and you wanted the finest, most expensive suite available," confirmed Mr. Sugton.

"Well, what the hell happened?" Junior asked, raising his voice and pushing his index finger into Mr. Sugton's lapel.

Sensing an altercation brewing, the desk clerk held up his left hand, reached for the house phone with his right, and said, "Let me call Mr. McArdle's office. I'm sure this is just a simple mistake, sir." Someone answered the phone at the other end, whereupon the desk clerk reached in his drawer and pulled out a wad of paperwork.

"Gentlemen, I'm not sure about this situation, but Mr. McArdle doesn't seem to recall a Mr. Junior Peck. I'm sorry, but all our suites are full. Won't you accept this voucher for a complimentary cocktail as our apology?" said the desk clerk.

"Hell, no. Get me McArdle. Hand me that phone," yelled Junior.

"Sir, I'm afraid he just left for the day," replied the desk clerk.

"Goddammit, Sugton, I'll get that McArdle," said Junior.

Junior and Mr. Sugton checked into a motel down the street from The Grand Petroleum Shannon Hotel. There they spent the night having fitful dreams. The first thing the following morning, the two returned to the lobby of The Grand

Petroleum Shannon Hotel planning to ambush Mr. McArdle as he entered the private elevator to the hotel offices.

"Here he comes, Sugton. I'm just gonna bust through those three security bodyguards and shake McArdle's hand. He knows me good. I bet he'll ask us up to his office and give us a free suite for all our trouble. The reservations people probably used your name instead of mine, and of course he's never heard of you," said Junior.

Junior pushed through the huge bodyguards and stuck out his hand to Mr. McArdle. The ensuing scuffle put a dead stop to all other activity in the lobby. Two of the bodyguards grabbed Junior and threw him on the marble floor, while the other one ushered Mr. McArdle into his elevator.

Once safe in the elevator, Mr. McArdle said, "Phew, that was close. You know, ever since I opened this hotel every Tom, Dick, and Harry has come in here claiming to know me and wanting favors. Thanks, boys, for keeping that bum away from me."

Junior picked himself up, straightened his coat and tie, and said "Let's get the hell out of here," thankful this incident had happened in Galveston, away from the prying eyes of Bullard society.

Neither Junior nor Sugton spoke during the drive home. When they got back to Bullard, Junior said, "This is just like the rejection by those goddamn Weldon boys. Never say a word about it, you hear me?'

"Yes, sir," promised Mr. Sugton.

To hell with any son of a bitch who thinks he's better than me, thought Junior, he hoped for the last time.

Junior started having nightmares. He often dreamt of his father and how he had never paid any attention to Junior's activities, how he hadn't really been a father at all. Then he remembered all the nights his mother had waited up for his dad to come stumbling home and thought of her now in the sanitarium.

One morning Priss shook him and said, "Wake up, Junior. You're having another bad dream. What is it?"

"Priss, it was about my childhood, how it was so empty. My papa was nothing but an absentee figure, and my mother had her hands full having to be both father and mother to me, trying to provide me with a safe and nurturing home. I'm afraid I've also been that kind of daddy to Bobby. I guess it's too late to get him into Scouts. Maybe I could take him fishing. I haven't been a good husband to you, either, and I am so sorry. Starting now, I will rededicate myself to you and Bobby," promised Junior.

"You are my true love, Junior. I see nothing but happiness ahead. I'm just sure of it," said Priss, taking Junior's face in her hands. "We can get through anything." She knew Junior wasn't the most ideal man or the most ideal husband or father. But he was her husband, and she vowed to stand by him. Maybe his nightmares would serve as a wake-up call for him to improve his behavior, she thought.

Despite rededicating himself to family life, Junior began to scheme about possible excuses he could use to get his hands on some of Priss's money to make up for the loss of his own. He remembered when Priss had bailed him out after he had lost $12,000 on the USC Notre Dame game in 1947. He knew she still had access to lots of extra money, and he needed to figure out how to get at it.

One day, out of the blue, Junior received a phone call from J. W. "Dub" Gilmore, his roommate from Weldon Christian Camp. Over the years, they had exchanged Christmas cards featuring photos of their kids, with the usual made-up stories about how their children were so accomplished. Junior had enjoyed making up stuff about Bobby. He had to. According to Junior, Bobby had been class president, had graduated magna cum laude, had been voted most popular student, had won the competition for raising the fattest hog in the history of the state of Texas, and had won a national science fair award—none of which was true.

"Junior, I wonder if you might want to come in on a new opportunity here in Fort Worth," began Dub. He had read about Junior's business accomplishments in the newspapers. The press had reported mostly good things about Junior's successes, afraid of any negative commentary pertaining to him since it might only induce him to buy the paper and shut it down. So for all Dub knew Junior was a fabulously wealthy, lucky, and honest businessman.

"What'd you have in mind?" Junior asked, shifting in his creaking leather chair.

"Well, we're expanding our family collection here at the Gilmore Museum to add a Remington sculpture wing. I thought if you could see your way to endow it, or at least a big chunk of it, you'd be most appreciated here in Fort Worth. I haven't actually visited East Texas, but from what I hear it's a little uninspiring."

"Let me check with Priss. Say, you think you could get me a membership in the Cattlemen's Petroleum Club and maybe waive the initiation fee?" queried Junior, his mind churning with possibilities. Bullard didn't have a Petroleum Club or a Cattlemen's Club, much less a Cattlemen's Petroleum Club, not that he could become a member, thought Junior. Now maybe he could obtain more status by becoming a member of such a club in Fort Worth, he figured.

"No problem," replied Dub as he made a red checkmark on his list of potential museum donors.

Chapter 20
Shaping Up and Preparing to Ship Out

 Junior hung up the phone from talking to Dub, let out a whoop, and immediately ran into Priss's arts and crafts room, where she sat knitting. "I just got off the phone with Dub. He told me about a wonderful opportunity in Fort Worth," he announced.

"It's not another racehorse, is it?" asked Priss.

"No, of course not. Honey, I know you're bored in Bullard," said Junior.

"Gee, how could you tell?" replied Priss.

"It might have had something to do with the fact that you have redecorated the living room three times in the last two months," answered Junior.

"What do you expect? You leave me home alone all the time, and what else am I supposed to do but look at magazines and fabric swatches. Plus, Bobby's hardly home anymore, which is frightening. I can't keep a close watch on him and all those floozies who are after his money," said Priss.

"Floozies is right. That last camp follower couldn't spell *cat* if you spotted her the *C* and the *T*," remarked Junior.

"Junior, stop making fun of the local girls. Who did you say was on the phone?" asked Priss.

"That was Dub, my roommate at Weldon. I've mentioned him before. The only decent man there," explained Junior.

"Doesn't he live in Fort Worth?" queried Priss.

"Yes, and how would you like to?" asked Junior.

"Like to what?" said Priss.

"Live in Forth Worth," replied Junior.

"Junior, have you lost your mind?" asked Priss.

"No, but you might if we stay here in Bullard. See, Dub's family owns the Gilmore Museum, and they are adding a Remington sculpture wing. And he asked if we would consider making a donation to help fund it. Then I thought, why not move there? We could get a new start," said Junior.

"Oh, honey, could we really do that? I hate it here. We've already donated to every possible charity in Bullard, and there's really only two—the Cammo Cotillion and Bert's Beagle Rescue. I gave up my place on the Women's Church Auxiliary and quit Book Club when you got rejected the last time from being in Rotary. I don't know why this town is so hateful toward you. They don't know you like I do," said Priss. She began imagining what life in Fort Worth would be like. She'd never been there but expected the ladies there, too, probably shopped in Dallas.

Interrupting Priss's daydreaming, Junior continued, "You know, honey, I'm pretty darn sick of this stupid town myself." Junior took a quick mental inventory of why they should stay in Bullard and could think of no good reason whatsoever. Besides, Dub's request for an endowment for the Remington wing at the museum could be a way to avail himself of more of Priss's money.

"I think we should seriously consider moving. I'll call Dub back and work on it some more. I was wondering if you might be interested in going in on the Remington investment. Most of my money is tied up right now, and I would take a huge hit on taxes if I wrote Dub a check out of my accounts," said Junior, hoping he could encourage Priss to make the necessary donation and then some. Junior figured that this Fort Worth maneuver would be just what the doctor ordered to get him back on track financially. All he had to do was ask Priss for a few hundred thousand dollars more than Dub needed for the donation. She'd never know.

Priss already had visions of herself in Fort Worth, free from the boredom she experienced in Bullard. "Sure, honey, how much money do you need?" she agreed.

"Do you have to tell your daddy?" asked Junior.

"Why, no. It's my money. I mean our money. You know, women in Fort Worth wear different styles than we do here. We just have the one store, and they only carry three different outfits in multiple sizes. Wow, I would love it," said Priss.

She went upstairs to ponder further what life might be like in Fort Worth. It was getting chilly outside, so she went to her cold climate closet for a sweater. "Oh my God," she muttered to herself aghast as she looked in the closet mirror. "This is a size eighteen, and it doesn't fit me anymore."

"Priss, where are you? Let's go celebrate our new future at the Catfish Basket," called Junior.

"Junior, I've been reading something and want to talk to you about it."

"Sure, but let's go eat," replied Junior.

"Oh, honey, I'm not hungry. Let me show you this thing I got at Bridge Club last week. There's a new kind of place for women to go and relax and feel better. It's called The Grand Petroleum Shannon Hotel Finer Figure Salon," explained Priss.

"What's that?" asked Junior.

"Marvene at Bridge Club called it a fat camp. You know, Junior, we could both use a little break from all the tedium around here. I was thinking I might just go to that figure salon for a month or so—you know, rejuvenate. Bobby's not home much, and you're not either. You've seen Jack LaLanne on television, haven't you?" said Priss.

"Yes, but what does that poofter have to do with what you're talking about?" asked Junior.

"He's not a poofter, Junior. He started a women's exercise program and sells something called a Glamour Stretcher for women to use at home. But if I go to The Grand Petroleum Shannon Hotel, they have all sorts of other machines for women. Plus, I would get all my meals there and I could shop in Houston. I'm gonna need all new clothes if we go to Fort Worth. And it wouldn't hurt you to buy some new suits, by the way. Why, Junior, wouldn't it be just divine?" remarked Priss.

"What would they do to you down there? I don't understand," asked Junior.

"Well, they have these machines. Look at this," said Priss, handing him the brochure she had been studying. Junior had little interest in looking at pictures of machines after seeing pictures of beautiful models in swimsuits, one prettier than the next and all shapely, like the girls in the Miss Texas contest.

"Hell, Priss, maybe I should go with you," he suggested, half-jokingly.

"Oh, Junior, you're so silly. It's only for women. Anyway, here's three of the machines they use. This one is the rolling machine, which rolls away fat. You sit on it, and it gets rid of butt fat. This other one is a jiggle machine. It has a belt on it, and you stand on a platform, put the belt around your thighs, and it jiggles so your thighs get smaller. And this one kinda looks like the conveyor belt at the checkout counter in a grocery. But who cares. Look at the before and after photos. Oh, and here's a machine you sit in with your hair up in a towel, and they turn it on and you sweat a lot; it's called a toning, reducing, and shaping bed. They give you water, so you won't get sick," said Priss.

"Priss, I haven't seen you so excited since Bobby was born. You just go ahead and go. I think you should take a girlfriend with you, though," advised Junior.

Priss arrived at The Grand Petroleum Shannon Hotel on a Monday morning. "Oh my, isn't this lobby fabulous," she said to the front desk clerk. The clientele were most impressive, similar to the patrons of the symphony in Dallas. In the afternoon tea nook there were a few ladies with greyhound dogs on leashes waiting for their husbands. So much for Bullard— this was way more her style, thought Priss.

She took the private elevator to the second floor atrium lobby and found the entrance to the spa. The smells of eucalyptus and mint were refreshing. This will be such a treat, she thought. Priss had signed up for a double session that lasted three weeks.

The next morning Priss began her sessions at the spa. The director of the program greeted the participants, saying, "Good morning, ladies. I'm Talford, the entertainment and fitness director here at The Grand Petroleum Shannon Hotel Spa. You can call me Mr. Talford. We are excited to have you as our special guests," continued Talford, in his mint green snap-front smock bearing the hotel monogram. "My associate Beryldean and I will run you through the basic program this morning. I personally trained with the great master of fitness, Mr. Jack Lalanne at his home headquarters facility in Los Angeles. I don't need to tell you how exciting that was, now do I, ladies?"

"No, you don't," interrupted Beryldean.

"All right, let's get to the machines. This first one is the thigh reducer. You simply step on the platform, wearing either sneakers or socks. Then you grab the handles, place the belt around behind your rear end just below your waist, and push the button to start the machine. There are two speeds—slow and fast—and one marked random, which alternates between speeds. I find it the most fun. Okay, here goes," said Talford.

Talford switched on the random button, and the machine whizzed into action as he stated, "Thisss onesss ffffour thhuh uuppper tthhys."

Then Talford asked Beryldean to demonstrate the butt roller machine. "Simply sit on the roller belt like this. Hheer's fffor thuh bbbuuht," said Beryldean.

"Thank you, Beryldean. Now for my favorite, the toning bed. You simply lie down, and we wrap you with eucalyptus-scented sheets and close the top portion, leaving your head sticking out. The treatment takes twenty minutes or so, but if you're uncomfortable just nod and call us—we'll get you out. Then, ladies, we're off to our private café on the third floor. Following a delicious meal of watercress and cucumber finger sandwiches and a lemon water cleanse beverage, Beryldean and I will meet with you individually and plan a special health program to suit your specific needs. Remember, we, at The Grand Petroleum Shannon Hotel, are here to serve your every need and make your stay relaxing and helpful. We want you to feel pampered at all times. Mostly we will be exercising in the mornings, and you will have the afternoons free to explore Galveston and the environs. We have a complimentary shuttle that departs every hour for designated historical sites and museums in Houston—and, of course, Neiman's and Sakowitz."

An audible sigh came from the ladies, who preferred leafing through the sale racks than sitting in a sweaty box. Priss spotted a couple of ladies who, she decided, would become her shopping buddies based on their stylish attire.

After lunch, Talford took Priss to the spa offices for weight and measurements.

"Oh, I just hate this, Mr. Talford. It's been so long since I knew what I weighed, and I don't want to know. I used to wear a size ten, and over the years—well, with my husband gone so much and our son in school all day—I just ate myself silly," explained Priss.

"Don't worry, Mrs. Peck. I don't have to tell you anything you don't want to know," said Talford.

"Please call me Priss. You seem like such a trustworthy and kindly young man," replied Priss.

"Okay, Priss. Let me tell you I've been through that situation personally myself. I invented a new form of entertainment here at The Grand Petroleum Shannon Hotel several years ago, and it started off with a bang."

"Goodness, what was it?" asked Priss.

"Believe it or not, it was an offshore drilling rig dinner theater," replied Talford.

"Really, I hadn't heard of it," said Priss.

"That's because it shut down," answered Talford.

"Why? It sounds, well, charming, or at least different," replied Priss.

"Mr. McArdle, the owner, asked the general manager to find ways to cut costs because, since the waters in the Gulf were choppy in the spring, the dinner theater could only stay open part of the year. Also the safety inspection people were always fining us for malfeasance in the kitchen. Once that news got out, fewer and fewer people came. The final straw was that the star, Miss Mary Martin, had to leave the show because she got acute tetanus from the rig," explained Talford.

"Oh dear. What a shame," said Priss.

"Yes, I was heartbroken and began to drown my sorrows in food. Why, I ballooned up to two hundred and thirty pounds, that's forty-five pounds more than I am now," confessed Talford.

"You mean there's hope?" asked Priss.

"Always. Now let's get some measurements. Just a secret between us two, all right? Cross pinkie fingers. Here we go," said Talford. He wrote: "Weight 162, Height 5 ft. 4 in., bust 42, waist 40, hips 40." Then he said, "I'll just note this here on your chart, and you can see the results when you're done— right, Priss? Besides, you'll see it's mostly water weight."

As the weeks passed, Priss made so much progress and felt so much better about herself that she signed up for three more weeks. By the end of her stay, she had lost 45 pounds and all her water weight and was a perfect size 8. Shopping had taken on a new and distinctly important role in her life. Thanks to her new "lift and separate" bra she also filled out a sweater nicely.

When Priss returned home to Bullard from the Finer Figure Salon, Junior answered the front door, and exclaimed, "My, who are you? To what do I owe this honor of such a beautiful woman at my front door?" Priss was pleased with his response to her new appearance.

The results from the Finer Figure Salon were unbelievable. Where there had been extremely large rounded curvy shapes before, there were now much smaller rounded curvy shapes. It was as if she had shrunk—that is, everything but her attitude. She had a new confidence, a straighter stance, and a surer stride.

She is just beautiful, thought Junior. "Why, my darling, I feel like a boy of eighteen with a girly magazine," remarked Junior. He caught a glimpse of himself in the hall mirror and realized he actually looked like a boy of eighteen with a girly magazine. Suddenly, Junior felt any and all new things were possible.

"Priss, let's get ourselves to Fort Worth. Wait till you see what I bought," said Junior.

"Junior, you look different to me now, too. What have you changed?" asked Priss.

"Dub took me to Beekmans, that men's store in downtown Fort Worth, and he convinced me to let my hair grow out. What do you think?" said Junior.

"I think we should go to our bedroom now!" exclaimed Priss.

Over coffee the next morning, Priss looked through the real estate brochures Junior had from Fort Worth. One home really stood out, and they agreed to buy it.

To help them with orientation, Dub's wife had sent a Welcome to Fort Worth package for Priss, listing doctors, dentists, hair salons, and other necessities she would need to get situated in her new city. Junior and Priss decided to make a small holiday out of their move. The afternoon after the truck came to collect their furniture, they set out with Bobby in the backseat with a Rand McNally map, charting an adventure through the Big Bend National Park before finally arriving in Fort Worth four days later.

As Priss looked at their new home for the first time, she remarked, "Oh, Junior, our new home is fifty times more fabulous than it even looked in the real estate brochure. There's nothing like this in Bullard, that's for sure." It was a 9,195-square-foot house in Gothic French style with a pool, situated on a bluff overlooking the West Fork of the Trinity River in exclusive Teca Heights. The property was separated from the main road by a fifteen-yard drive lined with crepe myrtles hidden behind a twenty-foot iron gate.

Soon after they had settled into their new home in Fort Worth, Junior sat down with Priss to discuss finances. He had a hard time getting her attention since the decorator was due any minute and she hadn't selected the swatches for the new upholstery.

"Priss, you know Dub told us about different levels of sponsorship for the Remington wing. We could limit our pledge to the lowest level. That would give us a plaque with our name on it, along with the other donors' names. Or we could go all out and endow the whole wing, and then they would name it after us. Imagine 'The Priscilla and Leland Junior Peck Wing.'" They decided to endow the entire wing.

Dub hosted a big gala to celebrate its opening, and all the notable people of Fort Worth attended. The Pecks quickly became accepted in Fort Worth society, leaving behind Junior's reputation as a nouveau riche nobody.

"I arranged a membership for you in the Cattlemen's Petroleum Club, Junior. And that group of men over there wants to ask you to join the Country Club," said Dub at the gala.

"Mr. Peck, we are right proud to offer you a membership in our Country Club. We need a strong fourth for our golf group. You do play golf, don't you?" one member asked.

"I haven't in years. But I grew up with the game, so I'm sure it'll come right back to me," Junior lied, knowing he could afford a private golf pro to get him up to speed.

Priss joined the Women's Auxiliary Club, became a docent for both the Bass Museum and Kimball Arts Museum, and qualified to be a member of the Daughters of the American Revolution, Fort Worth Chapter.

After a month of getting acclimated to Forth Worth society, Junior and Priss sat in their library over brandies. "Priss, isn't this a dream come true?" asked Junior, firing up a Cuban. "We've got to have your mama and daddy here soon. Have a nice party with all our friends. Take them to brunch at the club."

"I'm so happy here, Junior. I just knew our world would brighten once we left Bullard. Somehow we got off on the wrong foot there," said Priss.

"Don't talk about that anymore, honey. We're invited to all the events and involved in everything here," replied Junior, feeling that he finally had the social status he deserved.

"Speaking of events, I've been asked to cochair the Bluebonnet Ball," revealed Priss.

"Oh, that's wonderful. I'm so proud of you. Here's a toast. To the Bluebonnet Ball and to hell with Bullard," said Junior.

Junior and Priss had fit right in with Fort Worth society, but not Bobby. There wasn't much for Bobby to do. He wasn't accepted at Texas Christian University in Fort Worth or Southern Methodist University in Dallas, so Junior started checking out business opportunities for him. Of the handful of businesses for sale, Junior found what seemed like the least challenging one and bought it. In a hurry to get Bobby situated, he bought the land and the building, never thinking of the mineral rights. Bobby was now the proud owner and manager of Casa Bella Dinner Theater, located halfway between Fort Worth and Dallas on the west fork of the Trinity River and visible from the Pecks' new home in Teca Heights. At least the business had something to do with Bobby's interest in music, Junior thought.

Chapter 21
The Casa Bella Dinner Theater Fiasco

 It might have been sheer coincidence that Junior and Priss weren't the only people from Bullard to make their way to Fort Worth. Tim Teasle had worked his way to the Dallas–Fort Worth area as a result of his success as a landman. He continued his relationship with Elio Bouchene, who owned most of the mineral rights on small parcels of land from East Texas west through Fort Worth to Odessa, in the panhandle. Tim looked for land with evidence of salt on or near it, indicating the presence of oil reserves. Once he found promising locations, he would hire a local seismologist, who, in turn, would help him find an independent wildcatter to drill on the property. He was based at the Bed-You Hotel in Bedford-Euless while exploring land along the Trinity River between Dallas and Fort Worth.

One day as he drove along the Trinity River, he saw on the banks mostly rusted-out factories and rotted wooden shipping docks. Then he came across about a two-mile stretch of open water. He stopped the car and walked out to the edge of the river. There Tim noticed a line of white powdery-looking particles on the riverbank where the waterline had subsided. He wet his finger, swiped it on the white particles, and took a taste. It was very salty.

Nothing was there but a combination boat dock and bait shop with a handwritten sign that read: "We got double blade aglia, mepps marabou, cyclops lite, giant killer sassy shad, and timber doodles. We now carry worm ouroboroses!" Next to the bait shop was a large round dilapidated-looking building with a sign reading: "Casa Bella Dinner Theater. Now showing S UTH PA FIC." Tim reckoned some of the letters had fallen off. Nearby was a for sale sign identifying the agency as Purvis Realty and Petroleum and listing the agent as Maevis Purvis. The same real estate sign was in front of the bait shop. He copied down the phone number.

Tim hurried back to the Bed-You Hotel. He called Elio from the hotel lobby phone to ask if he knew anything about the Trinity River land where the bait shop and Casa Bella Dinner Theater were located. There was evidence of salt, so maybe oil was there, too, he told Elio. As it turned out, Elio did own the mineral rights to both parcels of land but not the buildings.

Tim thought his brother Talford might know something about the abandoned theater building on the Trinity River property since he had managed a theater in Galveston. The last time the brothers had talked, their conversation had been mostly about Talford's latest business, a high-end spa. Talford had had some success running the Casa Mer Offshore Dinner Theater, but it had closed when The Grand Petroleum

Shannon Hotel needed to cut expenses, after which he had stayed on to manage the hotel spa.

He called Talford from his room. "Talford, I've been explorin' for about a month around here. Some of the land-owners are cooperative, and some are not. If there is a home or business on the land, they don't want anyone drilling, so I just move on looking for parcels where nothing is built. Those landowners are only too happy to let us drill. Just yesterday I found some interesting land, but it had a bait shop and the Casa Bella Dinner Theater on it. Normally, I'd give no thought to land with buildings on it, but these looked like they'd been empty for quite some time. So this afternoon I'm calling the real estate lady about getting permission from whoever owns them to drill," explained Tim.

"You mean the Casa Bella Dinner Theater is for sale?" asked Talford. Tim realized Talford probably hadn't paid any attention to his concerns until mention of the theater had caught his attention.

"I guess so. There's a for sale sign underneath the bigger sign that reads "S UTH PA FIC," said Tim.

"Oh my goodness, Tim. That's where they staged *South Pacific*, starring Mary Martin, about a year ago. All I know is it was written up in *Variety* when it first opened. Some well-known Fort Worth actors were expected to perform there. Then there wasn't much more about it. There were a few ads in the *Houston Chronicle* offering bus package tours of Fort Worth that included a night at the theater. Sounded sort of lame to me," said Talford.

"Well, I'll keep you posted," said Tim, wondering what any of that had to do with drilling for oil on the property.

When Tim dialed the number for the real estate company, a perky voice answered, saying, "Purvis Realty and Petroleum, your prime choice for property and pumping. Maevis here."

"I'm Tim Teasle, and I'm a landman. Can you tell me who owns the property on the Trinity River, just west of town where the abandoned bait shop and the Casa Bella Dinner Theater are located?" asked Tim.

"We own the bait shop parcel and the adjacent one with the dinner theater, but the building itself is owned by a Mr. Peck. Why do you ask?" explained Maevis.

"In my capacity as a landman, I get paid to figure out who owns the mineral rights to land where there might be oil. Usually there's salt around that kind of land, and there's salt on that riverbank out there."

"Holy dashboard Jesus," said Maevis. "Do you think there might be oil there? We didn't sell Mr. Peck any of the mineral rights. He thinks that building's worthless and is only asking seventy-five thousand dollars, which is way below market value. His son Bobby tried to make a go of it but went bankrupt after the first season. I'm told Mr. Peck made his money in oil in East Texas. If he suspected there might be oil, he'd never sell the building. He's crooked as a corkscrew and mean."

"Well, ma'am, I have reason to believe there is oil there. Maybe you'd consider a contract to let a local wildcatter drill on the bait shop parcel, for which I'm prepared to offer you thirty percent of the net profits if we hit a gusher," said Tim.

"Can you meet me at the Amble Inn Dinette on Steer Street right away?" asked Maevis.

Once Tim and Maevis had ordered two sweet teas, they continued their conversation. "So, you're proposing that some wildcatter would drill just on the bait shop parcel and not on the dinner theater parcel?" asked Maevis, who wanted to figure out a way to drill on both parcels.

"Yes, ma'am. I think there's oil on both parcels, but the dinner theater owner might not cooperate if we ask about drilling. It's best not to stir things up," explained Tim.

"Hold on. Mr. Peck really wants to sell that building, but he won't if he thinks there's oil. He even told me to go down in price last week," said Maevis. She was ready to forget about her commission for the sale of just the building and gamble on the prospect of oil. "Why don't you talk to your people about this? If you could see your way to buying the building, then it's a green light for drilling on both parcels, with Mr. Peck none the wiser," suggested Maevis.

Tim made a few notes and called Mr. Bouchene from his hotel room. "Mr. Bouchene, this is Tim. I've got an unusual situation here." Tim described the bait shop and dinner theater parcels. "The bait shop parcel is free and clear to drill, but the dinner theater parcel is a different matter. Some man named Peck, who they say is an oil man, owns the building. The real estate agent said he made his money in East Texas and would never sell the building or allow anyone else to drill if he thought there might be oil there," continued Tim.

"Junior Peck?" interrupted Elio. "He's the biggest crook in the whole state. He cheated some fine folks out of great sums of money. Lots of people around here would like to shoot him on sight in broad daylight. Don't do anything right now. Find out what you can about how much they're asking for the dinner theater building. I'll call you tomorrow at the hotel," said Mr. Bouchene.

Tim found out that the dinner theater building had been empty for almost a year, and Maevis figured she could get Junior to come down in price by at least $15,000.

Mr. Bouchene called the next morning and said, "Tim, we've got to find somebody who's not in the oil business to buy that dinner theater building. Peck's smart enough to want to know who in their right mind would buy that flea-bitten property since it would appear to be worthless. Can you think of a third party we could put up as a front to buy it? Hell, I'll pay for it. I'd just have to do it as a silent partner."

"I've got an idea, Mr. Bouchene. My brother, Talford, works in Houston at The Grand Petroleum Shannon Hotel. He started Casa Mer, an offshore-drilling rig dinner theater in the Gulf. It opened with Mary Martin. It's closed now but was popular for a short time. Talford is active in theater in Houston."

Is that kid nuts? wondered Mr. Bouchene. But he asked, "How can I get in touch with your brother? What's his name?"

"Talford Teasle. He's at The Grand Petroleum Shannon Hotel. You got a pencil? Here's that number in Houston. I'll call him first so he knows what's going on. Wait an hour to make sure I've talked to him."

After Tim talked to Talford about the prospect of buying the Casa Bella Dinner Theater, he was once again excited about something—another dinner theater!

Chapter 22
The Will

 Junior and Priss had been living in Fort Worth a couple of years when her father died at his home in Bullard. They made the three-hour drive for the wake and service, as they had done for the service after Mrs. Mullin's death the year before A handful of people gathered for the reading of the will at 9:00 am the next day.

As the reading of the will was about to begin, Junior started perspiring and felt nervous, fearful that someone would discover he was using a lot of Priss's money.

"Junior, I think we should draw up a will," whispered Priss, suddenly aware of the importance of protecting family money and maintaining control of its use as she faced her new situation following her father's death.

"What the hell for?" asked Junior.

The lead attorney cleared his throat and began to read the will. "Ladies and gentlemen, we are gathered here today to remember a life well lived and review what Mr. Mullin has bequeathed to his family and loved ones. Mr. Mullin was taken from a life well lived, much too early. He was felled by an aneurism."

"I thought it was an embolism," interrupted Junior.

"No, it says right here on the death certificate that it was an aneurism," insisted the attorney.

"Oh, for Christ's sake," said the CPA there to witness the reading. "The man is dead. Can we just get on with it?"

The attorney removed a stack of papers from his valise. He gestured to the pile as he placed it on the table and said, "I will read each part of the last will and testament of Mr. James Wilke Mullin, dated August 4, 1959. This will also indicate where all the legal documents are located to avoid any form of testamentary trust challenges."

"What does that mean?" asked Junior.

"Sir, at this rate we won't get out of here for hours. Please refrain from comments. There will be time at the end of the reading for questions," said the attorney.

"Hush, Junior. I'm telling you, we need to have a will also," Priss insisted. Over the years of life with Junior, whose financial situation had sometimes fluctuated considerably according to sporadic investments, she had become increasingly aware of the usefulness of legal agreements.

"Bullshit. All that does is feed the lawyers and put their children through college," protested Junior.

"Moving along. The first source of income is the ACME lumber contract supplying lumber to the ACME construction company in perpetuity. This is valued at market rates. In today's pricing scheme, this contract represents approximately two million dollars annually projected to increase along with the price of lumber at an annual rate of three point seven percent as lumber becomes scarcer." The accountant fanned out the paperwork for the lumber contract, collected it, stapled it, and put it in a three-ring binder.

As the reading of the will continued, the binder grew to a thickness of two inches. It contained the documentation of assets totaling $17 million, half of which was to be put in a trust for Bobby Leland Peck and held until his thirty-fifth birthday and half held in interest-bearing financial instruments at the discretion of the board of directors of Mullin Lumber. Certain designated financial instruments were to be liquidated annually to yield an amount of $450,000 per year for the sole purpose of making Priss happy.

"I'll tell you what will make me happy, Junior. For me to be happy, we've got to put some written legal stipulations on that trust for Bobby lest some cheap tart gets her fangs into him. He doesn't show any kind of judgment when it comes to women," remarked Priss.

"Tell me about it. That last one looked like a poor man's Gina Lollobrigida, who, come to think of it, looked like a poor man's version of Sophia Loren," said Junior.

Priss motioned to the lead accountant and said, "We need a few minutes alone, please." They stepped out into the hall.

"Junior, this is serious. I'll set something up next week with these gentlemen. We've got to put together some sort of will and document our assets properly," insisted Priss.

"Why? You know good and well we have some assets, don't you?" Junior replied, trying to dismiss Priss's pleas and avoid any accounting or allocating of assets.

"Yes, but I don't know what they are," said Priss, determined to gain more knowledge of and control over their assets.

"You don't need to worry about money or anything else, Priss," claimed Junior.

"It's not me I'm thinking of. It's Bobby and that oil field trash he runs around with. Plus that damned dinner theater—our albatross. Every day I look out over our bluff, and there it is on that godforsaken stretch of the Trinity River. Bobby ran that thing into the ground in less than a year. There must be some sort of liability involved for all the equipment he bought, like expensive scrims, lighting, and hydraulic instruments for the motorized revolving stage, on credit. I bet he defaulted on all of it. And it's our credit he's ruined," complained Priss.

"Oh, sugar. Don't worry about that. I've got the whole thing up for sale for enough to cover the debt," said Junior.

"Who's gonna buy that rat trap?" replied Priss, skeptically.

"As a matter of fact, there's some sucker in Houston who is interested. It pains me to reduce the price, but that Houston man is a live one, and I want out from under that property," reported Junior, trying to reassure Priss that he had their finances under control.

"Okay, but I still think we need some sort of will," said Priss.

"Well, I don't. Here's your will," said Junior, handing Priss a legal pad on which he had scribbled a figure and drawn a line on the bottom where he and Priss were supposed to sign. "Now, that's that. I won't listen to any further talk about a will, you understand me, Priss? I do agree, though, that we need something to protect Bobby's inheritance—what did you call it?"

"Legal stipulation," said Priss.

"I'll get to work on that right away," promised Junior.

Priss and Junior rejoined the group even though Priss had not been entirely persuaded by Junior's reassurance.

That night Junior poured himself a drink and sat down behind his desk in the library. He took out his monogrammed Montblanc and started writing, "In the event some bimbo… In the event some trailer trash…" But unable to capture the essence of the problem, he thought, to hell with it, I'll pay someone to write the damn stipulation.

Priss still didn't understand Junior's reluctance to have a will. After all, her daddy's will was so tightly written there could be no misunderstanding of it. During Bridge Club, Priss asked the other ladies if they had a will and for their opinions about her dilemma.

"Good God, yes," they all said practically in unison. "Honey, you've got to get yourself a will. Otherwise, the state can come in and take over all your assets. Junior's a smart businessman—why on earth wouldn't he want a will? I actually overheard at the beauty shop these oilmen often have two or three wills, some to hide money from tax people," advised one.

"I have no idea. Every time I bring it up he avoids the subject. I'll just have to take measures into my own hands then. Any ideas?" asked Priss.

Another one of the ladies asked, "Have you noticed anything different about Junior? Has he lost weight, changed his haircut, purchased a new car?"

"What! Your insinuations are ridiculous. Our marriage is as solid as a rock, especially since we moved here," insisted Priss.

"You mark my words. If you go through his pockets and papers, you'll see something. There has to be an explanation for why a rich man doesn't want a will. Listen to me, Priss: I had a second husband who was not behaving properly. I hired a Pinkerton Agency man, who turned out to be the most thorough private eye. I think they call them gum shoes—I don't know why. He was able to get hold of pictures and all sorts of documents and copies of receipts such that I came away flush with money. I'll look him up in my file," said the woman.

The day before Junior and Priss were to meet the lawyers about adding the legal stipulation to her daddy's will, Priss picked up her pink princess phone and made a call.

"Pinkerton Agency, how may we help you? Oh, I see, well, since it's you, Mrs. Peck Jr., let me put you through to our finest detective, Mr. Thurber Mingus," said the receptionist.

"Hello, Thurber Mingus here. We find things you didn't even know you lost," the detective chirped into the receiver. "Yes, of course I know who you are. Well, I know who your husband is. Two o'clock tomorrow in our offices would work just fine. See you then."

"You must not, under any circumstances let Mr. Peck know about this," insisted Priss.

"I can assure you of the Pinkerton promise, Mrs. Peck Jr. Whoever pays the bill buys the privacy. Our fee is one percent of the discovery. What that means is, when I legally document your assets, our fee is one percent of the total."

"That's a little steep, don't you think?" asked Priss.

"May I remind you that the Pinkerton Agency was voted Best in the Country by the CIA?" said Mr. Mingus.

"Oh, all right. Daddy left me some personal happiness money, so I can just use that. When can you start, and how long will this take?" asked Priss.

"It shouldn't take too long to search documents, Mrs. Peck Jr. I'm sure everything's in order legally. I'll just start out at the Gregg County Courthouse for the drilling records. Anywhere else I should check?"

"We got married in Bossier City, so there may be some documents there," said Priss.

"Right-o, Mrs. Peck Jr. I'll leave first thing," said Mr. Mingus.

One week later Thurber Mingus called Priss and said, "Mrs. Peck Jr., I'm afraid I might have some unusual news."

"What do you mean? And stop calling me Mrs. Peck Jr. You can drop the Jr.," said Priss.

"Ma'am, I might have to drop the Peck part, too. You see, there is a marriage certificate in the court of records in the Bossier City archives that shows you married a Mr. Leland Peck Jr."

Priss let out a loud annoyed sigh. "Really, Mr. Mingus. You expect me to pay you to tell me things I already know?"

"Well, Mrs. Peck Jr., I mean Mrs. Peck, it seems you married someone named Leland Peck Junior, but it isn't the same one you are married to now."

"Have you lost your mind?" Priss screamed into the phone.

"The man you married then doesn't have the same social security number as the man you are married to now. In fact, neither do you," stated Mr. Mingus.

Priss dropped the phone. While bending down to pick it up, she felt light-headed. "Mr. Mingus, do you have any idea what you are suggesting?" she asked.

"Yes, I do, and that's just the tip of the iceberg. Would you be able to meet me at the Gregg County Courthouse tomorrow? There are a number of documents you need to see," said Mr. Mingus.

After agreeing to the meeting, Priss started pacing back and forth in the library. She seldom drank, but she now poured herself a cream sherry. She thought back to what her friend had said: "If you go through his pockets and papers, you'll see something." She checked the time. It was 2:00 pm, and Junior wouldn't be home for a couple of hours. There was time to go through his pockets. When she did, Priss let out a gasp. She found lots of used lottery tickets and quarter-horse racing chits. She now realized there was a great deal she didn't know.

The next morning, Priss drove with trepidation to the Gregg County Courthouse to meet with Mr. Mingus, telling Junior she was going to visit a sick friend back in Bullard.

Chapter 23
Circle of Deceit

Priss and Mr. Mingus took the metal stairwell down to the little office in the basement of the Gregg County Courthouse. Priss wore a tailored suit, gloves, and a hat with a small accent feather, attempting to appear very proper in the face of any allegations of impropriety. Mr. Mingus wore a single-breasted tan light-weight suit with a plain blue tie.

It was hot and stuffy in the basement. The fluorescent lights bounced off the speckled linoleum floor covered with thick yellow wax buildup, and the vending machines' noisy compressor kicked on and off relentlessly, making the atmosphere oppressive. Set out on a table were a large expandable green file and a cardboard banker's box filled with papers.

"Now what is the meaning of all this?" started Priss, wagging her gloved finger at Mr. Mingus. "I was told that Pinkerton was the finest detective agency in the country and that you were the best of the bunch in Fort Worth."

Mr. Mingus extended his hand to Priss in greeting. She ignored the gesture. "Ma'am, I'm going to need you to look at all these documents. It seems as if many, if not all, of the holdings your husband claims to own are not, in fact, his. Further, two of the companies he set up never existed," explained Mr. Mingus.

"Oh my God. You mean to tell me my husband Junior is a common crook, a thief?" Priss quickly took the powder compact from her purse and stared at herself in the mirror. She looked the same, but she was shaking so much from anxiety that the feather in her hat started shedding.

"I'm afraid Mr. Peck may have been involved in some shady business deals, Mrs. Peck. I realize it's a bit much to swallow. Are you still a member of the Rigview Country Club? We could drive out there. It might be more comfortable than this basement," suggested Mr. Mingus, trying to think of a way to minimize the shock he knew Priss would have to face.

"I don't know what I am or who I am anymore. Let's just go," said Priss.

Mr. Mingus packed up his large stack of files and ran after Priss into the courthouse parking lot. He had to exceed the speed limit to catch up to her car.

When they reached the club, Priss led the way into the Nineteenth Hole Lounge. Since it was a Tuesday, the golf course was closed. They sat down in the plush chintz-covered chairs under a gilded mirror.

"Bring us two sherries please, Jeeter. No, wait a minute. I'll just get the bottle from the ladies' locker room. Bring us two sherry glasses and some water," instructed Priss, reeling.

Then she said to Mr. Mingus, "Okay, let's go over this madness item by item, starting with our wedding—or what I thought was our wedding."

"Here is the certificate on file from the Bossier City County Record Hall. As I said, the man you married there has a different social security number from the man you're married to now," said Mr. Mingus.

Priss sipped her sherry and tried to take all this in. "Maybe that was just a clerical error," she suggested, sneezing at the sting of sherry as she gulped it down.

Mr. Mingus laid out a notarized document entitled "Official Seal of the State of Texas Land and Mineral Rights Records," dated December 14, 1942. "I'm sure this is not a clerical error, Mrs. Peck," he said, opening to the first page and reading: "On this fourteenth day of December, 1942, this court of records hereby registers and certifies that a Mr. Edward James Teasle transfers the deed and full ownership of the land and mineral rights to the oil play so named the Cherokee Lake well to Mr. Leland Peck Junior."

"Are you sure? Junior came home all excited to tell me his drilling company had struck oil near Cherokee Lake. Why, Daddy even took us to dinner to celebrate at Earnest's Supper Club in Shreveport—a far cry from where we married, or at least I thought we were married," said Priss, dabbing her forehead with her handkerchief and sighing. She was beginning to realize this information might indeed be true.

Mr. Mingus continued, "The Cherokee Lake well was discovered by a Mr. Edward Joseph Teasle. This record states it was Mr. Edward James Teasle who signed over the rights to Mr. Peck Jr. Furthermore, the signature of this Mr. Teasle does not match that on any of the other documents he ever signed for the various percentages of other oil wells Mr. Edward Joseph Teasle owned."

"Exactly what are you getting at, Mr. Mingus?" asked Priss.

"Exactly that your husband forged Mr. Teasle's signature. Probably at that time there were so many filings that no one bothered to check title transfers. And since it was notarized, the clerk date-stamped it and filed it away." Priss guzzled all the water out of her water glass and filled it with sherry.

"Then there's the matter of his last name and ancestry," said Mr. Mingus.

"His last name is Peck, Mr. Mingus," insisted Priss.

"Did he say he was one of the Kentucky Pecks?" asked Mr. Mingus.

"Yes, he did," replied Priss.

"According to the State of Kentucky Office of Residency Records, there was a family named Peck. They descended from a Mr. Elijah Peck and his wife, the former Miss Bledsoe. The last of that Peck family was a daughter, Miss Ila June Peck, who never married. Furthermore, for Leland Peck Jr., or whomever he is, there is no birth certificate on record, no baptismal record, and no listing in the Roots guide to family trees. Miss Ila June Peck died in 1919, a year before your husband was born, or at least a year before we think he was born," Mr. Mingus informed Priss.

"Good grief, of course we know he was born. I really think you need to clear up some things, Mr. Mingus. None of this makes any sense, and I'll thank you to stop with all this gibberish and get to the truth," admonished Priss.

Mr. Mingus coughed and said, "May I continue? It appears that two of your husband's companies never existed."

Priss went out in the hall and threw up. Then she ordered two dry martinis with a twist from the bar before returning to Mr. Mingus.

Seeing the martinis, Mr. Mingus remarked, "Let's not get too carried away, Mrs. Peck. We have a ways to go here. By the way, how did you know that's how I like my martinis?"

"I didn't. These are both for me," replied Priss flatly.

"Are you familiar with a company called Gulf Coast Cares?" continued Mr. Mingus.

Priss gulped one martini and replied, "No. Should I be?"

"There is a savings account in Bullard National Bank under the name of Mr. Alabama. It was opened in the spring of 1942 and has two hundred and seventy-two thousand dollars in it," reported Mr. Mingus.

"What does Mr. Alabama have to do with my husband?" asked Priss.

"We have reason to believe Mr. Alabama is your husband. The original deposit of twenty-five thousand dollars cash was traced to federal government bonds assigned to the state of Alabama and subsequently signed over to Mr. Leland Peck Jr. for purposes of cleaning up a hurricane disaster in Gulf Shores, Alabama. Our office in Birmingham tracked a trail that led to a record of some company named Gulf Coast Cares solely owned by Mr. Leland Peck Jr. of Bullard, Texas," said Mr. Mingus.

"What are you saying?" asked Priss.

Mr. Mingus tipped the end of his handkerchief into his water glass, dabbed it on his upper lip, and continued, "Your husband made up a company and bilked the state of Alabama out of twenty-five thousand dollars in federal disaster cleanup funds."

"Are you kidding me? Dear God, tell me that's all. If Daddy were still alive, this would surely kill him," Priss exclaimed, standing up, and throwing her gloves and hat on the table.

"Unfortunately, there is more. If you'll excuse me a moment, I need some fresh air," said Mr. Mingus.

Mr. Mingus walked out to the putting green and took several deep breaths then returned to a distraught Priss, who was sobbing in a corner of the room. As he took off his tie, he continued, "There was another nonexistent company, Mrs. Peck. The incorporation paperwork was drawn up by the law firm of Fleigh & Fleigh in Bullard. I believe you are familiar with them."

Priss nodded and put her head in her hands.

"The junior partner, William Fleigh, wrote the documents of incorporation. The company name was OLG, Our Lady of Guadalupe, and it only existed for a few months before it was declared bankrupt. Then Junior bought it back, took several hundred thousand dollars some twenty investors had put into the company, and created another bank account for that money."

Turning as white as the tablecloth, Priss asked, "You're telling me that the man I may not be married to is a common crook who lied about his ancestry and had companies that didn't exist but might have made a lot of money?"

"Yes, I'm afraid so. We're not clear on how much money he might have made, but this last bit of information we found is perhaps the most disturbing of all—possibly worse than the fact that he is not a Kentucky Peck. He is originally from Enid, Oklahoma, according to the only birth certificate we found. Leland Peck Jr. is the son of Leland Peck Sr., who died in jail in Enid, Oklahoma, serving a life sentence for murder. We found little information about his mother, but I can tell you that for the last ten years or so he has been sending monthly checks in the amount of three hundred dollars made out to a Daisy Peck at an address in Terrell, Texas. That address matches the location of the state insane asylum."

Priss fainted. An ambulance took her to St. Shepperd's Hospital, where it was determined that her blood pressure was off the charts. She was given a heavy sedative to help her sleep through the night.

The next day Mr. Mingus went to see Priss. Gone was the naïve woman he had originally met, replaced by a thin-lipped, wide-eyed, focused, and bitter woman.

"Mr. Mingus, I want you to draw up a legal document outlining all the information you have gathered about my husband, or whoever he is. If what you say is true, maybe he isn't my husband after all," requested Priss.

"Yes, ma'am, that's quite possible—in fact, it's legally true," stated Mr. Mingus.

"Could you get a Mr. R. E. Peppy Bailey on the phone? He's an old family friend and a damn good lawyer. He's with

White, Small & Johnson. Junior is out of town for a few days, so I have a little time to try to sort this out," said Priss.

The next morning in Counselor Bailey's office, Priss told him what she understood the situation to be. He phoned the district judge and said, "Your Honor, under the circumstances I believe we can ask for and get an annulment."

"We can't do that, Peppy. If she wasn't ever married, what is she getting an annulment from?" replied the judge.

"Oh, right. Now you listen to me, Priss," advised Bailey. "You go on back to Fort Worth. Don't even talk to that rat bastard of a husband—oh wait, not a husband. Can someone be there with you?"

"Yes, the Pinkerton detective, I suppose," replied Priss, dreading any encounter with Junior but knowing she would have to confront him to gain her freedom and regain her self-esteem.

Priss drove behind Mr. Mingus back to her home in Fort Worth. Junior was not there yet.

"Mrs. Peck, as a professional I feel I should inform you that Texas is a joint property state. That means Junior is entitled to half your net worth in any divorce filing," said Mr. Mingus.

"The hell with that. Two can play the hide-the-money game. He'll not see a penny. But apparently I'm not really married to that crook," replied Priss.

"I think that's smart of you, Mrs. Peck. Now, I realize now is not the best time to bring this up, but as you know our fee is one percent of discovery," said Mr. Mingus.

"Yes, I know, and it will be hard to calculate one percent of something that may or may not exist," answered Priss.

"Okay, how about a flat fee, Mrs. Peck?" asked Mr. Mingus.

"No, you more than earned one percent and then some. We can base it on the amount of money we think Junior had. Once we can sort this out, I'll write you a check from my happiness account, which I guess I'll have to rename the imminent divorce account. Why don't you call me Priss?" she said.

When Junior came home that afternoon, Priss didn't greet him at the door as she usually did, and he soon discovered she was distant and had company. "Junior, we need to talk," Priss finally said.

"What is it? Who is this strange man? Is he a policeman? Did Bobby get in some sort of trouble?" asked Junior.

"No, he didn't get in trouble, but you will," replied Priss.

"What the hell are you talking about? Pour me a drink, and let's sit down. What sort of bee is in your bonnet, Priss?" said Junior, concerned but believing he could take care of any kind of trouble he was in—as he always had—with money and power.

"Junior, you kept on resisting my wish to have a will. You gave me no choice but to take matters into my own hands. So

I hired a detective to get me information, and what he found is devastating to me, to us, to our good family name—whatever name that may be," said Priss.

"Really, Priss. Ever since you went to that fat camp you hardly eat anything. Are you just swimmy headed? Maybe I should make you a sandwich," said Junior.

"I don't want a sandwich. I want some answers, and I want them now," insisted Priss.

"What are the questions?" asked Junior, now hyperventilating with a beet-red face.

"One of my Bridge Club ladies found out her husband was running around on her—misbehaving, as she put it—and advised me to look into your behavior," said Priss.

"Surely you don't think I would do that sort of thing, do you?" asked Junior. "You are starting to chap my ass."

"I have no idea what you might do. Who exactly is Daisy Peck? Do you have another wife somewhere in Terrell?"

Junior broke down and said, sobbing, "No that's my real mama. She's in a sanitarium in Terrell. My real papa, he…"

"Stop right now. I don't believe a word you say about what's real. But I can tell you what's real from my perspective—I'm leaving you," stated Priss.

"No. Please, my darling. I can explain. You're all I have. All I've ever had," pleaded Junior, reaching out for Priss's arm, which she pulled away. Their dachshund, Shotsky, started barking and nipped at Junior's heels.

Priss yelled, "Come on Shotsky. Let's get out of here." Priss went into the bedroom and returned with a packed suitcase and the dog in a carrier. "You'll hear from my lawyer, you charlatan."

"Wait, Priss. Anything I did wrong I did for you, for us," insisted Junior.

"Well, what I'm gonna do for you, for us, is get a divorce. I'm leaving now," she said, storming out the door dragging her suitcase, the dog carrier, and Mr. Mingus by the arm.

Junior sat on the bottom step of the staircase, his thoughts jumbled and confused. He muttered, "Well, this is a fine kettle of fish." There had to be a way out of this mess. He began to scheme. Maybe he could tell her he was a twin, and that everything was the doing of his twin. That their mother had them out of wedlock, and that's why there had been no birth certificate, he thought. But then he realized that this scenario was too farfetched. He poured a brandy and paced around for about an hour then fell asleep in his favorite easy chair.

At sunrise, he woke up when he heard a car in the driveway. It was a Pinkerton Agency sedan pulling up outside the house. Mr. Mingus rang the doorbell.

Junior was sure it was Priss, coming back home to reconcile. But when Junior opened the door Mr. Mingus handed him a decree document showing the two different social security numbers registered as Mr. Leland Peck Jr.

"Could you explain this?" asked Mingus.

Junior was shocked. He felt like he had been kicked in the stomach by a mule.

Priss pulled up next to the Pinkerton Agency car and ran to the door. She had the look of a wild animal on a rampage, her nostrils flaring. "Who the hell are you?" Priss yelled at Junior. "I thought I knew you and now all this mendacity."

Junior wasn't clear about what was happening and didn't know what to say. Once again he felt rejected, belittled, small, and isolated, only this time he wasn't on the baseball field at Weldon Christian Camp but in his own home. He couldn't just run away. He felt a sudden increase in his body temperature and was emitting that musky scent of a frightened animal. Sure, he had done a few things outside the letter of the law—in fact, most of what he had done was outside the letter of the law. And he had thrown wild parties with unfortunate consequences for his family's social status. But no one had ever directly accused him of wrongdoing before and threatened his assets.

The air was dead still. For a long time, neither he nor Priss spoke in this vacuum of fear and hatred, each unwilling or unable to break the tension. Finally, Junior said, "I was just doing what I thought was right," as he stuck his hands in his pockets.

"Right? Was it right to forge title papers for the Cherokee Lake well? Was it right to marry me using an assumed persona? Was it right to leave your own mother in a sanitarium to die there, all alone? Oh, and how about screwing the whole state of Alabama and also using religion as a front for financial gain? Well, two can play the shell game. Maybe I can't do it as well as you, but I'm going to give it a try. You are legally entitled to nothing, you understand? You just try and get my money," yelled Priss.

Junior was flabbergasted by these revelations. He steadied himself on the stair bannister as he tried to think fast about how to counter them and regain control of the situation.

"Why, we've been married for twenty years. It took me that long to get us from nowhere to the high life in Fort Worth, and now it's taken you ten minutes to destroy twenty years. Not everything I do is crooked. I just sold that dinner theater legally for quite a tidy profit. As a matter of fact, I need to go sign the final papers right this minute," Junior shouted as he ran outside, jumped in his car, and drove away, his tires skidding on the oyster-shell driveway.

On the way to the closing for the sale of the Casa Bella Dinner Theater, Junior began to scheme about how to dig himself out of this mess. He supposed he could just buy the Pinkerton Agency and cast their detectives as incompetent fools. Priss would believe that, he was sure. She'd always love him, he convinced himself, since he was the father of her son.

After Junior signed the closing papers at the site of the Casa Bella Dinner Theater, he got back in his car and drove away with a glint in his eye and a smirk on his face. There was nothing like selling a pig in a poke to some south Texas fool, he thought. He cranked up the country music station and began to sing along with "Big Bad John." As he turned onto the main road, there was a twenty-foot open trailer truck stacked high with iron derrick pipe and three different drill bit heads turning into the dirt road. The truck was from Kidd Tool, Well, and Centrifuge, the largest oil field equipment supplier in Fort Worth. There was nothing down that dirt road but the dinner theater and the abandoned bait shop. Puzzled, Junior turned around and sped down the dirt road in the wake of the dust from the truck, needing to know what that truck was doing on the road. There, on the dilapidated dinner theater marquee, workmen were hanging a sign that read: "Future Home of Teasle Well #13." Recognizing the name Teasle, Junior suddenly realized that he himself had now become caught in a circle of deception that had started with his own blackmailing of Pop Teasle and was ending with a Teasle deceiving him regarding the existence of oil on property he had just sold. And the deception he had perpetuated to bring about his marriage had also now led to its dissolution.

Once everything registered in his mind, he went to the bait shop dock and gazed up at his former opulent home on the crest of the bluff in the distance. He recalled the lives of those Weldon campers who lived in a self-serving, self-perpetuating limited-perspective circle of life—like the worm ouroboros—not needing or wanting anyone or anything beyond what they had been born with. Now his own life seemed to reflect such a circle. He wanted to reach out to someone for comfort or broader understanding, but he had burned every bridge he'd ever built. His world of deceit was his own creation and had now become his ultimate undoing.

Junior walked along the rotting pier and kicked the bait sign into the Trinity River. A light rain began to fall. He watched the old wooden sign catch the polluted current bearing sludge, broken bottles, plastic bags, and old branches downstream. Through the drizzle, the top of the sign was becoming hard to see. He could barely make out the words "We now carry worm oroboroses."

About the Author

Margaret Mooney grew up in East Texas, graduated from the University of Texas at Austin, then moved to Chicago to pursue a career in advertising. There she spent thirty-five years working for three different companies. Procter & Gamble taught her how to understand consumer behavior, which came in handy for character development. At Leo Burnett Advertising, she learned what makes people buy the brands they buy. Her longest tenure was at Ogilvy & Mather Advertising, where she managed such accounts as The Chicago Tribune and NutraSweet in the US, Canada, and the UK. During her career, she received numerous accolades and awards including two Cannes Lions, five Effies for effectiveness in ad campaigns, and two David Ogilvy awards recognizing creativity.

In 2005, Margaret retired and moved to Santa Fe, New Mexico, where she immersed herself in the nonprofit world, preparing newsletters and ad campaigns for The New Mexico Cancer Institute, Equestars Therapeutic Riding, and the Grand Prix de Santa Fe. Margaret lives with her husband Larry Davis in the Cerrillos Hills, south of Santa Fe.